CLEAN-UP TIME

Poor Brad.

I wonder what his last thoughts were…

I realized I didn't care much as I set to work devising a plan.

People died all the time. It was how we all left this world. I just didn't want to be blamed for it.

Brad was a pretty big guy.

I'm strong, but not that strong.

I dragged Brad into the bathroom and flung him into the tub. I went back to my own apartment to get things that I would need….

Other books by Sèphera Girón:

BORROWED FLESH
THE BIRDS AND THE BEES
HOUSE OF PAIN

RAVES FOR SÈPHERA GIRÓN!

"Girón deserves a place beside the top mistresses of the dark."
—Hellnotes

"If Poppy Z. Brite and Nancy Kilpatrick turn your cold blood to hot, then welcome Sèphera Girón to the short list of dark mistresses of terror truly worthy of that title."
—Stanley Wiater, author of Dark Dreamers

"Girón at no time lets up on the horror quotient."
—Fangoria

BORROWED FLESH
"[Giron's] prose is rich and multi-layered."
—thecelebritycafe.com

THE BIRDS AND THE BEES
"An aesthetic experience that at once both celebrates and vivisects humankind's relationship with nature and himself. ...A straightforward, artfully rendered narrative."
—Cemetery Dance

HOUSE OF PAIN
"*House of Pain* is horror at its best."
—The Midwest Book Review

"A powerful and unflinching novel."
—Peter Atkins, author of Wishmaster

"Girón's prose is smooth as silk; the pacing is dead on. I devoured this book in a single sitting."
—Horror World

"*House of Pain* is a perfect—if far from safe—place to lose yourself on a stormy fall night."
—Fangoria

"Genuinely creepy."
—Cemetery Dance

"*House of Pain* rocks with good old-fashioned creepiness."
—Edo van Belkom, author of Teeth

JAN   2006

MISTRESS *of* THE DARK

SÈPHERA GIRÓN

LEISURE BOOKS NEW YORK CITY

A LEISURE BOOK®

December 2005

Published by

Dorchester Publishing Co., Inc.
200 Madison Avenue
New York, NY 10016

ISBN 0-8439-5547-3

The name "Leisure Books" and the stylized "L" with design are trademarks of Dorchester Publishing Co., Inc.

Printed in the United States of America.

Visit us on the web at www.dorchesterpub.com.

MISTRESS *of* THE DARK

CHAPTER ONE

Wednesday, August 10

She's watching me.

She's always watching me.

But that's OK. It gives me someone to talk to sometimes.

I put her in a chair by the TV so that I can see her. She looks elegant sitting there: black netted fabric loosely draped around her, eyeless face watching me, the white of her bones gleaming.

I've found that if I move her around too much, parts of her break off. She's even lost a couple of teeth over the years.

Well, I guess a skeleton can't help it.

I like having her around, though. She's like part of the family. I even give her a hat for every season. Right now, she has a wreath of sunflowers on her head, like a summer queen.

Sometimes I think it must be so nice to be dead. To be just a skeleton in someone's living room. Watching the world go by with no stress. No one telling you what to do and how to live your life.

Once in a while, though, I get lonely, which is also why I'm starting this diary. The big city is so different from the little town where I grew up. I was just a country bumpkin, I guess. It seems like that is how people peg me these days.

"Hi, I'm Abby!" I'll say, sticking my hand out, strong and firm like a big-city girl.

"Hey, Abby. Where you from?"

"Littletown, New York."

This is always followed by a pause from the big-city types. It's like they are doing a computer search in their brains, trying to figure out if I'm worth talking to or not. Some will be polite and stay for a bit to see if there's more there. Others will just plain dismiss me. I guess it depends on what they want, what they are looking for.

It's hard to make friends in this city.

Of course, it was hard to make friends in Buttfuck, Nowhere, too.

I guess I'm just not a good friends-making type, though when I have friends, I'm pretty good to them. I think.

When I looked in the mirror this morning, I could barely stand the sight of myself. I'm well aware that I'll never be beautiful. Just a gawky fat misfit.

That's me.

The face staring back at me didn't seem like my own. At the very least, it isn't the face I want representing me out in the world.

For starters, I have brown eyes and brown hair and

very dark eyebrows. We all know that guys don't care about us brunettes. They want the bleached blondes with blue eyes. They want thin girls with big tits.

Sure, I have big tits. Bigger than most people I know, but that doesn't mean a damn thing when you are fat. I break the scale at 125 pounds and no matter what I do, I can't get rid of these big hips and gut.

I even do a hundred sit-ups every day. Well, almost every day. Sometimes I forget. But for the most part, I do remember.

And of course I'm sooo lucky that I wear glasses. All the time. I'm not one of those people who only pop them on to drive or watch a movie. I'm one of the lucky souls who can't see the damn alarm clock two inches from my face. And we know for sure that guys just don't like girls who wear glasses. They all say they don't care, it doesn't matter, but the minute some dude tries to kiss me, he's pulling my glasses from my face. Maybe he's hoping that I'll like him better being blind. I mean, here we are in the 2000s and it's the same old shit.

Maybe it's even worse. The below-the-navel pants that all those lucky skinny girls get to wear with their high-definition abs. How many hours a day do you have to work out to get like that? And what happens when you stop? I wonder if Britney Spears will let herself go to hell like Liz Taylor did, especially now that she's a breeder.

Well, all I can say is that when I watched *Secret Window*, I was happy to see Johnny Depp wearing glasses. Actually he's worn glasses in a few movies. One of my favorite movies is his *Pirates of the Caribbean*.

I mean, how cool are pirates? Ghost pirates? I just

loved the special effects, how they were all undead skeletons swashbuckling their way around. And Johnny Depp is so hot, how could anyone not want to ride his ship?

I love skeletons. Like *Army of Darkness* had some rocking skeletons. I like skulls too. I've been collecting them for years now. There's something about knowing that there is something solid under our flesh, like tent poles propping us up, that fascinates me.

I wanted to go to college and take some of those science autopsy courses. Maybe be a forensics scientist or something. But of course, being from Buttfuck, Nowhere, killed that idea dead in the water. My stupid parents barely made ends meet, let alone put anything away to make sure I would get educated.

Luckily I'm one of those bookworm types. So even though I didn't get to go to college, at least not yet, I learn tons by reading and cruising the Internet.

But, of course, cruising the 'Net doesn't get you the sheepskin you need to get a job.

So I'm stuck waitressing at one of the tourist traps til something better comes along.

Ooolala. It's owned by a couple of rock stars who think they can grab some cash from the Big Apple's worms. It's kind of a cross between Hard Rock Cafe and Planet Hollywood. An eclectic collection of celebrity underwear. Corsets, bras, slips, thongs, even stuff going back to Bettie Page. There are a lot of shoes and boots. You know how rock stars love their platforms and stilettos. There's a whole room dedicated just to celebrity footwear, which I guess is also more of a family room then other rooms would be.

There's more men's underwear then you would think. Tank top, bikini briefs, Speedos (yikes!), glittery diaper-type things that I guess they tie over their leather pants onstage.

At night, there are fashion shows and a couple of times a month a burlesque act, complete with larger-than-life drag queens.

The drag queens kind of scare me. They are so big and intimidating with their layers of makeup, giant boobs and wafts of perfume. When it's slow, I'll watch the show from the bar, marveling at how they balance on those giant shoes, and wondering why it is that so many men look better as girls then girls do!

I guess the key is that they take great pride in what they do, whereas those of us born as the fairer sex just take what life throws at us and seldom try to improve so dramatically. Of course, those that try to emulate the drag queen persona look like drag queens themselves. I've seen it with my own eyes here in the flesh, and back at home on Maury when he plays "guess the drag queen."

I've only been here a couple of months, and the shock of all the big-city newness is starting to fade.

I'm still not comfortable around the queens too much; I'm always afraid I'll say something wrong or not politically correct. Maybe I'm not even supposed to call them drag queens. Maybe they are something else now.

There are a couple, though, that have been nice to me. They ask me how I'm doing and tip me when I bring drinks to their dressing rooms.

One of them, Storm, is more of a gothy queen. I've

seen her as a man, kind of cute, but boy, once the eye-liner and long black wig go on, she's stunning. She's nice to me. She tried to give me makeup tips once and I ended up walking around all night looking like the Addams Family's lost little sister. Storm dances around to Rob Zombie and Sisters of Mercy and some other stuff like that. I'm not an idiot; I cruise the 'Net. But there are no goth clubs in Buttfuck, Nowhere, and so the whole deal is new and intriguing but kind of Halloween-like to me.

Another one is Mavis. She hangs with Storm, but she does the Judy Garland shtick. Mavis is one hot guy without the Garland crap. He's a tiny little blond man. Kind of looks like Eminem or someone like that. Walking down the street with his duffel bag, you'd think he was some rapper from Chicago. Add on some false eyelashes, the dark wig and some fishnets and my god, he'd send almost anyone over the rainbow. And with those platforms on, he could just step over the rainbow. My lord!

Backstage really does look like a rock star hangout. All the booze and drugs and groupies hanging around. You'd never know it, really. Ooolala tries to be fairly normal looking at the front of the house. Especially in the family shoe room. But what lies behind the curtain is more magical then the Wizard of Oz himself.

A lot of the other waiters don't like the drag queens, or they're just college kids trying to make a quick buck and don't really care about people or giving good service.

Being a waitress isn't my idea of a dream come true either, but at least I meet people.

When I'm really lucky, I meet the same people over and over again.

You know, the other day this really hunky guy came into the restaurant. He had that Johnny Depp thing going on. You know what I mean. Dark hair. Smoldering dark eyes. Quirky grin. Man, I thought I was gonna soak my undies bringing him a beer. I even put one of those stupid souvenir stir sticks in his beer glass, just to show him he was extra special. I think it only succeeded in making him wonder if I was nuts.

He looked at that stir stick in the glass, lifted it out and stared at the curvy boobs of the plastic lady, her big round lips making the O in Ooolala. Then he looked at me, fixing me with a dark-eyed Johnny Depp stare.

"You trying to kill me or something?" he asked, pointing the stir stick at me.

"It's a souvenir!" I told him cheerfully.

"Yeah . . . right. It's a danger. You shouldn't do that."

He put the offending stick down and lifted the beer bottle to perfect lips. I guess maybe I was staring, because he put the bottle back down and snapped at me.

"Don't you have other tables?"

"Yes, I just wanted to make sure you were OK," I said to him. He looked me over as if trying to figure out if I was worthy of his presence. His gaze traveled from my glasses down to my tight Ooolala scoop-neck T-shirt. I know my nipples were hard; I've noticed whenever I see a cute guy my nipples take on a mind of their own. It's embarrassing, but I guess it's not as bad as being a guy getting a hard-on and trying to hide it. He studied my nipples too long; then his gaze traveled down the rest of my body, where I guess he was offended by the ripple of fat at my belly, which I hoped was mostly covered by my money pouch.

"Yes. I'll call you over when I'm ready to order." He waved me away, turning his attention back to his beer.

Why are the cute ones always so arrogant?

You know, it's hard enough to get up in the morning sometimes without having some man, a man who probably has the world at his feet from his beauty, sneering at me.

He had many drinks and nothing to eat. He just sat and stared at the wall of thongs and drank his beer. I noticed in my rounds that his right hand was below the table. I wondered if he was jerking off to the underwear. It wouldn't be the first time. Despite the all-ages advertising for the restaurant part, it was a fetishist's fantasy. Almost everyone who worked here had a story to tell about catching some pervert jerking off under the table.

That got me to thinking, though, of Mr. Johnny Depp Look-Alike sitting there beating his meat while everyone around him ate theirs, none the wiser to his little hijinks. How easy it would be to drop something on the floor, crawl under there and slip his delicious pole between my lips. Who would know? Just a quick hummer and off I go.

But of course I don't have the nerve to do such things.

And I don't think he was stroking, either, but I'll never know for sure.

As my shift was closing, I returned to his table and asked him to settle his bill. He nodded, the beer giving his eyes a glazed look. He tossed a few bills onto the tray.

"You got nice tits. Too bad you got glasses."

I stared at him, stunned.

I fumbled in my apron for change.

"No change. Just get your eyes fixed. You'd make more money."

Mr. Johnny Depp stumbled towards the men's room. I hurried back to my locker to change out of my uniform. I took my hair out of the ponytail and freshened up my lipstick. I raced back out to the front.

As I had hoped, he was just leaving the restaurant and going out into the street. He wore a black leather biker jacket and I could see how nice his ass was as I followed him for several blocks.

Again with the glasses.

Why were people so shallow?

My fingers clenched and unclenched in my coat pocket.

Following cute guys had been a hobby of mine for many years. I'm not a stalker. I just appreciate a good ass and want to be near it. I like looking at a pretty face as much as the next person.

I guess it started back in second grade. My parents—well, I should say my mom, because my dad had moved out by then—my mom couldn't get her shit together in the morning, so I had to walk by myself to school every day. It was kinda scary and it was a pretty long walk.

Looking back on it all, it might even have been close to a mile. There were ways to make the walk more interesting. Especially when you were shy like I was. I spent much of my time walking, staring at the ground. It's amazing how much you notice when you really take the time. I used to like it when it would rain and the worms would all be crawling along the street. Long and stretchy, inching along, oblivious to cars and kids. There were always kids that found sticks and would scoop up the worms, chasing each other with them dangling from the ends. Almost always the fate of the worm was predetermined. If it weren't flung into some prissy girl's hair, then it would be tromped on or dissected or stretched into several parts until the novelty wore off and it was abandoned.

There were always the dogs at certain houses. Some would bark ferociously, as if little kids were going to come in and steal the family jewels. Some waited expectantly, wagging their tails, hoping someone would pet them. I often did.

Dogs are a funny thing when you think about it.

So loyal, in some ways. You could kick a good-natured pet in the head repeatedly and it would just stare up stupidly at you, accepting its punishment.

I wonder, sometimes, why they call cheating bastard men dogs?

I guess they mean the other type of dog. Wild roaming-in-a-pack scavenger dogs.

Dogs that sniff through garbage and hump your leg if you're on the rag.

Dogs never scared me, ever. Even as a little kid.

In walking, I was always looking to see who could be potential friend material. What was the secret code to making friends in this little town?

I don't know how it started, but I do know who the

first boy I followed was. Billy Fishmen. I made quite a game of it. I would follow the boy beyond where I lived, pretending I had to go to the store or something. I'd walk a bit behind him, memorizing his gait, checking out his jeans, wondering if he knew I was even there, or if I was invisible.

I'd figure out where he lived and would spend much of my spare time walking by his house. I'd spy on him when he was at the park, hiding behind the recreation shed, as if he didn't know I was there. No doubt the kids saw me there and figured I was doing something that they didn't know about. Which I was.

I'd sit against the wall, drawing lines in the mud, while stealing glances at the boy playing on the swings or kicking a ball around. I don't know if he knew I was following him or if it was just a coincidence that I always seemed to be where he was.

There are no coincidences.

So I followed Mr. Johnny Depp Look-Alike to an apartment building and hid as he took a jingling ring of keys from his pocket and opened the security door.

Now I knew where he lived.

I wonder what made him come into a tourist restaurant instead of one of the little pubs. Maybe he was staying with someone and using his or her apartment.

It would be interesting to find out.

I took note of the address. I realized that I was only a few blocks away from Vicki's house, so I figured it'd be rude of me to be in the hood and not make an appearance.

Vicki was a friend, but not really. I don't know if I'm really capable of making friends. She's someone I hang

11

out with, and that day she was home. We sat around smoking dope and talking about how nice it would be to meet Prince Charming and be taken care of for the rest of our lives. Vicki had it made better then me, however. She was one of those pretty girls who knew the secrets of the universe. She had the knack of meeting men, and they fell instantly in love with her. Much of her apartment was furnished by pining suitors she had scooped up and dumped over the years. Her problem wasn't meeting men. It was hanging on to them. She grew bored so quickly with guys, and yet they were willing to jump through hoops for her. I never understood it, except that she must give really good head or something.

I didn't tell Vicki about Mr. Johnny Depp Look-Alike. There was no need. I never told her about any of my crushes. I know what she would say. She would wonder why I didn't just ask him out or give him my phone number or something like that. She didn't understand how hard it is to be shy.

She doesn't understand a lot of things about me, but then again, most people don't.

Vicki used to work at Ooolala, but now she works at a strip club. She started off as a cocktail waitress, but one night, amateur night, she had been goaded by a bunch of her customers into hitting the stage and I guess she got hooked. She says it's way easier to bump and grind for three songs then to lug trays of drinks all over the place. The money is better, and certainly there were men willing to pay cash for her services. She said she never accepted money for sex from her clients, but I don't know if I believe her. I think she fucks customers but just doesn't want me to know.

Well, that's OK. We all have our secrets. She's entitled to hers and I'm entitled to mine.

At some point, the phone rang. Of course, it was one of Miss Vicki's pining suitors. I rolled another joint and lit it while she teased the poor boy on the other end. She laughed lustily, with that low throaty voice that some women are born with, and others acquire after years of chain-smoking. I'm not sure which way it went with her.

She waved me over to her and had me listen in to Romeo uttering promises and lies, remembrances of some mystical night they shared. Vicki kept putting her hand over her mouth to cover her giggles.

I wasn't sure what to think. He sounded like a big dumb goofball to me, but what did I know? I couldn't really pass judgment since my batting average with the opposite sex sucks pretty bad.

Stupid men and their stupid superficial bullshit. I bet Romeo wouldn't like Vicki if she wore glasses. How can such a stupid little thing like some glass and wire make all the difference to some people? It makes me mental.

We giggled and laughed and she even had me talk to him for a bit.

Sure, why not?

I told him how I like dark guys with big dicks and he assured me he had the biggest. I laughed and dared him to show me.

Well, shit, doesn't he say to turn on the computer and he'll reveal all?

I watched him waving his winky on the webcam and found myself all hot and bothered watching it. He wasn't lying about being big. Or at least he looked pretty big to me. Maybe I didn't have much experience, but I've seen some teeny weenies in my life, and even on a webcam, that wasn't one of them.

"Wanna suck on this, baby?" He grinned, stroking himself. Vicki had set her cam up too and was fondling her naked breasts for him. Damn, but she had one luscious set of cans on her. My eyes darted from Romeo's growing pocket rocket to Vicki's cherry-topped mounds. I wanted to lick them all, but instead took another haul on the joint.

"Why don't you?" Romeo was saying. Vicki stared at me.

"Wanna?"

"Wanna what?" I asked. I didn't know what she was talking about, since I was obviously spacing out in my little lewd daydream while they were discussing something.

"Lick me, baby," she cooed. She held her breasts up towards me. She didn't have to ask again as I teased them with my tongue. Romeo beat his meat twice as hard, watching me lick Miss Vicki. I rubbed her breasts in my hands and stared into the camera while I gnawed on her nipples. Romeo couldn't believe his good fortune and was shouting words of encouragement. Vicki was saying something or another back to him, but I wasn't paying attention. I was enjoying an unexpected moment of heaven.

And that's one of the reasons I hung out with Vicki. You never knew what was going to happen. There were no expectations, no hang-ups. It was like what the hippy days had been rumored to be; only now we were on cruise control at the dawn of a new millennium.

After Romeo blew his wad, Vicki lost interest and, quite frankly, so did I. I liked looking at that big throbbing baseball bat, but now it was back to its little ludicrous size, all limp and blah looking. Vicki logged off the computer and turned to me.

"So . . . what do you want to do tonight?" she asked.

"Well, shit, now I'm all hot and bothered," I joked, pulling my blouse away from my chest and pretending to fan my face with my other hand.

"Me too. We need to go out and find us a real man."

"Dancing?" I asked. I loved going dancing with Vicki. She was so hot on the dance floor, which was why she probably was raking in the loot as a stripper.

"Sure. Let's go down to Boingo's. Drink some pints and sweat on the dance floor."

"I'll need to go home to change first," I said. "I came here from work."

"Of course. Be back in two hours," she commanded. "Here, take one for the road."

She tossed me a joint as I left her apartment.

As I walked along the street, I was excited about the idea of going out. I liked seeing people, especially at night, in their skimpy little outfits. I liked to watch the mating rituals, how women preen and men steal glances. How each hopes the other is receptive, not misinterpreting them . . . how each hopes to meet a soul mate, a connection that could last a few hours, a few years.

By the time I made it home, I was tired. It had been

a long day, and I realized I was starving. After a while of poking around in the kitchen, I managed to cobble together a meal of cheese and crackers with a bowl of chips. I took my meal to the living room and planted myself on the couch to scarf it down while wondering what to wear. Idly, I flicked the channels until I landed on the news.

"Wow." It was indescribable, the images being played from one of the war-torn countries. I had missed the intro, but it didn't really matter. What mattered was the anguished look on people's faces as they ran through mayhem to find sanctuary. Bombs scattered dirt clouds so high that they disappeared into the sky. Blood was evident on clothes and flesh as these poor people scurried for shelter. I looked over at her.

"It's terrible, how people can hate so much."

As I stared at the TV, something else seemed not quite right. I put down what was left of my dinner and went over to the skeleton.

"Sliding away on me, aren't you?" I pulled her up very gently. Over the years I had managed to pull off her arms and had to rewire her. It was a pain in the ass and I didn't want to break her again.

I propped her back up so she could see the TV better. If she could see. I'm not sure, since she had no eyes. But I think they see somehow with other senses. If they have senses. They have no nerves, so maybe they don't have senses. At any rate, it doesn't really matter. It makes me feel better for her to be able to see the TV, and that's all that counts when all is said and done.

In the end, I wore a black leather miniskirt and a

black T-shirt with a plunging neckline. It would be a cold day in hell before Vicki went out without her assets showing, so I had to play the part. When I first met Vicki, I was still wearing country-girl clothes. Rock-and-roll T-shirts and jeans and the odd knee-length jean skirt. It didn't take long to discover what a mistake that was. As is my custom, I quickly learned to adapt.

The night was spent in a haze of rye-and-gingers, cigarettes and thrashing bodies. At the club, we danced until the lights came on. By the time we stumbled back to Vicki's place for an after-hours—or should I say good-morning—cocktail, we had acquired a nice young man named Brad.

The first moment I noticed Brad, Vicki and I were gyrating on the dance floor, and he was leering at us. I liked the way his eyes glittered like a predatory animal's in the flashing lights.

We sat on the couch, drinking beer and passing a joint around. Candles flickered before us even though the early morning sun cast a reddish hue around the room.

"I can't believe it's morning already." Vicki sighed.

"No, me neither."

"Anyone have to work today?" Brad asked.

"I have the dinner shift, but that's not for, well, shit, eleven hours or so . . ." I said. Part of me was begging to lie down but the other part was curious.

They say curiosity killed the cat, but I disagree. This kitten is alive and purring.

Brad sat between Vicki and me and had started to give us power-tokes by holding the joint with the lit side in his mouth and blowing it into ours. At some point, he spit it into the ashtray and we were all kissing one another.

For the next few hours, we explored one another inside and out. It was the most fun I've had in years, if ever.

There was no time for more then half hour of lying in a semidaze, and then it was time to shower and get to work.

Imagine my surprise when Mr. Johnny Depp Look-Alike himself came waltzing in a couple of hours into my shift. He made a point to sit in my section as well, I could see. I wondered what it was that had so captivated his interest over there the other day. He barely acknowledged me as I went over to take his order.

"Coffee, please," he said.

"Sure." I smiled as I walked away. I wondered if he had had as rough a night as I had. My legs were so shaky I thought I was going to collapse in a heap of quivering nerves from lack of sleep, too much sex and now this. . . . I went over to the coffee station to prepare his order. I put one of the Ooolala stir sticks in and chuckled.

He eyed the coffee and the saucer of creamers and sugars.

"Trying to kill me again, are you?" he said, picking the stir stick out of the coffee cup with long, slender fingers. He reminded me of some sort of bird. Maybe a heron or a crane. I chuckled. Ichabod Crane from *Sleepy Hollow*.

"No. I'd chop your head off first." I scurried away and returned with a menu. He waved it away.

"I'm not eating." He looked up at me. His eyes were

black pits of coal, warm yet uninviting. He looked down at his coffee and then quickly glanced up at me again. "I hope that's OK. I'm just not very hungry right now."

"Whatever floats your boat."

He sat there for about an hour, drinking four cups of coffee, playing with a pack of matches and staring at the walls. Though I didn't think he was staring at the walls at all. I think he was dreaming beyond the walls, pondering some puzzlement I'd never know. He paid his bill and left me five bucks tip. No smart-ass comment this time.

When I was cleaning up the table, I saw he left a book of matches behind. They were from Boingo's. The idea of it sent a chill down my spine. I opened them up, hoping he had scratched his phone number on there. No such luck. They were just an empty remnant from his pocket, along with some gum wrappers and a couple of Life Savers with debris stuck to them.

The rest of the night dragged, or maybe it was just me. There was a steady pace of people, but it was never crowded. The thought of the matchbook was playing on my mind. And still, this very minute, it haunts me. Had he seen me there the past night with Vicki and Brad? And if he did, was he jealous? Why had he come in tonight?

She has no answers for me. She thinks I'm reading too much into it. He just liked the ambience, the thongs, or maybe he was a restaurant critic or travel writer. Maybe he liked me. Who knows? I have to agree that it could be anything, so there's no point in losing any sleep over it. And sleep sounds really good right about now.

CHAPTER TWO

Friday, August 12

I had a bunch of weird dreams, but that's pretty typical for me. Dreams don't really mean much in the scheme of things, but when you are stuck in the middle of them, it can be a really big drag. Especially when you're stuck in a dream you don't want to be in.

I mean, really. I could have had some nice, fun, sexy dreams like other people seem to have, but no, I have to have crappy, scary dreams. Even dreams that start off like they might be some kind of fun turn out to be a big drag by the end. Worse is that I can't seem to wake up when the going gets rough.

I dreamt about this dog. I don't know if I ever knew this dog in real life; however, I've always known this dog in my dream. He or she's there all the time. Sniffing around in the corners, following me from a distance, barking at the moon. I don't know what his deal is, but he's always there.

Often, I feel the dog before I see his golden fur. Not

really feel, but sense. It's like once I slip into the dream world, all my senses are heightened. I feel and smell things like I don't in real life. There's another sense that is awakened in my dreams. It's hard to describe, but I guess it's like some sort of psychic energy. I know things without knowing them, but not only do I know them, I know what will happen. But what is going to happen often changes just by me being aware it's going to happen. Then there's a slant, like a sideways floor in a fun house, and my fears start to be reflected in the chain of events.

With my heightened senses, I become more instinctive then logical. I go into a hunter mode, where I'm waiting and watching and ravenously hungry. It's not my stomach that's hungry, but all of me. My blood crawls, my brain aches, my teeth yearn to tear and rip. But I'm also usually paralyzed with terror. As if I can't quite fulfill the hunger that drives me.

There are places that I go in my dreams that are as real and familiar as everyday places. I fall asleep and there's that house on that street again. Will I go into it this time? Will I fall through the attic floor? Will dead babies come crawling after me?

The house changes in location and structure. But that house still harbors something that lurks in boxes and ceiling boards. The dog pants in the corner somewhere.

Whenever I enter a new room, there is shuffling and rustling, as if something is trying to escape from my presence.

The floorboards sag beneath my weight, popping as I walk quickly along them. This house has no firm foundation. This house is a soggy, rotten structure filled with nightmares, ready to crumble.

I make my way around and through rooms, plugging my nose against foul odors that cling heavily to the air. Behind the walls, the dog pants and whimpers. It doesn't matter where I go; the dog is there.

I crawl along exposed attic beams, hoping that if I can just shimmy across, then I will lose the animal.

I jump down to the next level and run, more boards falling away beneath my feet. All I want at this point is to get out of the house.

It doesn't matter which way I turn, which way I run; the house has endless rooms.

Rooms with beds and ornate dressers. Rooms piled high with newspapers and other clutter. A pile of skulls. Meaty carcasses hang from hooks from the ceiling in one room and I have to run through them and beyond them.

At last, I find a window and without even seeing where it goes, I jump.

I land in a Dumpster full of rotting meat. Flies buzz around in thick clumps, disturbed by my sudden arrival. I scramble out, screaming, and as I leap to the ground, I find myself face-to-face with the dog.

At least I think it's a dog. It might be a wolf. In that murky dream way, the dog ripples and doesn't quite take form.

Yellow eyes glow at me, the only static image on the beast. It snarls and slobbers as I crouch down, my hands over my head, to protect myself from an attack.

Quick as a blink, I flip from ducking a dog to walking through a damp, foggy meadow. The day itself is bright enough, but the fog is thick as moisture from the grass, hanging heavy in the air.

Clawing my way through the fog, I'm grateful only that the ground isn't snapping and shifting beneath my feet. At least, not like the house was.

I walk until I come to the edge of the earth. Below me, through the dense fog, lie the rolling swells of the ocean.

As I stare at the waves, the sounds of the ocean reach my ears. Distant growlings and rumblings are gone.

I wandered from my reveries into the living room. Monica sat there. I fixed her hand where it had fallen from her lap. For a moment I flashed on her hand with warm flesh wrapped around the bones that I straightened.

Monica alive and breathing. I laughed.

I checked my e-mail, read through all the horoscope columns I subscribe to and chuckled. They were all so different and it amused me. However, no matter how the authors worded it, today was going to bear an element of surprise for me. It was just a crapshoot how I would deal with it.

I clicked through some porn ads and looked at miniclips of people having sex. It aroused me in one way. The idea of people fucking their brains out with all those people in the room watching them was a turn-on. But the act itself was so boring. Even looking at interracial or gay sex was so ho-hum these days. I knew clicking over to weird insertions or even the S/M sites would show posed people doing the same old thing. Sometimes I wished that there were new ways to experience pleasure. The yearning that had snuck up on me in the past few years reminded me of that movie *Hellraiser*. Poor Uncle Frank was searching for the ultimate pleasure. And look what he got for his trouble: a trip to hell.

Surely looking for pleasure wasn't a one-way ticket to hell? If we weren't meant to find pleasure, why would God put it in us to want more and more? And why would he punish us because we dared to find more?

I didn't think that even if there were a God, he would get too upset with the idea of people searching for the ultimate pleasure. Sure, people point to Adam and Eve and the apple to show that pleasure is a sin. But didn't God create the apple and the idea of choice? And wouldn't he cut us some slack after a few thousand years to see what we would come up with next? After all, he ultimately created us for his amusement, didn't he? Or she? Or it?

Later that day, I went to work and hoped that Mr. Johnny Depp Look-Alike would show up. He never did. I didn't relish the idea of going home to watch TV with Monica, so I went over to Vicki's house.

She was lying on the couch, smoking a joint when I walked in.

"You shouldn't let just anyone in," I scolded her as I came through the door. "You didn't even ask who it was? You just heard a knock and said, 'Come in.'"

"So what? The only people that come over are those that want to fuck me. And I'm horny, so who cares?"

She held the joint out to me. I took it and sucked on it.

"You're always horny," I said.

"You come over to fuck me?" she asked, opening her gown a bit so that I could see part of her right breast.

I grinned.

"Sort of. I thought maybe we should give Braddy-boy a call."

"Why the hell not?" Vicki said and reached for her cell phone, which was cradled between her legs in the flaps of her long silk robe.

Brad wasn't doing anything, either, so he came over. We all knew what we wanted and didn't waste any time with boring old chitchat. We started to kiss and cuddle. Vicki's housecoat slipped right off.

One thing about the three of us: we were like a well-oiled machine. We worked in constant unison, mouths and hands expertly touching and stroking. I guess that's one of the good things about really enjoying pleasure. You just focus on the moment and forget about everything else.

I remember a time when I couldn't focus on pleasure. When sex seemed just plain wrong, and even at times nasty. Nasty because it seemed to me that sex was a power game. It isn't news to anyone who's thought about sex for very long. Sure, there is loving sex, pleasure sex, urgent sex and power sex. I was in such a bad place in my life that I thought all sex was about power. And power was something that I didn't want to lose. So I kept it to myself, all rolled up in a tight, festering ball.

I remember the first time I realized that I didn't have to be thinking a million thoughts during sex. I gave myself permission to just hang out in the moment, to really feel HER tongue lapping my most sensitive areas. That flesh upon flesh was warm and wet and that warm and wet was a very good feeling indeed.

SHE was good for me in that sense. How could you ever leave a lover who teaches you pure pleasure for pleasure's sake?

Yet life is funny. I've seen it happen before with other people. It's life itself that gets in the way. All that crappy life stuff. When you live in Buttfuck, Nowhere, it's easy to have crappy life stuff rain on your parade.

She made my body sing. I ached for her when she wasn't around; I smelled her on my clothes when I went about my day. I throbbed for her, heated for the moment I would see her beautiful face again.

A face filled with lies.

Her tongue was so wonderful when it was a toy, an instrument of pleasure. Yet that same tongue cut me like a knife.

And so a perfect lover once more falls by the wayside. I'm not the first person to experience betrayal, nor will I be the last one. My story is everyone's story. Yet the pain always feels fresh.

I turned myself over to the moment with Vicki and Brad. I would never let myself love either one of them. Their talents lay within the writing forms of their flesh. Why complicate one with the other?

People who love aren't people who give pleasure. Those that love pleasure are like vampires: giving and taking vital life energy with a joie de vivre that belies any chance of being a decent human being in any other aspect.

Brad was one handsome man, though, and he could last for an hour or more. Vicki and I never had to worry about being left behind; there was enough for everyone.

Brad was thrusting into Vicki doggy-style while I suckled on her large, pendulous breasts. He stopped and stood up.

Vicki turned around.

"What's wrong?" she asked.

"Nothing. Nothing at all." Brad smiled. He leaned over to the floor and picked up Vicki's bathrobe belt. He waved it in the air.

"I was thinking of spicing things up a bit." He smiled as he hog-tied Vicki. She squealed and I watched as he positioned her so that her butt was naked in the air, while her hands and feet were tied to each other. He smacked her a couple of times with his hand on the quivering cheeks of her butt.

"Now what do you think?"

"I-I . . ."

Brad grabbed his underwear and stuffed them in her mouth.

"Shut up, bitch," he said. I watched as he looked at the round globes of her ass. He played with himself to a size that I had never seen before. He impaled her repeatedly as she moaned and cried. A twinge of jealousy surged through me, as I had no access to touch her at all now. Brad didn't last long and collapsed in exhaustion.

I untied Vicki. Her eyes were glazed with pleasure.

"Wow, that was amazing," she said. "So forceful."

"It was great."

"What did it look like, Abby?" Vicki asked as she rubbed her wrists and ankles.

"It looked hot," I said as I reached for my cigarettes. I lit one and exhaled. I didn't know why I suddenly felt uneasy. I had come my brains out about fifteen times between the two of them. Yet I suddenly felt like I was left out of the loop. Like they had experienced a pleasure that I wasn't part of.

"Next time I'll tie you both up and work from one to the other," Brad said as he lit up a joint.

"Yeah," I said, not sure if I believed him.

Later on, Vicki proposed an idea.

The three of us should live together.

And for some strange reason, we all agreed.

I won't get rid of my apartment. They don't have to know that. I'll just bring over a few things and play house until we get sick of each other.

Wouldn't it be cool if we actually could all get along? Imagine how low rent would be?

But I don't see it. I really don't.

Monday, August 15

At work, I sat with the drag queens, Mavis and Storm. They were between sets and I bought them drinks. I had a break myself.

"Do you have weird sex?" I asked them. They laughed at me with typical haughtiness. I almost regretted asking, but if I didn't ask, I wouldn't find out.

"What do you mean by weird sex, honey?" Mavis asked.

"Like, group sex. Sex with your own sex. Any of that sort of thing?"

"Group sex, yes, I've tried it a couple of times," Mavis said.

"Not me. I'm strictly girl-on-girl," Storm replied, taking a dainty sip of wine.

I leaned forward. "But really, Storm, you have a penis. So it's guy-on-girl, right?"

"Well, if you put it that way, I guess you can say that. But dildos are a wonderful thing too."

"I guess. But they aren't the real thing. They don't have the same power."

"Power?" Mavis laughed. "I don't call that thing between my legs power when I'm dressed like this. It's a burden."

"No. It's not. You have the power to penetrate."

"So do you. Fingers, tongue . . ."

"It's not the same and you know it."

"Sounds like someone is having a bit of penis envy to me," Mavis said.

"Maybe I am. So what girl hasn't?"

They looked at each other and shrugged.

"I don't know."

"Do you think you can have sex with someone and not feel anything at all?" I asked them.

"Why, sure, honey, those are the times where we yawn and ask, 'Is it over yet?'"

"What about sex that is really great? Can you feel nothing for the person?"

"What do you think one-night stands are?"

"But that's just one night of meaningless sex. What about time after time?"

"That's why people have affairs. They want the sexual thrill, but they don't want to deal with the person as a person."

"Do you think? I thought people had affairs to get something. Like money or holding some kind of power over another person. The thrill of the game of getting caught."

"And there are affairs where no one is attached. Where it just goes on and on and you realize one day that you really are just fuck buddies. For some reason, affairs of that sort often get ruined by one party or the other wanting to have some sort of commitment. Too bad."

"What about a threesome, though? Can you love one person and hate the other one?"

"I can imagine that, sure. Why not?"

"Humans are a complicated breed. Maybe the person that hates the other person wants something. Maybe the person they hate actually has nothing to do with what they want. They are just in the way."

"I've never seen the attraction of polygamous relationships. They just seem so complicated. As if relationships aren't complicated enough."

"I suppose." They didn't tell me anything that I hadn't already puzzled through on my own. But their answers reassured me on some level. It is obvious to me that Brad is in the way. I'm not sure yet what it is that I want with Vicki, but Brad is in the way.

I'd better get packing. The sooner I haul some stuff over there, the sooner I can figure out what is going on.

Tuesday, August 30

It has been a long time since I've recorded my thoughts. Looking back on my past entry, I can see that it's been nearly two weeks. Life has been busy.

I moved some clothes and a few boxes of personal stuff over to Vicki's. So far, things are going pretty well. We are all pretty busy with our jobs, so sometimes a day or two will go by before everyone is together and ready to play. I think there is some unspoken rule about no one playing without everyone present, because when I'm alone with either Vicki or Brad, we don't do anything.

The sex continues to be fantastic. We've been playing more with bondage ideas. Brad tied us both up one night as he had promised, and it truly was mind-blowing to be so helpless while he worked his magic on me. Sharing the experience with Vicki made it even more special.

One night, Vicki and I tied up Brad spread-eagled and dripped hot wax all over him. He was sore for a while, but he's back in action again.

In the meantime, I saw Mr. Johnny Depp Look-Alike again. He came into my section and sat at the same table. He sat staring at the paraphernalia and looked sad. I wanted to say something to him, but I didn't know what. I brought him several cups of coffee while he scribbled some sort of notes into a notebook. I wondered if he was a writer, a restaurant critic or just keeping a diary. He could have been making a shopping list for all I know.

I followed him home again, watching the sway of his hips in front of me. He wore tight jeans that showed off his ass. He also had on a leather jacket. There was a bit of a bite in the air that day. The weather is so changeable. One minute it is so hot you want to throw on a pair of shorts; the next you are freezing to death.

I felt nippy in my thin coat. I stood outside his building, having a cigarette. I wondered which apartment was his.

Imagine my surprise when he came back out again. He had changed into leather pants and his hair was combed back as if he had thrown his head under the sink for a few minutes. He had a slight grin on his face and he walked with a swagger. My stomach clenched. He had a date.

I followed him a few blocks until he turned into a bar. I continued walking to my own apartment since it was only a couple of blocks away.

He had gone to a nightclub.

I quickly changed into nightclub gear. I didn't think for a minute of going to Vicki's house or even telling them that I was going out. In fact, for a while, as I hopped into the shower, I forgot I even lived at Vicki's house. It was a very quick shower; there was no time for dreaming. I told Monica how I saw Johnny Depp Look-Alike go into a nightclub. My heart was pounding as I pulled on my nylons. I was going to track that man down. I was going to finally talk to him.

I hurried back to the nightclub and paid the hefty cover. Of course, cover is hefty wherever you go in this city. I don't know what we're paying for, since drinks are even more once you get inside.

I grabbed a double rye-and-coke and sucked it back quickly. I ordered another one and set to work walking around the first dance floor area. It was on the third floor, in the old rock-and-roll area, that I found him. He was leaning against a bar, talking to a blond girl.

I stood observing them for a very long time. The

way she tossed her hair and touched him when she laughed spoke of intimacy. I wondered if they had fucked yet.

A slow song came on, some long-winded rock ballad from the seventies, and they hit the dance floor. They held each other closely as lovers do. Mr. Johnny Depp Look-Alike's eyes were open, staring with that sad haunted look as he held her close. I wondered if she was the cause of his misery. Or if he was just one of those gentle creatures that is haunted by sadness no matter what is going on.

No matter what it was, I thought she was one damn lucky woman to be holding him so close. I wondered how his body would feel pressed against mine. Would I feel his warmth through his clothes? Would he press his pelvis against mine in a suggestion of what could happen?

After they danced, she went to the ladies' room. I followed her in. As we stood in line to use the stalls, I looked her over. She wore a tight black dress. Her figure was tiny and shapely. Her hair was teased a bit too much, almost like eighties hair. She had on pancake makeup that was a little too thick. It was running a bit as sweat trickled down the side of her face. I wondered if she was horny. I resisted the urge to tell her to blot her face. She asked the woman on the other side of her for the time. Her voice was high and I realized it was one of those annoying Jennifer Tilly voices. How could he stand to listen to that for very long? I guess that's where the power of being a man could come in very handy. When she starts nattering on, just grab her by the hair and plant her face between your hips. I couldn't see any other reason that a man could stand to listen to that except for knowing that he could shut her up and enjoy it twice as much.

I didn't pee when I went into my stall. I just pretended to blow my nose and came out quickly. She reemerged in a few minutes and studied herself in the mirror. She spotted the sweat streaks and set to work refinishing the pavement. Many minutes later, layers were reformed and retooled and a fine coat of powder was dabbed to set it. I had to admire her handiwork. I could never take so much time troweling my face. I always wondered about women who used so much makeup. What did their men think when they saw them without it in the morning? Did the woman look totally different or was there some semblance of the makeup queen there? Did this girl have some horrible scar or acne holes that made her cover herself so much, I wondered.

I looked at my own face in the mirror and compared it to hers. I think I was younger. Maybe that was why she piled on the makeup. Maybe she was trying to hide her age.

I had on a bit of eye makeup and some lipstick. No rouge. Nothing else. There were bags under my eyes, but that was because I had been spending my nights having sex instead of sleeping. As far as I was concerned, a few bags were worth all the pleasure.

I realized she was talking to me.

"Do I look OK?" she asked.

I nodded.

"Good. Because I thought there was something wrong because you were staring at me." She snapped shut her powder case and slid it into her purse.

"I'm sorry. You just look like . . . someone I used to know." I lied.

"Oh?"

"My cousin Brenda. She looked a lot like you. She died horribly in a tractor accident. She was driving and . . ."

"That's quite OK. I don't need to hear the gory details." The woman stood up and smoothed down her clothes. She checked her hem in the mirror and clicked away on stilettos. I watched her go. She was not the type of girl he should be dating. She would just use him and throw him away. A sensitive man like him deserved a woman of quality. Someone who could understand his morbid thoughts. Someone who saw life just as dismally and darkly.

For the rest of the night, I watched them flirt and dance and drink many martinis. Once in a while, I'd lose myself in the dance floor, catching glimpses of them out of the corner of my eye. How she laughed in his arms as he stared at her with dark, foreboding eyes. His intensity and sadness washed across the dance floor in waves, hugging me in comforting caresses.

I knew he wasn't the one for her. She was captivating in a way you watch an annoying commercial endlessly because it's familiar. She was familiar.

It dawned on me why she grated under my skin so. She reminded me of someone I used to know. A girl who was in my third grade class. That girl followed me throughout grade school and well into high school before she finally disappeared.

Kimberly Evans was her name. How precious. Kimberly with her curly blond hair that hung in loose ringlets down her back. Little Kimberly Evans, whose bright blue eyes were easy to fill with tears. She was such a little suck, that Kimberly. You could do almost anything to her and she would burst into tears. Untie her sash, bend her book, pull one of those ringlets. She was a sitting duck.

Normally I wouldn't have bothered with a girl like her. But she was always in the way. On the first day of school, she sought me out and, like a duckling imprinting on the first thing it sees, she stuck to me ever since.

Sure, I was nice to her at first. But as I realized what a suck she was, I grew to resent seeing her. I took different routes to school to try to avoid her. But there she was, at least three times a week, waiting for me with that stupid grin on her face.

Now here was the image of that girl, all grown up in front of me. I went outside to have a cigarette. As I smoked, I watched people come and go from the club. So many were couples, giddy with laughter or sullen from a fight. The sight of so many couples sickened me. It didn't seem right, how so many people had found each other and here I was alone.

I sucked on my smoke and thought about it all. I wasn't alone. I had my friends, and they kept me amused with their strange and wondrous games. I was living a life most people only dreamed about, and I should revel in it. Yet there was still something inside of me that ached. A void that never seemed to be filled.

I threw down my cigarette half-smoked and returned to the club to see what the lovebirds were doing now. At first I thought I had lost them, but then I spotted them through the crowd, sitting at a table. He had loosened up a bit, and a grin even flashed across his face now and again. I hoped it was one of those grins that guys give you when they aren't really listening at all, but are just trying to figure out how to get into your pants. The thought of them wrapped around each other in naked bliss turned my stomach and I had just about enough of the whole scene.

I decided to return to my own love nest and wandered down the dark and dreary streets until I returned to my second home.

They were watching TV when I came in. They looked at me, half-stoned from whatever it was they had been smoking.

"Hey, you're home, Abby," Vicki slurred, reaching her hand out towards me.

"I certainly am." I planted a big juicy kiss on her lips. I went over to him and did the same.

"So what's going on?" I asked. I turned my gaze to the television set. There was a light bondage porn film playing.

"We're trying to get some pointers." He grinned.

"Pointers? I thought you two were the masters."

"You can never learn too much."

I watched as the man tied up the woman. She struggled against his firm grip, yet her face showed she was loving every minute of it.

"It's such make-believe," I said, sitting down. "Why don't we play instead of watching other people play?"

"I'm kind of tired," she said. "I just want to relax tonight. It's late, Abby."

I looked at the clock. It was two thirty in the morning. I had spent far too long at the club. I realized that there was no way I was going to entice these two into any sort of scene, so I cut my losses and went to bed.

In the darkness of the night, I wished that I had just gone home. If I was going to lie alone in bed, with my thoughts racing, I wanted to be around my own belongings.

They never did come to bed that night, and in the bright light of day, they were still in their same spots on separate couches.

I woke many times during the night, hoping to feel the warmth of flesh sliding in next to me. I didn't much care about making love; I just wanted to savor the heat of another human next to me and plot how to entice Mr. Johnny D. Instead, I had to plot alone. Maybe the next time I saw him I would be bolder. After seeing what he had trapped himself with, I knew I had to be daring and clever. It would be hard to untangle those octopus arms from him, but I was up to the challenge.

When Brad and Vicki woke in the morning, I had coffee made and was reading the paper at the dining table. Vicki woke first, yawning as she creaked and cracked her bones.

"Wow, I must have been tired. Falling asleep on the couch . . . no wonder I feel like a truck hit me."

"I guess you guys must have been partying pretty hard," I said, looking at the joints and cigarettes in the ashtray.

"Yeah, we were having a smokeathon. You shoulda been here. Where were you anyway?"

"Oh, I just went dancing, that's all."

"Without me?" Vicki pouted.

"I figured you could use a break. You dance all day long."

Our chatter must have disturbed Brad, for he stretched and blinked his eyes sleepily. There was something kind of cute and helpless about a guy waking up.

"Hey, Abby." Brad smiled. "You missed quite a party."

He stood up and stretched more, and I could see a partial erection through his silky boxers.

As he went to the bathroom, I turned to Vicki.

"So did you guys . . . ?" I asked. Vicki reached for her cigarettes and flushed slightly. My heart sank.

"No . . . no, not at all," she said. She looked me in the eye and dropped her gaze.

"Ok . . . so we did. . . . We fooled around a little. Nothing kinky."

"I thought that we weren't supposed to. . . ."

"I know. Even while we were doing it, we were going to stop and wait for you. But we figured, hey, we've done it together before, what's the difference?"

I didn't say anything as my heart pounded rapidly.

"Would you rather it was just you two?" I finally said. Vicki looked shocked.

"Oh, no. Not at all. I don't want him for myself."

Brad emerged from the bathroom. He looked at our faces.

"What?" he asked.

"Nothing . . ." I said.

"I told her about last night, that's all." Vicki sighed.

"Is there a problem?" Brad asked. "You know I want you too, Abby. You weren't here and the pot was good. . . ."

"I know. It's OK." I went into the kitchen to get another cup of coffee. Brad followed me in and wrapped his arms around me. He rubbed himself against me and for a moment I almost fell into his spell.

"It's OK. Really," I said, breaking away from him. I turned to face him and in that instant, I realized that I didn't like him very much. In fact, I didn't like him at all. He took my Vicki from me and it pissed me off.

I took my coffee into the bathroom, where I took a shower. I left the door open, and as I suspected, soon I was joined by Vicki and Brad. The three of us kissed under the running water. As my soapy hands fondled Vicki's breasts, I felt placated for the moment. They took care of me, their tongues and fingers removing the worries of Mr. J.D. and his rancid girlfriend from my mind. The solace that I had been seeking had come to me at last.

Feeling much more energized, I was able to get to work on time and have an OK shift. My two drag queen friends were hanging around a lot that day between shows, which always makes the time pass more quickly.

After my shift was over, I decided that I wasn't going over to the apartment. I wanted to be alone with my thoughts. With my things.

I went into my apartment and looked around it. How I had missed my possessions. I sat on my couch and lit a candle. As I watched the flame flicker, I felt her watching me.

"Monica, you need to get a life." I laughed. I lit a cigarette and stared into the dimly lit room. A thousand thoughts and memories flitted through my mind and I had a weird dream.

In the dream, I was walking through a forest. It was spring and there were snatches of flowers growing here and there in pockets of pine needles. Beneath my feet was a mixture of dirt and dead leaves. As I walked, I was acutely aware that I was younger. My mind was naive, like that of a child. A squirrel ran around in the bushes and the rustling sound annoyed me. Here and there, I heard creatures scattering as I walked. Every time something moved, I would hear a rustling, and it startled me. There seemed to be a lot of creatures running loose today.

It dawned on me that there might be no squirrels or raccoons. Maybe something was following me.

The idea took hold and wouldn't let go. As the rustling sounds increased, so did my paranoia. I started walking faster as images of wolves and bears popped into my head.

What big eyes you have.

The better to see you.

I scurried along. I didn't even try to look for the rustling noises behind me.

What big teeth you have.

The better to eat you.

I ran, and as I ran, the rustling grew louder. There was definitely something following me.

I tripped and fell, and cried out. My hands covered my head. But there was nothing but silence.

As I pulled myself together, I looked at what I had tripped over.

It was the half-decomposed remains of a young girl. I screamed as I recognized the face as my own.

I woke with a start on my couch. The candle had burned down into a pool of melted wax, the flame dim as it flickered weakly.

My nerves were shot. I clicked around the channels until I saw a music station playing Jay-Z and Linkin Park's Collision Course concert. I jumped around for a while to wake up and sang along. At last I had shaken the clutches of the dream enough to get my head straight. I made sure all the candles were out, and I splashed some water on my face. That made my eyeliner run, and my eyes stung, so I had to do some emergency repair.

At last I had my act together and had decided to go back to see Brad and Vicki after all.

It was only around nine when I reemerged into the bustle of the city. Since the weather was nice, people walked briskly to the places that people go on a pleasant evening. I took my time, trying to push the images in the dream from my mind.

My eyes kept glancing at the bellies of the girls wearing low-slung jeans and tube skirts. This seemed to be a trend that would never die. Sometimes I yearned for the days of girdles and corsets. Some people were never meant to walk around with their bellies hanging out, and others should be arrested for looking so delicious.

In front of me was a strange-looking man, or maybe it was a woman walking a small dog. The person had long, bleached blond hair, and the shirt being worn exposed the back and covered most of the front. The back looked decidedly masculine, but the person wore big Hollywood sunglasses so it was hard to tell. I followed the person for a while, sometimes racing ahead to try to decipher the sex. The person suddenly broke into a smile and embraced someone on the street. The man blushed and stepped back. I saw it was one of the drag queens, Mavis, from my work. I scurried by before he spotted me. It was too late. Mr. Emimen Clone with his do-rag and red tracksuit waved at me and called my name.

I turned back to look at him. Next thing I knew, I was being dragged along to a gay bar, where we had several drinks. It was fun hanging out with Mavis and Steve. The owner of the bar happened to love dogs and took little Angeline to the back to play with his Chihuahua, Lala. Steve was a drag queen as well, big surprise. They talked about gigs and wigs while I perused the eye candy. The place was packed though it was Sunday, and many shirtless hunks in leather pants cruised back and forth. Mavis was a hit in her workout gear. Her androgynous face had just the right angular shape that you had to do a double take. Her blue eyes had the faintest touch of black mascara; bits of short blond hair peaked out from her do-rag.

Mavis had jogged about four miles since getting off work. I sighed and sipped on my drink, thinking of all I had done since getting off work. Nothing. Absolutely nothing.

Eventually I figured that Mavis and Steve wanted to be alone. Angeline was returned at some point and needed to be walked. I excused myself and returned out into the warm night.

Ahead of me, a girl walked briskly, her ass tightly

swaying with every *clip-clop* of her heels. She wore a tiny pink crop top that was mostly covered by a mane of blond ringlets. I wondered if she had a belly ring and quickened my pace to get in front of her. A glint in the streetlight told me my suspicions were correct. Her breasts were large and very smooth, as if she was wearing one of those padded water bras. They bobbed as she walked, but they didn't fascinate me as much as her belly ring did. I stopped in my tracks as I saw the shape. Large pointed teeth glinted with rhinestones.

A sense of déjà vu washed over me.

Someone else had a wolf's-head belly ring.

The thought sent a shiver through me.

The better to eat you with, my dear.

The blonde disappeared into the night. I looked up at the street signs and realized I had gone too far. I doubled back and found the right street.

I could smell incense and pot smoke as I walked down the hall. I wasn't too surprised to see Vicki sitting on Brad's lap while he blew pot smoke into her mouth. They looked over at me with half smiles.

"We've been waiting for you," Vicki said as she slid from Brad's lap. I stared at her; she was wearing one of her stripper costumes. She hardly ever did that around the house. Her large breasts were practically bursting from her tiny PVC bra. She had on a fringe skirt and mile-high white stilettos.

She wrapped her arms around me and blew the smoke from her mouth into mine.

I inhaled both the smoke and her bright ruby lips.

"Am I interrupting?" I asked, noting that Brad wore

only his briefs. He was bulging from where Vicki had been sitting on him.

"No." Brad stroked his crotch. "We were waiting for you, as Vicki said. We were hoping you'd be home tonight. It is Sunday."

"Sunday is a day of rest," I said, putting down my purse.

"Exactly. And we want to rest with you."

Vicki led me over to Brad's lap. Brad and I shared a joint while Vicki removed my sneakers and socks. As she licked my toes, I was glad I had showered earlier.

"Vicki wants us to dominate her tonight." Brad winked. I looked down at her and she stared back up at me with puppy-dog eyes.

"Keep licking," I said as I nodded to Brad. "Well, you'd better prepare the equipment while I get dressed."

I pushed Vicki away with my foot and went into the bedroom. A wave of dizziness swelled through me and I thought I was going to pass out for a moment. I had probably stood up too fast. I sat down on the bed and stared at myself in the dresser mirror. I looked pale.

I pushed at my hair as memories of my nightmare flashed through my mind. I didn't want any more bad dreams. I wanted life to be peaceful now. I wanted to start fresh in the city, far from Buttfuck, Nowhere, and all the annoying people there. Here in the city, I could lose myself. I could be free from watchful gazes and live my life in whatever manner of decadence I chose. Freedom to be whomever I wanted called to me, and as I stared at my image, I saw a geeky girl with glasses who yearned to one of the cool kids at school.

What would the cool kids think of me now?

I chuckled as I thought of cheerleaders and football stars long past their glory. Too young to be has-beens, too old to recapture past glamour.

I'm sure many of them were out of college, if they ever got there, and were now living the life of the mundane, with spouses and kids and minivans. At least I was tasting what life had to offer before I settled down. There was so much to do and see. So many people to do and see that I couldn't imagine being with just one.

Except for that one.

I'm not going to think about such things; I'll just say that I stripped off my clothes and found a saucy leather halter top and a matching miniskirt. I pulled my dildo from my underwear drawer and went into the living room. Brad had already set to work tying Vicki to a chair. He had put a ball bag in her mouth and was now tying her arms and legs. Her pussy lips were stretched past the thin strap of her G-string.

I waved the dildo at her. "I'm going to be doing you good tonight, young lady."

The fun and games went on for hours. We teased and tormented poor Vicki, flogging her arms and legs, tickling her until she nearly choked on her spit. I made good use of the dildo and watched as she tried not to beg for more. Brad wrapped rope around each of her tits so that they stood out even more, engorged so full of blood that her nipples were practically purple. They were the best part of the night and both Brad and I took full advantage of their suppleness.

As I pleasured Vicki, I couldn't help but notice a certain look in Brad's eye. Even though I didn't have my glasses on, I felt certain that he was hinging his every movement on a private dance with Vicki. The idea of them having a blossoming romance behind my back was upsetting, but I feigned ignorance as I continued to worship Miss Vicki with my tongue.

At long last, Vicki was released from her bondage and collapsed in a happy but spent lump onto the couch. When I tried to cuddle next to her, she said she needed room to stretch out, that her limbs were sore. Even my offer of massage didn't meet with any sort of warmth. I slunk over to the easy chair and watched as Brad sat down, his erection still protruding.

"So Brad," I said coyly, still warm and hungry from our play. "What do you say we finish things off. . . ."

Brad stroked himself, looking lasciviously first at Vicki and then me.

"Why don't you girls get me started up again. . . ."

Vicki groaned reluctantly while I settled myself at his feet. I set to work reviving him, but he seemed uninterested as Vicki lounged. When I looked up at his face, I saw him watching her.

"Am I doing something wrong?" I asked.

"Not at all," Brad said. He stretched out. "I am a little tired. Work tomorrow and all."

I stopped sucking, feeling as though I were suddenly the third wheel on a two wheel bike.

"Am I bothering you?" I asked, standing up.

"Of course not, honey." He drew my face close to his and kissed it. I kissed him back, reaching again for his dick. This time, he let me plant myself on him

48

while he sat on the couch. I knew he was watching Vicki; I could see his blurry image in the glass reflection of the frame. Vicki was playing with her tits as he fucked me or I fucked him. We fucked each other, bouncing on the couch. I drove thoughts of Brad and Vicki and what they were probably doing when I wasn't around from my mind. The main thing was that I was here now, with Brad's firm strokes sending pleasure jolts through my body. Who cared who was filling the void in the moment?

Things were much less tense after Brad and I had our fill of each other. Vicki was already snoring lightly and I crept away to use the shower and fall into bed.

Monday, September 5

The next few nights I made sure I came right home from work, so that I couldn't give them a chance to grow any closer.

We found harmony once more, finishing each other's sentences like a triad, anticipating each other's needs as normally as any married couple. It took my mind off my worries for a while.

I barely thought of my strange customer for quite some time.

We set to work making the apartment ours. We bought some new dishes, a cheerful yellow, and lots of fancy glassware. Since I worked in a restaurant, I was always happy to make them the latest drinks. I'd whip up some sort of frothy fruity thing and we'd settle in front of the TV. Sometimes we'd fool around; sometimes we just went to sleep since we all had jobs and you can only be bohemian for so long before it takes a toll on your body.

As we settled into routines, I forgot about my suspicions with Brad and Vicki. In little ways, it seemed as though my Vicki was coming back to me. She had started to confide in me again, and I tried like hell not to be distant.

In the meantime, I had acquired a little hobby to take my mind from my worries.

I did one hundred and fifty sit-ups every morning, sucking in my gut so hard that I thought I would suffocate or burst like a balloon with every crunch. I started to do light hand weights too, especially while I was watching TV. It suddenly seemed like a good idea to build a bit of strength. After all, I lived in the big city now, and who knew who might be around.

Every day, I added a new exercise to my routine until I was doing an hour a day, not including walks. Some of my exercises seemed weird to the others, so I tried to do them in private in another room. I'm sure they thought I was experimenting with different forms of pleasure, when in reality I was only interested in amassing strength and fortitude.

When I wasn't exercising or watching TV or having sex, I cruised the Internet and decided on a new diet. I figured food that would help me combat osteoporosis and other problems was a good way to start. It was with great resolve and regret that I cut out desserts. I cut out alcohol too for now. I knew I'd have a few drinks on a special occasion or even just on a Friday night, but while I made frothy fruit drinks for the others, I started to imbibe more water. My smoking increased a bit too, especially with the wacky weed. I guess I needed a bridge between no booze and straightness. At least toking doesn't build calories, although you have to be careful you don't get the munchies and eat everything in sight.

The goal of having clothes, a uniform, one size smaller appealed greatly to me.

When I was on the Internet looking for diets and exercise, I also looked into laser eye surgery. It still seemed so risky, so strange and daunting, yet I was drawn to the idea of never having to wear glasses again. I wouldn't have to feel the sting of remarks like Mr. Johnny Depp Look-Alike's or wonder if a guy would find me more attractive without my glasses. I wondered what it would be like to see the clock in the middle of the night or to see the face of my lover clearly.

The price of surgery is beyond me at this point, but things have a habit of changing. Especially in my business.

What I really need right now is a change. A good change. For the better.

CHAPTER THREE

Tuesday, September 13

The universe holds great balance. Science and math can try to explain some aspects, but the only other way to explain others is karma or maybe even God. Whatever you do will come back to haunt you, no question.

Whenever you believe you've put to bed some nagging thought or doubt that has been plaguing you for months or even a lifetime, you can bet it will come creeping back into your thoughts at one time or another, skittering towards the light, ready to be exposed.

I never liked the idea of Pandora's box. Of secrets unleashed to an unsuspecting world. Most of us can't fathom the ideas of the average human. To think too long or hard about a subject can lead to questions and questions often lead to answers, but sometimes there are no answers. Why is something the way it is? Why do some things bother some people but not others? How can it be that you can feel alone in a crowd, a city, a relationship?

Are we really keepers of our own demise, or can we blame fate?

Fate has to bear a hand in all this. We all know this. There have been songs written about fate, cruel fate, lucky fate, serendipity and coincidence.

I wonder if you can count serendipity and coincidence as fate. I imagine most people do. And I guess it depends on what fate means to you.

Sometimes I feel like fate is the only thing that has the script to these pathetic lives of ours. Those scripts are all locked up somewhere in the big filing cabinet in the sky. It's not for us mere humans to know or understand our own fate in order to prepare for it. Oh, sure there are religions that claim if you meditate long enough, God will open up one of those filing cabinets and let you take a peek inside.

But how can you make a life plan with only a bit of information?

It's like getting a road map with only half the streets on it. It might be just what you need or it might be totally useless and stupid.

I like to get my fate fix from listening to songs. Sometimes I think that people get hooked on a song because there's a message in it. Fate might have a hand in that. Maybe fate is saying to listen to the music. Be part of what you need to be a part of. Why else do songs suddenly pop into our head? Why do we find ourselves suddenly singing a snatch of something and then we walk into a store and hear it playing on the radio? Are we psychic? Or is someone giving us a message? Are there coincidences or are we all just chess pieces in someone else's game?

I can't pretend I'll ever keep the same opinion on the subject for more then a few minutes. I just know that the other day, I woke with a song in my head and it haunted me the whole day through.

It was there playing over the speakers when I got a coffee at the café. I caught a snatch of it blaring from a passing car. I saw the flicker of the image of the video eight times in store windows. When I got to work, it was being played in the more upbeat section of the club.

Mavis was singing along with Ludacris, telling everyone to "Get Back." It's a catchy tune from that *Red Light District* CD, but it's old, so I couldn't figure out why I kept hearing it all day long.

I wanted no one near me that day: my mood was intense.

I'm not sure what brought on the sudden darkness. Usually Ludacris songs make me smile, and that particular song had a funny video that went with it. But the sense of the song this day was that I was a PMS time bomb ready to blow.

It was fate—or maybe not fate—that brought Mr. J.D. Look-Alike sauntering into my section. I almost laughed when I saw him scurry in, clutching his paper the way a rat would hoard cheese. He seemed eccentric, not glamorous or even captivating. His movements were nervous and jerky and he wasn't as groomed as he always was. I wondered, not for the first or last time, why he would pick Ooolala to have a coffee when there were surely many cheap diners that would have given him an entire breakfast for what we charged.

Maybe he was rich and didn't care about prices. Maybe he was hoping to befriend me by constantly sitting in my section and therefore attain friend status and maybe score a free cup now and again.

Sometimes I think that I think way too much and need to give my brain a rest.

I watched him nervously twist a little piece of paper around and around his fingertips. He pulled and scrunched until my amusement in watching him wore off and I wandered over to see what he wanted.

He looked up at me and gave a little frown.

"Still no contacts?" he asked.

Unsure how to take his audacity, I blinked at him. "I don't like to wear contacts. They are painful and I don't see as clearly."

"Too bad. You have beautiful eyes. The world should be able to see them." He tapped on the table and looked around.

"I want a cup of coffee. Just a cup of coffee. I'm not hungry just yet, but I don't want to get you in trouble if you're supposed to serve food."

I realized he was giving me an out for kicking him out of my section. I chose not to take it. I wanted him here, no matter if I got into trouble. We were supposed to have guests having more then coffee in our busy times, but for now, Mr. J.D. could pull fake movie star status and still come out on top. Sometimes I fancied that it was the real deal, but little things about him told me he wasn't. Besides, the real Mr. Johnny Depp was raising a family somewhere far from the prying eyes of the likes of me. And that was fine. This wonderful fake Johnny Depp was amusing me greatly, and for the double bonus, he was single. For now.

His attention to my glasses yet again pissed me off. Actually it didn't piss me off so much as hurt. How could I help how I looked? I was born with crappy sensitive eyes and contacts hurt like hell and I was pretty much blind without my glasses. It must be nice to be handsome like him and not have to worry about looking like a square or a nerd. I wondered what it was like going through life never having to worry if you looked like a geek or a nerd or a spinster librarian all because you are cursed with glasses.

It seemed to me that someone with any dignity or common sense would realize that people wear glasses because they have to, not by choice. In fact, I bet that more famous people wear glasses than regular people, but no one ever knows it except on awards night when contacts fail and the actor has to pull out a pair of specs.

I brought Mr. J.D. his coffee and a glass of water. I put a lemon slice on the water and placed it in front of him.

"What's this?" he asked, eying the water suspiciously.

"I just wanted to do something for you. I thought maybe a glass of water would hit the spot. You seem, well, not yourself today."

He nodded and stared at the glass.

He looked up at me.

"You gonna watch me drink it too?"

I blushed and hurried away. Damn him and his smart mouth. I was always full of sarcastic comments but today just didn't seem worth the effort. There was nothing brewing in the old sarcasm pot anyway. And Mr. J.D. deserved no less then the finest of barbs.

I pretended to polish silverware while I glanced at him. He was scribbling furiously in a notepad. I wondered if he wrote lewd little stories about events that might happen in the room after closing time. Little did most people know that he would be right. Most restaurants have their torrid little affairs where the best place to get jiggy is at the ol' workplace after drinking a few brews and dimming the lights.

It mattered not to me what he wrote; Ludacris was singing that damn song for the fifth time today and I was beginning to wonder if I should be paying attention.

"You're going to have him imprinted on your retinas, honey," a soft voice drawled beside me. I turned to see Judy Garland/Mavis standing beside me, batting large false eyelashes and stroking me with her feather boa.

"Who?"

"Why, that delicious specimen you're gawking at. You might want to wipe the drool from your lip."

I hurriedly wiped my mouth and realized that she was pulling my leg.

"Funny," I said.

"You have the hots for that one, don't you?"

I nodded.

"I don't wonder if he has the hots for you too. He's been sitting there quite a bit the past month or so."

"He hasn't asked me out," I said, not wanting to volunteer that I knew that he was seeing someone. Not just seeing someone, but banging someone. I thought of that woman, that giggly shriek demon, and shook my head sadly.

"Maybe he wants you to ask him out."

"No. He doesn't want to go out with me. He usually picks something apart about me when he comes in. He either complains about what I serve him or he laments the fact I wear glasses. He's made comments about my weight."

"It's just like us ladies, isn't it? To be attracted to someone so callous, yet so perfectly delicious."

"He's not so hot," I said, watching as he scratched his head.

"You know he's the best-looking thing that comes in here. You think I haven't been watching? I see all the lovelies, my dear."

I looked around at the rest of my section. There were mostly older people in their fifties and sixties, obvious tourists with video cameras and plastic bags filled with postcards and T-shirts. If I worked in a different room of the restaurant, there would be children running loose as well.

"Maybe you need Mavis to cheer him up, get the old wheels greased."

"No . . ." I tried to stop her, but it was too late. Mavis sashayed over to Mr. J.D. and waved her pink boa in his face. He sneezed and looked up with both disgust and horror.

"What the hell are you supposed to be?" he asked, brushing stray feathers from his shirt.

"Why, I'm the entertainment here. I'm playing over in the dance hall in half an hour. You should really come in and hear me sing."

"I don't think so."

"Not today."

"Well," Mavis buzzed on cheerily as she opened her little silver pocket book. She plucked out two tickets. "Why don't you come by sometime and check it out. I gave you two tickets so you can bring a friend."

Mr. J.D. stared at the tickets and then pushed them back.

"Thank you, but I don't know anyone who would be interested in seeing a drag queen show."

"Well, keep them and think about it. You could even come alone. No one bites." She wandered off, waving her boa in glee. I watched her disappear back into the dance hall.

Mr. J.D. turned around and waved me over. He held up the tickets and for the briefest of moments I thought he was going to invite me to the show. How I had misread his intentions. He pushed the tickets into my apron.

"Tell that . . . that person that I'm not interested and I don't wish to be hassled again. I'm a red-blooded male and intend to stay that way."

I pulled out the tickets and smoothed them as I spoke.

"A drag queen show is like comedy, and there are impersonations of celebrities. Just because you go to a show doesn't make you gay. It's just supposed to be fun."

"Yes, I'm well aware of that. Believe it or not, Miss"—he peered at my name tag—"Abigail. I have seen many a drag show in my time. There is nothing Miss Garland out there can show me that I haven't already seen."

"She was just trying to be nice. She knows you are a regular."

He stared at me with large brown eyes. I wanted to fall into them so badly. I thought I caught a glimpse of a frightened boy, of a deer in the headlights, and the image made me shivery.

"A regular. I see." He turned to stare at his coffee cup. "Well, it does appear that I have become a regular of late. And you know, Abigail, I'm not sure why. I feel drawn to this place. It has a haunting feeling, like I'm supposed to know something when I come here. Yet, I can't for the life of me figure out what it is."

I didn't know what to say, and he continued to stare into his cup. I left him to his moody musings and continued to stew over my own. This enigma had me confused. Fate had surely brought him here, and we had a dance to dance. He didn't know it yet, but his fate was already sealed.

I left the tickets on his table and when he left, they were gone.

Thursday, September 15

An e-mail came for me out of the blue. It was from Mom. When I saw her name in my in-box, I wondered what she wanted from me. She never bothered with me unless she wanted something.

Dear Abby,
   (She always got some perverse pleasure in addressing me as Dear Abby.)
   Today is a happy day. I've finally found a new

job. I am working in a gentlemen's club as a cock-tail waitress.

I went by your place the other day, but you weren't there. Have you moved or something? No one has seen or heard from you in months.

I had been hoping to see you, as there was something I wanted to ask you. Maybe we can get together sometime?

—Mom

I sighed. When I left that wretched little town, I didn't tell a soul. No one knew I was lost in the big city. No one from my past life knew that I worked at Ooolala. I imagine they could find me on the Internet or through my Social Security number if they really wanted to. No one would bother. No one ever cared enough about me to do such a thing.

Which was a relief. I didn't need anyone haunting me from my past, least of all my mother. I thought about blocking her e-mail, but I decided to just delete it as if I had never read it at all.

After I read the e-mail, Brad emerged from the shower. He towel-dried his hair, his naked, smooth body damp from steam. He watched me, his eyes bright.

I always appreciated a naked Brad in front of me, though as time went on, I grew to resent him opening his mouth. I waited for him to say something stupid, and he did.

"Checking your e-mail?" he asked.

"Just finishing up. Want to use it?" I stood up, offering him the chair.

"No . . . not that." He wiggled his hips a little, and his dick grew a little firmer.

He was a pretty boy. A nice looking boy.

What a big dick you have. . . .

"I was thinking, well, since Vicki and I had a solo gig the other day, maybe you'd want to even the score."

He stroked the side of his thigh and studied me with a wicked gleam in his eye.

I admired his dick. I admired his audacity.

I don't remember exactly what I said, but it was spicy enough to both please and torment him as I flounced past him and into the bathroom. I locked the door.

As I stood under the hot pelting shower, I wondered what my mother wanted to ask me. She probably wanted to borrow money again. It was either that, or she wanted some gossip.

My mother thrived on gossip. She was the type that wouldn't rest until she knew what everyone she knew or even was acquainted with was up to at any given time. She especially enjoyed pain. She wallowed in divorce and death the way a pig wallows in mud. Her face positively glowed when she heard rumors of illicit love affairs and torment wrought upon unsuspecting families. She herself had been involved in more then a few scandals, as had I.

The apple never falls far from the tree, but sometimes the apple is lucky enough to find a hill and roll the hell away.

When I finally had the opportunity to ditch the party animal called my mother, I took it. There was no need for her to know that I was following one of my dreams.

To live in New York City.

I asked for extra shifts at work. It's expensive to keep one apartment, let alone pay part of two. I was going to work tonight. It was one of the special drag queen show nights, the Burlesque Masquerade.

Burlesque Masquerade was popular with all ages. It gave both tourists and regulars a chance to don fetish gear and dance and watch a stage show.

A section of the restaurant was usually closed off for a dance floor, with walls and doors sealed off from the rest of the area. Rich people who wanted a banquet hall for special occasions could reserve it as well.

I had been to a few of the Burlesque Masquerade shows, but I had never worked one. It would be much different from serving lunch and dinner to tourists on the go. This should be a rowdy crowd that would stay for hours and have fun.

Part of me wanted to do the handsome man on the other side of the door. I had heard him try the handle a few times. He was probably puzzled and sad that I had locked it.

Anyway, I'd better get going. Time's a wasting.

CHAPTER FOUR

Saturday, September 17

Wow . . . I can't believe how the night went. I'm too fucked up to write about it now. I drank waaay too much.

Later

In the cold light of day, I can better examine what is and isn't relative to my life.

Noisy children in restaurants are annoying but constant. They are part of the furniture.

Noisy boyfriends are annoying but constant. If they have the looks, the noise can be tolerated.

Noisy girlfriends are annoying and inexcusable. No one should have to put up with a noisy girlfriend, man or woman.

Sometimes I can't believe I get paid to do what I do. It's so easy. You talk and chat with people like you are hosting the world's best party. They order drinks and tip you. It's all good.

That night at the Burlesque Masquerade made me realize I was wasting my time doing lunches and dinners. More money was to be made at night, and it was easier too. Vicki worked a lot of nights, so it wasn't like I'd be missing anything. For a couple of days now, I've worked days and nights.

The Burlesque, of course, isn't a normal event, but I still find the night crowd more easygoing, and better at tipping.

That Storm and Mavis sure know how to corrupt a girl.

During the night, they pulled me back into the dressing area. I was astonished at how many people were back there. It was almost as crazy as I imagine it is backstage at a rock concert. People were actually smoking dope and doing cocaine openly.

"Aren't you afraid of getting busted?" I whispered to Mavis as she snorted a line.

"Nonsense, sweetie. Don't forget who the owners are. They know what it takes to put on a good show."

Watching all the fun made me consider going into showbiz. These girls were in New York City, partying like it was 1999. It made me remember what it was like to be alive.

During the course of the night, they twisted my rubber arm to have a few lines and a few tokes. I waitressed up a storm and by the end of the night had three hundred bucks burning a hole in my pocket.

After I had changed from my uniform, I was ready to leave when Storm found me.

"Don't go yet. There's a party."

I don't remember much about the party except that

it was large and loud. Instead of spilling over into the restaurant, it leaked down to the basement. I quickly discovered why basements were fun for fetish people. There were couches and chairs and little tables set up. Obviously this was a common area for parties. I had never known about it before. I remember watching a couple fucking on the couch until Mavis pulled me away and told me it's not polite to stare.

Storm and Mavis kept me under their wings most of the night and I met some celebrities, even a big hip-hop star. He was tall and muscular, dark-skinned and gleaming. He had a ready smile and I know I flirted with him a few times. He laughed at me, lamenting how I wore glasses, that I had pretty eyes except for that. It sort of turned me off.

I fell asleep on one of the couches. I wasn't the only one, though. When I woke the next day around six thirty, there were other people sprawled around, on couches, on chairs. One couple lay naked, passed out midfuck. It was all pretty comical and I steadied myself to face the light of day.

I liked walking in the early morning. There were a few taxis on the road and the telltale signs of a city getting ready for the day. My walk home was uneventful, as was sinking into bed for a few hours until I had to work again for the lunch shift.

I crawled into the king-size bed with Brad and Vicki, who were both wearing pajamas. I wondered vaguely if they had fooled around while I was gone and decided I didn't care one way or the other.

Monday, September 19

Another e-mail from Mom. She's getting smarter. This one had one of those check-if-you've-read things on it. I clicked it off and chuckled. Fuck her.

Wednesday, September 21

It's late and I'm still sitting here, waiting and waiting. Outside, the neon lights of the city flicker, bathing the room in a reddish hue. I hate waiting. It makes me crazy.

It's Vicki that I'm sitting here waiting for. She finished her shift about half an hour ago and told me to wait for her while she serviced someone in the back.

At first I sat here patiently, waiting and smoking. The club was closed, so I could smoke all I wanted. The staff stuck behind cleaning were smoking and drinking, and played tunes for a while. When they were done, they shut off the music and the lights.

I knew Vicki screwed some of the guys on the side. She never admitted it, but you could tell. How could she make so much money all the time just stripping?

I didn't see the guy, just the back of his head as Vicki had dragged him into her dressing room, signaling for me to wait for her.

The hum of the jukebox, the clicking cycles of the beer fridges and the occasional outside blare of taxis were all I heard at first.

After a while, I heard more.

There was talking. Loud talking. At first I thought it

might be some waiters left behind, and then I thought it might be the tenants that lived above the club. But it slowly dawned on me: I was hearing the man yelling at Vicki.

I had gone to her, knocking on the door. She opened it, a sly look on her face, her breasts hanging free. After she had assured me everything was fine, I returned to the bar. I helped myself to a pint of beer from the tap and sat drinking it, smoking yet another cigarette.

Later

A few minutes ago, there was banging and slamming. Rhythmic pounding. He was giving it to her good. She cried out many times, and still does, but I'll wait. I figure by this point, she knows what she's doing and I'm not going to stop her.

Later

The sad part is, I was wrong about that. There was pounding and crying all right. The bastard left quickly, slamming Vicki's dressing room door and then the back door to the club as he ran. I saw his shadow disappear down the street. Instead of Vicki emerging, all grins, waving her wad of cash, I had to go find her. She was beaten up pretty bad. Her face was bloody; her breasts were scratched. She didn't want me to call the cops, though. She was one of those pathetic people who believe that she got what she deserved.

Sometimes I want to smack her myself, but I wouldn't leave her bloody and crying. The pervert had still paid her for her troubles. He had stood over her, peeling off bill after bill as he kicked her curled-up body. She had wept, telling him to leave her alone. At last he had.

Nice bodyguard I was.

I helped her gather up her money and wash her face. She wasn't as bad as she had seemed at first. Still, it was a rough night. Much rougher then Brad and I ever got with her.

The crazy woman actually laughed about it at one point. She said he had a nice hard dick and she had found it hard not to give into the pleasure of it. I pointed out it's hard to feel pleasure when you have a bloody nose. She didn't seem to agree.

We smoked a joint as we walked down the street. She didn't want a cab. She wanted the night air. So we walked and passed the usual late-night types. There were beggars and bums and crazy people. There were stoners and drunks and people just getting off work. The city was alive with the shift of the night children.

Vicki didn't even seem to care after a while about what she had been through. She was more interested in wondering if Brad was still up.

I told her she just got fucked, but she said something about wanting to get fucked properly, not by a client. I've never been a hooker or a stripper or whatever it is she fancies herself. I've never had sex for money, so I guess it's different. She must just close her eyes and wish for it to be over instead of getting into it. Maybe that's what the johns want. Maybe that's why some of them liked to smack her around on top of it all.

The sex trade was strange and I was learning all sorts of things. All the different levels and weirdness.

There were no fetish clubs and barely any strip joints where I was from. Sex was something regular folk did with regular folk, and if anyone paid for anything, well, I imagine it was a big joke. I didn't even know anyone who had paid for it. Yet here, almost everyone had paid for it in some way or another, whether it was buying a video, seeing a show or shoving bills down a stripper's G-string.

For the second time in a week or so, I ended up back at Ooolala in that party room.

I guess smoking that joint made Vicki want some coke, and she knew where to find it. In a way, I was a bit hurt that she knew all along about the private VIP room at Ooolala. Why was I so out of the loop that no one told me anything?

But then again, I did know about it when she wanted to go down there. I had just found out, but in time not to act surprised that it existed, as I would have a week ago.

She found Storm, who she said always knew how to hook her up. Apparently it was true, because Storm was strung out on something, and her gothy makeup was running in cakey smears down her face. Her eyes looked larger and more lost than ever with the black rings dripping and smearing. I didn't know who looked more like an assault victim, Vicki or Storm.

Before long, Vicki found her happy place, snorting lines with some of the other queens. This was a different crowd from the one burlesque night had drawn. There were more queens and hard-core partiers here than when there was more of the general public hanging around.

Some of the queens had bad tempers at this late hour, and I could hear snatches of drunken outbursts, like little fires that needed to be stomped out quickly and efficiently before they spread, flare up around me.

As Vicki sought solace in powder, I saw that the rap star guy was there again. This time he had a bit of an entourage with him. There were several big black men in suits surrounding him. As well as the men, there were a couple of black girls that looked like ads for a fitness infomercial. They looked like they had stepped out of a rock video, with their hardened abs and rounded triceps. I marveled at the beauty of their ample asses, how they wore expensive skirts perfectly cut to hug and lift them. On the drag queens, I knew there was the magic of padding and other theatrical flairs. But on these girls, you could tell by skimpiness of their clothes that their asses were real. Apples, pears, you name the fruit—I was awestruck and envious of those asses.

I thought about one of those girls, teetering on her stilettos, bent over that couch over there. Her ample apple ass high in the air as Mr. Hip-Hop Rapperman plowed her with a rod like something off a porn site. Nothing like that ever happens when I'm looking, but I had enough pot to dreamily imagine it all the same.

I wasn't too impressed when I emerged from my daydream to see Vicki kneeling below one of the tables, sucking off a guy. I knew it was her by the way her heels stuck out from underneath. I knew she was sucking him good from the spaced-out stupid idiot look on the guy's face. I marched over there and dragged her by one of her heels.

"Vicki?" I said. She crawled out, pouting. I shook her, wanting to slap that puffy, still blood-smeared face of hers.

"What the hell are you doing?" I asked her.

"Just trying to forget my troubles," she said.

"You are just trying to start new troubles is what you are doing. Come on, let's go home and see Braddy-boy. I'm sure he'll appreciate you. Better then some random stranger getting your work for free."

"But he's cute. . . ." She gave a feeble wave as I dragged her over to a chair. I made her sit still while I found her purse. We carefully made our way up the stairs and back out into the street.

I could tell by the sky that it was only an hour or two before dawn broke again.

Funny how you can tell by how the stars and moon seem to slide off to the side to make way for the glow of morning. Vicki was babbling on about stars and wishes, cluttering up my thoughts of what I wanted to wish on the big twinkling star to the right.

When we got home, Brad was snoozing on the couch. There were many candles lit, most of them burned down. He was naked, his hand lightly cupped around his balls. He snored lightly as we stumbled in the door. There was a large note on the table. It instructed us to wake him when we got home, since he didn't have to work in the morning.

Vicki looked like hell, but I guess she's like the energizer bunny, because she keeps on going and going. She lost no time in crawling over to Brad on hands and knees, wiggling her butt at me. I could see her ass cheeks perfectly: Her tiny PVC miniskirt did nothing to cover her. Brad stirred as I slipped off my own clothes. Once, Vicki and I had come home to a note and we didn't believe that he really wanted to be woken up. We let him sleep, and the next day he was hurt and surprised we didn't rape him.

So we had our way with dear Brad, who relished that fine line between dream and fantasy, between embracing the moment and giving back to it too.

Once were we finished satisfying our base needs, we all sat around smoking. Brad was awake by now and noticed Vicki's face for the first time.

"My lord, what happened to you?" he asked. He reached to touch her, but she pulled back like a wounded animal.

"It's nothing."

"She got slapped around tonight," I said. "Don't ask. It's not important."

"Of course it's important," Brad said. "I love you." He stroked her hair and reached out to me. "I love you too. I love both of you and I want both of you to be safe."

I listened to the rapid beating of his heart while his hands stroked my head. I believed him in that moment. I believed he loved us both.

"Were you hurt, Abigail? What happened?"

"It had nothing to do with me. Don't ask anymore. It's over. We'll move on."

"Vicki?" Brad lifted her chin and looked her in the eyes. She blinked a few times, tears glistening at the corners of her eyes.

"Abby's fine. She did nothing wrong. Everything will work out fine."

Brad finally seemed content that we weren't going to spill the beans. He finished his cigarette, hugging us and patting our heads as if we were going to dash away on him. He finally sighed deeply.

"Look at the sun." He stood up and pulled back one of the heavy curtains. It was positively morning out. "That's it. I'm going to bed."

Brad went into the bedroom. Vicki yawned and stretched and followed him in. I heard her fussing in the bathroom for quite a while as I idly watched music videos and made notes.

I don't know why I make notes, really. I wonder who the hell I expect will read them when I'm dead. Or maybe someone has been reading them while I write them. I doubt it, though; I'm very careful with my journals. Who would want to read about my boring life anyway?

Well, I guess it's not that boring at first. From the outside, it must look glamorous, all that sex and all the booze and drugs I could ever hope for if I chose to be that trashed. But working is hard. The job I have requires a lot of physical stamina. You have to be able to walk really fast without spilling stuff, you have to remember a thousand things at once, you have to make out checks with one hand and put whipped cream on a cake with another. You have to be able to concentrate.

Sometimes I have to give myself little concentration exercises to practice with before I get to work. Especially if I'm really trashed, like I am tonight. Well, this morning, I should say. It's close to seven thirty now. Most people are up and on their way to work by now.

Children have to be fed and groomed. Dogs have to be walked. Husbands need to be kissed.

Well, I just have to drag my own sorry ass out of bed each day and hope for the best. I'm not in a hurry to get married and have kids. Who needs to deal with all that nitty-gritty shit anyways? I like this loose arrangement. A husband and wife of my own. We are trying to divide up our chores in an even way that matches our personalities. Of course, there are chores that everyone loathes, such as laundry. There is no way to get out of laundry; everyone does his or her own and that's that.

But washing dishes and cooking—you can take turns with those. We all have such crazy hours that half the time no one is home to eat a dinner, should someone be home in time to cook one.

I tend to eat a lot at Ooolala since we get our meals half-price. I eat better there than if I was cooking for myself. I hate making salads, but I try to eat at least one small one every day at work. I actually like them there. My favorite is the chicken salad with grapes and mandarins in it. Sometimes there are chunks of walnuts too, which rock, all tossed together with real mayo. Of course, that's not really a salad; it's more like a meal. On the days I have the big chicken ones, I don't each much else. Most of the time I force myself to have some of that green leafy crap. Man, I could use one of those mandarins right now. It would be so sweet and juicy.

Juicy like Vicki.

Juicy like HER.

I must still be pretty messed up, so I'd better get to bed.

Thursday, September 22

Mavis invited me for a coffee after work. I was glad to see him dressed as a guy for a change. It unnerved me when he towered over me in platform shoes. He wore jeans and a nice blue cotton shirt that set off his eyes.

It turned out that he just wanted someone to kill time with until his date with Steve. He prattled on about Steve and drank three cups of coffee.

I watched him. I found his conversation banal but enjoyed watching his face light up in animated grins. His happiness was infectious, and soon he had me laughing.

"You've been so sad lately. What's wrong?"

I laughed. "I'm not sad. I'm having the time of my life."

"I don't know. . . . Sometimes I sense that you aren't happy. What are you looking for?"

You know, I sat there wondering just that. I'm still wondering. I don't really know what I'm looking for. I have a hole, a void that needs to be filled. I said something clumsily about feeling empty. I didn't say it in a sad way, just in a way that made me feel naive. I knew there was so much more to life, and only age would bring me that knowledge. Sometimes I yearn to grow older more quickly so I could understand things better. Then I look around me and see people far older then me acting just as stupid. I wonder how those few people that seem to have found it, did it? How did they fill that emptiness?

When it was time for Mavis to leave, I hit the bathroom and went out into the evening. I wondered if there was anything going on at Boingo's tonight. My veins were coursing with caffeine and I felt an urge to dance.

The club was still pretty empty when I went in. It was a weeknight, so that was no surprise. Sometimes the club didn't fill up at all during the week.

I wandered around the two floors that were open. The other floors were closed since it was a slow night. I bought a rye-and-ginger and sipped on it as I looked around the room. There were a few faces I recognized from other times I had been here, but no one I knew enough to talk to. It didn't take long to sip my drink, and one led into another before I remembered that I'm not supposed to be drinking. I'm supposed to be on a diet and doing a hundred and fifty sit-ups a day.

Well, the best rules were made to be broken. I was told I was sad this day, and I needed to digest it. I don't know if I am. I didn't know then and I don't know now. I know that I'm not brimming with joy and delight. But what would I be sad about? I'm free and doing what I want when I want to as long as work allows.

I had been working a lot too. I think I did doubles four times last week.

No wonder I'm sad.

I'm not sad when I see that I'm paying for two places to live. I'm going to have to stop by to fill the cat feeder again. Too bad Vicki is allergic to cats. I can't bring mine over to the new place.

I guess some people would think I'm a crazy woman who rents an apartment for her cat. But that's not it at all. My treasures are there. If I ever get sick of being here, I can always go back. I like having a safety hatch. Everyone should have one. For all I know, the others have safety hatches too.

I spent the night drinking rye-and-gingers and eventually felt bold enough to dance by myself in the crowd. Dancing was good for me. It shook free aggressions and tensions that nothing else did. A few drinks in my system didn't hurt either. The aches and pains of my joints were forgotten as I danced the night away.

Of course, when I got home, my friends were waiting up, eager to play with me. Ever since that one time they did it by themselves, they've been certain to greet me, wanting sex every time I come through the door. It's as though they are trying to make up their betrayal to me. Or maybe they are boffing each other all the time and are fucking me out of guilt.

It didn't really matter to me. Of course, I would prefer that they were groveling, but no one has ever thought me worth groveling over before.

Their attention exhausts me, though. On one hand, it's great and I seldom say no. Yet on the other, I'm tired all the time, and I'm starting to screw up at work. It's hard to remember things on four or five hours of sleep. Some days it seems like all I do is work and fuck. There's nothing else.

So it felt good to dance by myself in the crowd.

That was, until I realized that I wasn't dancing by myself anymore. Mr. J.D. was dancing in front of me. He smiled and I smiled back, paying more attention to what I was doing.

He tossed his hair so that his bangs slid from his

face. He hadn't shaved in a while and the scruffy look only endeared him to me.

I wondered how long he had been there. I blushed, examining my behavior and pondering over whether I had done something stupid or weird. I couldn't even remember what I had been doing except dancing. I looked around at the faces of people dancing beside me. Some had their eyes closed, some were trying to seduce their partners with their eyes, some clung to each other as if this were a slow dance and not some endless boppy electrotech song. Breasts were bobbing up and down to the music, as were round, shapely asses. A sea of heels and flats and men's dress shoes flooded the dance floor.

In the brief instant that I became fascinated with the pink bobbing tits of an enormously endowed woman, Mr. J.D. disappeared on me. I combed the crowd for him for a long time, but he was gone.

I think that really sucks, that he would dance with me and then disappear like that.

But then again, he did dance with me. If he's with that shrew, he's probably under tight lock and key. He may have been happy to see me there at all. Maybe he had stolen a dance while she was in the bathroom, and then they left right away.

I know it's a stupid excuse, but I'm sticking with it for now.

It's better then wondering if I'm losing my mind. I'm positive it was him, but maybe it wasn't. Maybe I had just hoped it was him. I've done that before. I've actually talked to people thinking they are one person and not another. Only when the person starts explaining himself do I realize how far off the mark I am.

It's a creepy syndrome, to be sure, but the shrink said that some people have it. The inability to recognize faces. However, I don't think I have that. Some faces are chiseled right into my head, like they have always been there and always will be.

He was gone. If he ever was there.

I'm glad I saw him, whether it was wishful thinking or not. It reminds me that there are challenges in life that we have to meet.

I hereby make myself a challenge that Mr. J.D. will be mine before the year is up.

CHAPTER FIVE

Saturday, September 24

Bad news. Real bad news.

So says my mother. She is trying to entice me with e-mails. She holds me little crumbs, as if I'm supposed to come sniffing around like a dog. But I won't. I refuse.

Sure, I read every little cryptic remark she makes, but I won't reply. No sirree. I plain old refuse and no one can make me.

Sure, I guess if there were some really weird family reason, I might let her know my whereabouts, but I can't think of anything at all in our white trash family that would lead me to betray my secret.

She keeps alluding to a secret. There must have been ten e-mails sent one day alone. She was manipulative and creative in her messages, though. It was an interesting puzzle to see what she might be talking about as I unlayered each thin sheet of information as though it would float from my fingers at any time. And, in ways, it can do just that.

I wondered if Mom was going to try to blackmail me. She didn't have anything, though.

There was nothing, no trace of where I am or if I'm going somewhere else.

Dear Abby,
It is imperative we get together. I have some questions.
Mom

Dear Abby,
Please respond. I promise not to abuse your e-mail.
Mom

Abby,
Did you know that each day we die a little bit? How are you doing, Abby? Are you rotting from the inside out, or are you growing and thriving?
Mom

That's my mom. The drama queen. Then there's Mom the detective.

Dear Abby,
I went by the restaurant today and they said you quit months ago, and from what they gathered, you left town. No one has seen you in weeks and your phone was disconnected long ago.
Where are you, Abby? I need to talk to you.
Mom

Dear Abby,

Are you OK? Of course, if you're not, and you're lying dead somewhere, I would never know, would I? I hope you're not suffering from depression again. If you are, you'd better make an appointment to see Dr. Maxell.

I need to discuss something with you.

Mom

Dear Abby,

I just know you are feeling lost and lonely without your mom to talk to. Give me a call or e-mail. I promise I won't say anything to piss you off.

Love, Mom

The last e-mail caught me off guard. It almost sounded like something a mother would say. Not quite, but pretty darned close, and I liked it. For a moment, my hand hovered above the keys, as if daring them to push the buttons that would allow me to answer.

She was trying her control tactics. I had over thirty or forty e-mails from her. She would rise and fall in tone like the ocean. First she would be sweet and caring, then slowly during the course of a day, or two, or three, she would build up anger and frustration.

She was up to something and I didn't care.

Even though I deleted the e-mails, now and again I would go and read them in the trash can.

Tuesday, September 27

Vicki was in a strange mood. I think she does too much cocaine, and her view on the world is odd and warped to say the least. But the thing I like about Vicki is how she will try anything once. Brad was always eager to try new things, or at least things that were new for us all to do together, so tonight we experimented with cellophane. We bought one of those large industrial-sized cartons of plastic wrap where you could take a finger off with the slicing thing on the side. I tore off large strips as Brad wound them around her. He started at her feet, and as she squeezed her legs tightly together, he sealed her shut.

Brad and I spent quite some time wrapping Vicki up like a giant cocoon. When he got to her head, I was getting worried that she might pass out or asphyxiate. Brad seemed to know what he was doing as he layered the plastic around her head and face. Carefully, like he was forming a doll, he pressed the plastic down on her eyebrows and around her closed eyes. By the time we were finished, she was hot to the touch. In fact, I worried that the plastic would melt right into her skin.

But it didn't.

She lay there for some time, breathing through a straw Brad had wound into the plastic. I wondered if she felt claustrophobic. I would hate to be all swaddled up like that. Plastic. Blanket. Straitjacket. It all seemed bad to me.

Even thinking about it now gives me the heebie-jeebies. I guess that's why Vicki was the wild one.

Brad enjoyed running his fingers along her plastic

body. He stroked her plastic head, caressed her plastic boobs, tickled her plastic toes.

It made me think of those dreams where you can't move. Where you know everything that is going on around you, but you are powerless to do anything about it. Why anyone would willingly want to experience that sensation at all is beyond me. But who am I to judge?

I placed my hand on that warm, breathing, plastic body. She felt so strange. The texture was similar to a penis in a condom, yet more intense, more vibrant. More alive.

It was addicting, rubbing my hands along her smooth form. I understood now why Brad was doing it. Together we ran our hands along her body, kneading and touching, tracing lines and forms.

The body was a marvel. How did your cells know how to grow a hand or a foot? The idea of it always puzzled me, and I was sure it was one of the mysteries I might have finally understood if I could ever save up for school.

Vicki was a modern-day mummy, wrapped in plastic instead of cloth. I wondered how long she would stay preserved if she suffocated in there. I imagined the straw slipping from her lips, and none of us noticing. I could see a flap of plastic lodge over her mouth as she tried to breathe. With no one to lift it for her, she would die.

These were dangerous games for dangerous times.

The long cocoon shape put me in mind of summertime. I thought about all the bugs that gathered in the forest. How they laid their eggs in dead things, how squirming white larvae twitched to life among rancid meat.

Vicki was no maggot. She couldn't even move or eat.

I'm not sure what the point of the exercise was, but both Brad and Vicki were incredibly excited by it all. After we cut her free, Vicki took a bit of time to compose herself. She drank lots of water, and we sponged her sweating body down gently with soft white towels. When she seemed ready, the three of us had wild unbridled sex for a good hour. Vicki seemed spaced-out, or maybe transcendent. Maybe doing weird things to your body gave you another view on life, or at least on life at that moment.

What did it matter, though?

It wasn't like she was going to write informative essays on her findings. She was just a stripper in a club in the big city. One of many who did strange things to feel alive.

There were all sorts of strange things to do. I knew that even growing up.

The body could be lured to the point of ecstasy in so many ways. What seemed odd or strange to one person could be total bliss to another. This is why fetishes exist. They give people a chance to put a label on behavior that can't quite be explained. There have been books and degrees written on ecstasy and fetishes. Many a fictional character has met disaster trying to capture that perfect moment of ecstasy.

I guess I was still naive enough or new enough to find adequate ecstasy through regular sex. Other activities gave me a rush too. Some activities are more practical then others in that elusive quest to fill the hole.

After Vicki and Brad went to bed, I stayed up, staring

at the wad of cellophane hanging out of plastic bags in the kitchen. I retrieved one, repulsed at first by its dampness from Vicki's sweat. I returned to the couch and wrapped it around my arm. I didn't like the sensation at all. I smoothed a piece over my breast, feeling it heat up almost instantly. How did she stand being in all that heat for so long? On top of that, we were stroking her with our own hot hands.

It must be an experience like a sweat lodge. I'll ask her tomorrow if she had any hallucinations.

I really should go feed the cat soon. It's been a long time since I've been over there. In fact, I'm not sure when I last went over, but I do remember pouring a whole bag of food into the cat feeder before I left. The cat should be fine still. And if not, there were always mice to eat.

This city certainly has it share of vermin. But then, I imagine every big city does. Hell, the place I lived before here had cockroaches. The cockroaches from my past had nothing on the ginormous roaches taking up residence in this city.

It always made me queasy to think of the secret bug life going on behind the walls, under the floors, in the ceilings. How many bugs a day were scuttling back and forth along drainpipes, peering from apartment to apartment looking for food.

In their travels they probably laid eggs or procreated in some fashion, which means more bugs, more rats were being born on a daily basis. It was a wonder that entire buildings didn't collapse from the addition of so many insects.

Bugs disturbed me on some levels but not on others. I wouldn't freak out if a cockroach scurried across my shoe or ended up in my chocolate cake.

I pulled the plastic from my tit and returned it to the garbage can.

Wearing garbage bags on a rainy day was the closest I ever came to being wrapped in plastic. When I was a kid, it was all the rage to slice open the top of a garbage bag and wear it as a raincoat.

Some of the other kids who didn't come from very good families also donned the garbage gear. Sometimes we were made fun of, but most of the time the other kids envied us because they either had outgrown their fancy rain gear or were forced to wear outdated cartoon characters.

It was sweaty wearing those garbage bags. It also trapped your hands. However, it still didn't take away the thrill of hunting down those worms. They were so big and cumbersome. It made you wonder why they even existed at all.

Garbage bags probably aren't the most practical solution when the weather gets rough. As an adult, I carry an umbrella and pretty rain shoes. I do take my rain gear more seriously than I did when I was a kid, that's for sure.

Now when I looked back on packs of kids wearing garbage bags, I shuddered. It must have been weird seeing lots of bubbles skipping along the roadway to school.

I worry about Vicki sometimes. I worry that she's going to get hurt in all these fun and games. It's mostly Brad who does anything.

Vicki grabs life by the balls and that's why I love her. Who doesn't love someone so infectious, so pretty and so good-natured? She could convince almost anyone to do anything. Look at the guy who had wanked off over the computer for us.

I hope that Vicki and I can be friends for a long time. In fact, she is my only friend. If I didn't have Vicki and Brad, I'm sure I would lose my identity.

Friday, September 30

Went by the apartment today. Man, the place feels foreign to me. It doesn't feel like home anymore. I've grown used to my harem and enjoy the rattling around of other people in the house. The need to be alone hasn't been with me in quite some time. In fact, the whole time it took me to feed the cat and check a few things was less than ten minutes.

I know the cat would have enjoyed some company, but that's not on today's agenda.

I had been hanging around with Brad and Vicki too long. I wanted to go dancing and let off some steam. I couldn't be bothered to see if they were up to it, had no patience for waiting for clothes to be chosen and acquired. I was halfway there just by stepping out of my apartment again.

I walked for a long time in lieu of taking the subway. It always seems better to me to walk briskly no matter how far you need to go. That way you aren't a sitting duck for any strange subway incidents.

Yes, I'm still nervous about the subways. There are no such things where I'm from, and to me they seem a dark and dangerous labyrinth that can only lead to pain and electrocution.

However, I realize that I have been groomed on far too many horror movies, and I bet no one else thinks of their home as a labyrinth, nor of their friends covered with maggots.

When I was at my apartment, I did take the time to weigh myself. I was a hundred and twenty-three, lost two pounds. I felt proud about that.

Going into the bar, I wondered if he was here tonight. It was funny, but once I planted the thought of Mr. J.D. into my head, he seemed to be lurking around every corner. I caught glimpses in the shadows, from across the crowded room. Images of the back of a head or a briskly paced walk.

Every time I was deluded. It was my mind playing tricks on me.

I don't know why it happened, like some sort of fate thing, I guess, but here was Mr. J.D. and his squeaky girlfriend sharing a few drinks.

I watched them for a long time before the music called to me. I had come here to dance, and dance I would.

When I lost myself dancing, I lost them.

Saturday, October 1

Whenever I think about her, I get depressed. It's been a while since I actually wrote about her, but I can't help myself. Today my body was full of yearning. It was an ache to see her once more. To touch her pretty blond hair and hold her soft, supple body next to mine.

But it would never be again. What we had once is gone from me. Has been gone from me for far too long.

Sunday, October 2

The woman just never gives up. I know where I get my tenacity and persistence, as if there were any question at all about it.

Mom sent more e-mail, and I had barely had a chance to do any cruising before I saw her numerous entries to me.

There should be none of these veiled threats or even downright blackmail coming my way. I've lived my life as fast as I could in spite of my mother, and I'm not going to let her bring me down.

Monday, October 3

This time I spotted Mr. J.D. He was going into Ooolala just as I was getting off my shift. They had sent me home early because I was going in a lot at night lately, and it was beginning to take its toll on me more than before. I was always tired, of course, from the sex and drugs, but I was never tired from life.

He did a double take as he saw me leaving. It crossed my mind that maybe he had gone there to see me and only me. However, I knew that wasn't the truth. He hadn't been by in ages, and if he wanted to ask me out, he would have by now.

Thursday, October 13

He sat down at his usual table, and my heart skipped a beat.

He did his usual coffee song and dance and attempted some kind of small talk by making a joke about something. I don't even remember what, because I was trying to keep my gaze from revealing too much.

I had to leave before he was finished, but at least I got to see him again.

Saturday, October 22

For a long time, I sat near the lions and stared over at the fountain.

The library had always appealed to me. I guess it was because I had seen it in so many movies that its icons were imprinted into my subconscious.

The first day I had stumbled across the library, a fantastic sense of déjà vu and homecoming struck me. I've never been a big reader, yet I felt compelled to enter this magnificent building. I walked up the marble stairs, read inscriptions and admired busts and statues. My senses were alive as I stared up at the amazing paintings on the ceilings.

I sat down on one of the little benches and stared around me, taking in everything and nothing. My mind was in overdrive.

People came and went, came and went. They carried books, read books, shuffled books, looked for books. Books were a lifeline for so many people. It fascinated me, this simple thread that bonded together so many different types of people. I wondered why the library had the opulence of a palace. Why was the library supposed to be so regal, so amazingly huge, a palace for pages?

I would kill to have an apartment like one of the smaller rooms in that place.

It always amazes me how churches, libraries and government buildings are designed with such magnificence for temporary guests. What do books care if they are surrounded by ceiling paintings and stained glass? Do books need lions guarding them?

Can't I just look up the information on the Internet anyways?

These ancient customs would drag down modern times, but lucky for me, there were still studious bookworm types lured to the library like a PMSing woman is lured to chocolate.

I first spotted her a couple of hours ago, when I was sitting on that bench, where I had sat the very first time I had ever come here. I watched her golden ringlets bobbing like an angelic halo. She had pale porcelain flesh and very fine makeup, if any at all. Maybe she was one of those girls who spent hours putting on makeup so that she didn't look like she had anything on.

At any rate, she had a glow, that special glow about her that I recognized.

She was mine.

I knew I would be invisible to her, just another student scribbling frantically in a notebook. What was I writing? A poem? A story? An essay? Maybe I was drawing a picture of her.

I watch the Angel, for that's what I named her, walk into one of the research rooms. She was shapely in that way I adored and hated. Like Kimberly Evans.

She had large breasts that made her washboard stomach seem even flatter, and a plump ass that gave her a Marilyn Monroe hourglass figure, only she was probably about twenty pounds lighter then dear Marilyn ever was.

My Angel was tall for a girl, maybe five seven or so, and she wore chunky white heels to accentuate her height. Why anyone wore all white this time of year was beyond me, and that's why I knew she was my Angel.

Her belly ring, the only cover for such bare flesh, glittered. She wore a tiny white crop top with a little white half blazer. The funny part was her low-slung white jeans. I didn't think anyone wore white jeans anymore, especially after Labor Day.

But the world is strange, and people are even stranger. My Angel had no idea what kind of strange she attracted.

The luminescence of her face cheered me up as I dared to move from my bench and into the research room. Now I had found my Angel, I didn't want to lose sight of her.

It's difficult to find angels in the city. Angels in America, like that play.

I had my own personal angel now. She did her research or her homework or whatever it was she was trying to do. A very normal, tedious task to be assigned to an angel. Yet that was part of the training, I'm sure.

It's not that often I spot an angel, or a demon for that matter. Most people are ordinary; some carry extraordinary features or skills. Most are average.

Like me.

Charisma? Beauty? A glow? A joie de vivre?

It was impossible to put a finger on how to spot an angel.

You just knew.

I just knew.

And the rare time I found an angel, I wanted to bask in his or her glory. The closer I could get to my Angel, the more I could draw in her energy.

Her pretty blue eyes were staring up at the ceiling painting. She was probably wishing she was in those clouds. I didn't sit at the table in that room for very long. It was too quiet.

The sounds of mouth breathers and fluttering pages were getting on my nerves.

I went back to my sentinel on the bench.

Eventually, echoey chitchat and scraping, shuffling feet up and down the stairs drove me back out to the lions.

I didn't know if there was any other way to leave the building, but I decided my Angel would leave through the front door. She would have to pass by security, open that pale pink knapsack that obscured her wings, and leave.

I could tell by how the water flowed from the fountain that this was true.

The lions would keep my instincts honed. I am putting a few of my thoughts down as I wait.

I see a flash of white.

The doors open and shut.

She is near.

I can feel her.

I can smell her.
I can taste her.
There she is.

Sunday, October 23

My Angel, how she disappointed me with her human frailties. It wasn't hard to seduce her. It never is with girls like that. You have to appeal to their dark side, make it clear that you are bumbling along in this life too. But oh, this pot is making me horny, and your breasts look like they are aching to be touched, to be licked, to be sucked.

When she came into my apartment, she was a bit spooked by Monica, but it didn't really matter. Once she was here, I locked the door.

Then I locked my lips on hers.

We had a few drinks, a few tokes. We ended up naked, locking our legs around each other's heads.

My Angel did a valiant job, and quite truthfully just the thought of touching her large angel breasts made me come more than anything her tongue did.

After we fooled around for a while, we were hungry.

I was ravenous.

I handcuffed my Angel to the bed so she couldn't fly away while I ran out for subs.

She was pretty funny expecting that I would un-handcuff her upon my return.

I buried my face between her legs again when she started to make noises about getting home.

Angels have no homes.

If you are lucky enough to capture an angel, are you really going to let her go?

CHAPTER SIX

Monday, October 24

That Mavis makes me laugh. One minute he's a tiny Eminem look-alike and the next she's doing Judy Garland only twice as tall as Judy probably ever was with those shoes. I love those old fifties stars, and the week before Halloween there's a show every night. I'm working most of them, but tonight I managed to just hang out and chill. Since Vicki had to work, I brought Brad with me.

Wouldn't you know how fickle fate is?

Mr. J.D. himself showed up, and without the Queen of the Banshees. Maybe they broke up. Maybe it had just been a fling. A terrible mistake that filled both of them with regret.

My Angel must be looking out for me.

Yet, as always, my luck was sloppy luck. Mr. J.D. would no doubt think I was with Brad. We live together and fuck, but it's Mr. J.D. I want.

He saw me after he sat down. He raised an eyebrow

as if to inquire why I wasn't working. Mavis was going to open the next set and I didn't want to miss it.

I excused myself from Brad and plunked myself over with J.D.

"Ditching your date?" he asked.

"Not at all. He's a friend. One of my roommates." It was the total truth. No lies here.

"I see."

The set opened and we watched the show. During the next break, Brad came over and introduced himself.

"I'm Brad," he said, shaking Mr. Johnny Depp Look-Alike's hand.

"Jimmie," my J.D. replied.

The men eyed each other, and I excused myself to go to the restroom. When I returned, Jimmie was gone.

Well, it was good that I got to sit beside him for a little while, at least.

Tuesday

There was a window display of angels and devils. Of course, with Halloween coming, it was just part of the landscape. Something in the mannequin's dead eyes caused me to stop and study the scene.

It was nothing remarkable. In fact, the more I studied the scene, it seemed downright garish.

Red-horned male devils were lusting over white-lingerie-clad angels. The window was draped in glittering red and black foil.

One of the angels looked like she had fallen, her hands raised as she lay on her back, her legs wide and definitely unangellike. Her fluffy white halo was askew; her wings were lopsided.

I loved her wings.

They were made from real feathers. In fact, as I studied all four naughty little angels, I saw that they all wore feathered wings. I decided that I needed to buy a pair of wings. My Angel should have wings.

There were several sizes and styles to choose from. Wings even came in black and red. But I wanted white.

White would be lovely.

I proudly took my purchase home to show to my Angel.

She didn't seem too interested or enthusiastic about the wings, but I slipped them on her anyways.

She looked very pretty wearing her white angel nightie, lying in repose on my white bedspread.

She was like a piece of heaven. An oasis.

I slipped the halo onto her head and felt exultation as an artist does when they create a masterpiece.

After admiring my handiwork for a moment, I went over to my second home.

Wednesday

Sometimes I like to go to the train station and people-watch. It's a weird little ritual that I've noticed with myself.

If I have a day off, like I do today, I like to spot the wide-eyed tourists who have never been to New York before.

Sometimes they travel in packs, pulling out maps

and cameras, their high-pitched voices lost in the steady hum of a bustling city.

Sometimes there's a loner.

You can spot a writer guy or starlet girl, dressed in what they consider a big-city funky look, carrying a knapsack. The odd one will be clutching a guitar.

The single girls are fun to follow. I see one right now that has that annoying Teri Hatcher deer-in-the-headlights look. I'm going to follow her for a while. They never are too sure if someone is following them or not, and get downright paranoid if they feel eyes on their backs.

Even if they think someone is following them, they would never suspect a normal-looking young woman with glasses.

Thursday

Jimmie hasn't been in for a while. I wonder if he's avoiding me, or maybe he's just so busy with that girlfriend that he doesn't even want to drop by anymore. After my shift was over, I decided to go for a walk. It was still pleasant out, yet the slight nip in the air reminded me Halloween was coming and not long after that, the snow.

I'm not the first nor last to gripe about my disdain for winter. I know once the snow hits, I'll wonder why I ever moved to New York City and didn't pick Florida or California.

But I know why I came to New York, besides the fact it had always been a dream for me. Once I landed in the big city, I felt like I was home. The humming, the vibration, the air embraced me. My blood rose to the surface as if awakening for the first time.

Although everything was foreign, it was familiar at the same time.

Like Halloween.

Like Christmas.

Thursday, November 3

Halloween night has come and gone. How quick and strange it all became. Shadows and flickering lights, screams and laughter, yet when it was all over, one lay dead on the ground.

At first it didn't seem real.

We stared at him, just lying there, his face smeared from his vampire makeup, his cock firm and lovely for the last time.

"He really was, you know. . . ." I remember stammering gibberish at Vicki, who stared at me with wide-eyed disbelief. I tossed away the stake that I still held in my hand. Blood ran down the wood and along my arm.

"What?" Vicki could barely get the words out. I don't know how long it was before she remembered to breathe again. My own head was spinning. Whatever we had smoked that night sure packed a wallop. That and Brad's frightening behavior.

Vicki boo-hooed and blathered on, at one point crawling onto him as if she could bring him back to life with her tears. How quickly she forgot the threat that nearly left her the one lying in a pool of blood.

I remember watching an episode of *Six Feet Under* when the cop shoots a man squabbling with his girlfriend. Even though it looked like the man was going to kill her, she was devastated that he was shot dead on the ground.

This reminded me of that moment, only I was the cop who overreacted. Or did I?

Like that work of fiction, I don't know if I overreacted. I've played the scene over so many times that I don't think I'll ever forget how it went down.

The day started out good enough. I worked lunch that Halloween day. I had been looking forward to it. I wore my new angel wings and a white corset and those long-legged pantaloon underwear things. I was working in one of the racier underwear rooms tonight. This room was known for having intimate drinks and snack food. There were several little areas with small love seats and a fireplace. Even in broad daylight, couples would come in to cuddle in front of a never-ending roaring fireplace. There was a bit of romance in the room, and the underwear consisted mostly of frills, lace and satin.

Sometimes I imagined the room somewhere in Paris. Maybe it was supposed to be. I don't know. I just knew that I liked working in there, and Halloween day was busy and fun.

Well, it was all fun and games until things shifted.

It all started when a lady in one of the booths screamed loudly. The sound pierced through my head and caused me to drop my tray of beer. Kaboom. Straight onto the floor.

Sharon and Diane, who were working with me, giggled as they set to work helping me clean up the mess.

"Boy, are you shaky. It's Halloween. You gotta expect it."

"I know. . . . I don't know what's wrong with me." I knew what was wrong, though. Things just felt wrong. There seemed to be a thunderclap of sadness rolling my way, and I was helpless to stop it.

The joys of manic depression.

I can't believe I was close to tears as I wiped up the broken beer-glass shards. Sharon pushed me away with a mop and had that mess cleaned away faster then it would have taken me to even figure out where to start.

When I realized the mess was under control, I strolled towards the woman who had screamed. She was still squawking like some damn parrot, pointing at something. The guy she was with had a rat on his shoulder. This was no cute little mouse. It was a huge brown rat. As it lazily climbed along its owner's arm, I saw that it was a huge male rat. The rat was pretty gruesome, but not worth screaming about. However, this was a restaurant, and Halloween or no, it wasn't good for business to have a rat hanging around.

"I'm sorry. You're going to have to leave the rat outside," I said as firmly as an angel in underwear can.

"Hey, it's part of my costume, man. I'm Willard, and this is Socrates."

"Still . . . there are health regulations. Snakes and dogs aren't allowed, either. I'm sorry." I decided against the friendly touch I almost gave him. He looked pretty angry, and I wasn't surprised when he knocked his beer over and stomped off in disgust.

Two beer accidents.

Things always come in threes.

Around four, a couple came into my section. They were dressed as *Pirates of the Caribbean*, and I nearly laughed when I recognized Jimmie under his garb. Of course, Ms. Shrew couldn't pull off a pirate look with that brassy hair and heavily coated face. But she wore her do-rag thingy at a jaunty angle and leered in a natural fashion at me. I saw that she leered at most of the women in the place except for the over-weight ones. Those ones she sneered at in true pirate fashion.

I wasn't too happy to see him with her, but in a per-verse way I guess I was happy to see him. Why come here of all places on a Halloween afternoon?

They cuddled and smoochy-faced on the couch, careful not to mess their makeup. That was when the third beer went down.

It was no accident. I delighted in watching Ms. Shrew's pretty features curl up in disgust as the beer dripped down her ragged pirate miniskirt. The way the beer trickled down her legs, it looked like she peed herself. I had to cheer quietly about Jimmie ordering a large draft. Sixteen ounces of Heineken was flowing down her skinny little body.

"I'm so sorry," I said with mock pity as I started dab-bing at her legs. She tore the rag from my hands and looked at my face. A light of recognition shone in her eyes, yet she crinkled her brow. I knew my blond wig and long glitter lashes were throwing her off. She would never know me from the club without my dark hair. I had taken off my glasses when they came in, since angels don't wear glasses.

"Don't I know you from somewhere?" she asked as she dabbed herself.

"Do you come here very much? I work here a lot," I said.

She shook her head.

"I don't know. It doesn't matter." Wilted from her former splendor, she trudged unhappily to the bathroom. Jimmie stared at me.

"You did that on purpose," he said.

"What?"

"I know you did. I've watched you serve drinks a hundred times, and you've never had a problem with just one drink."

"Well, for your information, I'm having a klutzy day. That was the third drink I've spilled in less then an hour."

"Right."

I went to get them replacement drinks. I would have bought them drinks for the rest of the night if I could relive that moment the drink sloshed all over her one more time.

They drank their drinks quickly, their amorous mood shifting towards shallow bickering. I waved good-night at them as they left with her bitching about her beer-soaked dress. He left me a ten-dollar tip. I wasn't sure why, but I guess because it's Halloween.

Vicki, Brad and I went to a costume party. Brad wore a vampire outfit; Vicki was a cheerleader. I changed from the angel costume that I wore at work to a more risqué angel. This angel wore a push-up bra and garters. A sheer skirt-type thing started under the bra cup and ended just above my thighs. I hoped that it took away attention from my stomach.

I did have to say that all those sit-ups seemed to be working. Even between the time I bought the outfit and the time I wore it, I had toned up a bit.

A few more months of waitressing and sit-ups and I could be a contender. If I didn't wear glasses.

We had a good time at the party. In fact, we had gone to the party expecting just a regular Halloween party. We were all pleasantly surprised when the booze and drugs kicked in and everyone started to feel the love. The three of us stayed in our core group but we invited other people in. At one point, I remember staring blurry-eyed across the room, seeing a sea of tangled legs and thrusting hips. Everyone was connected to everyone else. It was as if we were performing a magic ritual. Maybe we were. I didn't waste the opportunity and made a quick wish. I'm not going to write it down, because then it won't come true. I don't expect it would anyway. However, stranger things have happened.

The three of us arrived home, and due to the heady intoxication of an orgy and party drugs, Brad was ready to go again.

"Come on, ladies, let's get our Halloween kink on."

Vicki sighed a little bit.

"We don't have to. I feel pretty good right now."

"Besides, it's not Halloween anymore. It's the Day of the Dead."

We all chuckled at the thought, then stopped. My

head was swimming. I was full from the orgy; yet I also hadn't forgotten that it was my first Halloween in New York City. I wanted to end it with a bang. Literally.

To get our second wind, we all decided to smoke a joint. I'm pretty sure Brad did something to that joint, because it seemed kind of different then the usual toke. However, it was hard to tell, since we were already trashed from the party.

As we smoked, talk lazily turned to gossip about people at the party to other, stranger things.

"What's the weirdest way you've ever come?" Brad asked us. His eyes were glowing as he toked the joint. He looked true to his costume, vampiric and deadly. Suddenly I didn't want to play his games. I didn't want to tell him my deepest, darkest secrets. I wanted to skip straight to the sex and stop talking about it.

Vicki took the bait.

"I guess it was back when I was 'bout fifteen. I was on a date with this guy. We had dated for a little while, I even fucked him a couple of times. He found out that I had fucked someone else, though to this day I say it's none of his business. Neither guy had a claim to me as far as I was concerned. He got really pissed off. First he swore and cursed at me, then he slapped me around for being a slut. To prove it, he tore down my jeans and started fucking me. We were in the front seat of his car and there were gearshifts and the steering wheel and all that shit bruising me as he took me. He had his way with me and didn't even give a shit. He was furious. With every hard brutal stroke of his cock, he wrapped his hands around my throat. It was strangely arousing; I had never felt him so big and forceful. He was cutting off my air. I don't know if he really wanted to kill me or not. But somehow, through the combination of sensations, I came my brains out."

I laughed. "People really come when they're suffocating?"

"Sure they do."

"I know people have been found dead trying to come like that. Do you think they made it?"

"Without a doubt. I think that if you're going to die, coming the most glorious come in the world is the way to do it."

"Which brings us back to the topic. Have you ever had the most glorious come you think you can have?"

"I go through phases where I think every time I come, it's the most glorious come I've ever had. I like to live in the moment," I said.

"What gets you off, Abby? Really and truly?"

I tried not to grin too wide. My secrets would be safe inside of me, not splayed open for the others to see and examine and judge.

"Being with you two gets me off. Seeing what new strange and interesting ideas you have gets me off."

Satisfied that I had answered the question adequately, I lit a cigarette. They bantered on for a while, finishing the joint and making plans.

I never listened to them as they discussed the wherefores and how-tos of any session. I liked to live in the moment and see what surprises lay in store for me.

The room was turned into a makeshift dungeon. Dracula had us in his lair. I was the fallen angel; she was a cheerleader who skipped a game and fell into bad times. We were both shackled to a spank bench.

We wailed and lamented as any good actresses should do. Considering the night, it was more like howling at the moon.

Dracula teased and tormented us, threatening to suck our blood as he made us suck his dick. We rattled and clattered and eventually turned to each other for comfort and more. Brad's gaze wasn't quite so steely when he saw me with her, such as today, tonight.

We all managed to work ourselves up to a fuckable frenzy, and Brad started to do me. He kept experimenting with putting his hands over my mouth. I hated it. I didn't see how this was nirvana or even on the right track for it.

He slammed into me doggy-style, alternately playing with my breasts and wrapping his hands around my throat. He knew I was going to come; he could play my body like a violin and read it too. As I approached the blast-off point, he tightened his grip around my throat.

"Too hard," I choked. It was, too. I wasn't trying to be a baby about it.

The warm wonders of orgasm slipped through me and I caught a glimpse of what it was like to come while you die. I could see how people were found dead. It was easy to lose yourself in the moment, but I was smart enough to know how to pull back.

I wouldn't recommend doing it by any stretch of the imagination, but I'm glad I tried it once. Like I said, Brad knew me better then any other lover, and he pulled back immediately. He unshackled me.

I lay back, catching my breath. I with dizzy with pleasure and exhaustion. That had truly taken the last ounce of energy left in me.

Or so I thought.

I watched him with Vicki. She lay on her back, her legs spread wide. He started off maneuvering her hips to the pattern he liked.

She played at being panicked about being shackled, which excited him all the more.

I grabbed a bottle of water from the kitchen and idly sat on the couch, watching them. My pussy ached, but it was a delicious feeling. I was nearly close to being filled up this wonderful Halloween evening.

At least, it should have been a wonderful Halloween evening.

Brad was holding her by the throat, and she looked up at him. She looked hypnotized by white makeup and ruby red lips.

Her legs quivered with pleasure. I could tell she was getting close.

I took Brad's wooden stake off the coffee table and played with it while watching them fuck. I was too tired, too lazy, to suck her tits.

After a few minutes, I saw that Vicki wasn't looking so good, zombie makeup or not. I realized that she was slipping past that point of no return where little deaths can mean big ones.

"Let go of her throat!" I yelled at him. He continued to pump away at her like she was some sort of pleasure toy. Her eyes were bulging. I got up, ran over, and lunged the stake at him in a fit of rage.

His eyes opened wide in horror as the stake slipped into his chest. I'd never been very strong in school, but you never know when you might need it.

I was too strong, I realized as I stood up. As the sudden slashes of pain filtered into Brad's drug-addled brain, I released his grip from her neck.

Vicki's eyes rolled back in her head, lost on the tidal wave of delight she had looked forward to.

I pushed him off of her and set to work trying to revive her as best as I could. She coughed and gasped as I unshackled her, while beside us on the floor, Brad lay in a growing pool of blood.

I didn't have to look twice to see that our friend and lover had bit the big one in the sky.

"Holy fuck, Abby. What are we going to do?"

"I don't know. I need time to think."

I wasn't at all sure what to do about the corpse.

I did what any normal person would do in my situation: I told Vicki to go to bed. She had to go to bed. She had to stay out of the way while I decided what to do about Brad.

Poor Brad.

I wonder what his last thoughts were. . . .

As I set to work devising a plan, I realized I didn't care much.

People died all the time. It was how we all left this world. I just didn't want to be blamed for it.

Brad was a pretty big guy.

I'm strong, but not that strong.

I dragged Brad into the bathroom and flung him into the tub. I went back to my own apartment to get things that I would need.

It took many hours, and it was exhausting, but between an axe, a chain saw and a couple of knives, I was able to cut ol' Brad up pretty good. I gathered parts of him in garbage bags, then shoved those bags into a couple of suitcases.

I wasn't too sure what I was going to do with those suitcases, but I had lots of time to think about it. Vicki was going to be sleeping for a long time, I knew that. She slept forever when she wasn't freaked out, so I felt confident that she would be sleeping even longer with all the booze and drugs coursing through her system.

I took my first load of Brad out for a walk. This one was in a little suitcase I wheeled behind me. I think it was arms and legs. Even that little bit of him weighed quite a bit. I walked along the sidewalks, marveling at how many revelers were still out and about, even though morning was fast upon us. I got a kick at how the little wheels clicked and clacked on the pavement. How normal it was to be walking down the streets of New York on the morning after Halloween with a bit of Brad in a suitcase.

It took a long time, but I managed to stash Brad bit by bit around the city. I returned to Vicki's apartment and gathered up my tools and took them back to my place.

When I came home, I went to the bathroom and took a long, lovely pee. My period had started. Oh boy, more blood to contend with . . .

CHAPTER SEVEN

Sunday, November 6

Vicki is a basket case. She misses Brad. She can't believe that he is gone. She asked what I did with his body, but I didn't tell her. She has sworn that she won't tell. For a while there, I thought she would, and that wouldn't be good at all. How would I explain where his body went? How would I explain it was all just a drug-addled accident? That he nearly killed my friend?

I told Vicki that I'm moving out. I've had enough of all this craziness, and I want my own place and my own life. She looked at me as if I was abandoning her. Yet when she finally spoke, she agreed it was for the best.

I've put most of my stuff in boxes. They are stacked by the door, and every time I come to see her, I take one with me. I'm glad I never did move all my stuff over. I'm really glad I kept my own apartment.

Nothing in life is easy. It just goes on and on.

Sèphera Girón

Tuesday, November 8

I am sitting on a bench at the Museum of Natural History. I really enjoy coming here now and again to think and stare at all the dead animals. My favorite has to be the whale, although there are some pretty impressive dinosaurs too.

When I see the size that some of these creatures were, it makes me feel so insignificant. Every day, one animal kills another to feed. I guess in some ways humans are the same; we just don't usually see the animals we are eating. By the time we have a burger or a steak, the animal doesn't look like anything anymore.

That makes it easy for most people to be carnivors.

I wonder if, when a whale scoops up a school of fish, can he feel them swimming and fluttering in his belly?

A few weeks ago I saw some show on chimps. Those things are really vicious. If they get pissed off, they'll rip you to shreds. There were some people who had raised a chimp from a baby. He was in movies and commercials and they treated him like a son. However, an animal is always an animal, and something bad happened one day and he was sent away.

His owners came to visit him for his birthday and brought a birthday cake. The other chimps went nuts with jealousy, broke out of their cages and went on a rampage. Fingers were eaten; lives were taken.

I think that humans evolved from apes.

Wednesday, November 9

Today I thought I'd celebrate the fact that I brought the last box home by cranking some tunes and drinking some sparkling wine. It felt good to be home. Maybe it would give me a chance to sober up and assess my game plan.

What was my game plan?

I hadn't considered my options in a very long time. I'm thinking that now had better be that time.

My dream was to move to New York and lose myself.

I guess I did accomplish that already. I've really lost myself at this point. Vicki saw me kill Brad, and God only knows if she's going to keep my secret. I tried to keep her drugged up for a few days, and dragged out getting my boxes so that I'd have excuses to see her and get her high and work wonders on her body. I was hoping that Halloween night would be just a blur. Just one more crazy drug-addled night. Maybe I could convince her that Brad had just left that night. Maybe he was angry that we didn't want to play his games, and he took off.

I wondered how much she remembered.

She's never mentioned if she heard the chain saw going when I was dismembering dear Braddy-boy. That had been quite a poetic moment.

I remember staring at him as he lay in the bathtub. I had donned a pair of large sunglasses since none of us had any goggles or other eye gear. They were a joke from Ooolala. The sunglasses were huge and purple with rhinestones dotting the outer frames.

Anyway, Brad was lying half naked in the bathtub. I had removed his cape because it kept tripping us up when I was dragging him into the bathroom. I couldn't decide the best way to start the project. I figured his head might be a good beginning. It would be a simple task, and I'd get the feel for the chain saw.

The chain saw was old. It had once belonged to my grandfather. I rarely saw my grandparents, and they died when I was young. They lived on a big old farm, and in the barn were treasures for miles.

One of my cousins saw me poking around the barn, and he spied the chainsaw first.

Terry was only about fifteen at the time. He picked up that chain saw and swung it around with glee. It was old and rusty. He pulled on the chain and it roared to life. The force of the motor running caused him to lose control of it. It fell from his hands and gashed him in the thigh a good six inches.

The chain saw bounced to the ground as we stared in horror at the blood flowing from him. Though I was only about ten myself, I reached over to that chain saw and picked it up. The vibration in my hand felt soothing. I swung it in the air a few times and considered what it would be like to slice through Terry's leg. Images of blood spurting as he screamed played through my mind. The separation of meat from bone, of leg from body would be fascinating to see.

He screamed as I fiddled with the chainsaw, trying to figure out how to turn it off. Terry nearly died from blood loss that day and still walks with a limp. The last time I saw him, he looked like a huge bloated walrus that washed up to shore. He had one of those horrible handlebar mustaches that women loathe, and he was splotchy and shaky. His voice was as weak as his countenance as he sat like Jabba the Hutt in his easy chair. There was always a beer in his hand and a story to lament over. Nothing was worse than the day he got bitten by the chain saw.

You have to be careful with chain saws. If you treat them right, then they will behave as they should.

When I left the farm that weekend, I hid the chain saw in my belongings. At the time, I didn't know why. I couldn't imagine what use a girl like me would have for a chain saw. Yet I have to admit, it has come in handy once in a while.

The head came off easily enough. I stood holding Brad by the hair and examined his face, frozen wide eyed and slack jawed forever.

"Poor, dear Brad," I told him. "You got too close that time. You pushed it too far."

For a moment I mused on the loss he would be in my life; then I put his head in the sink. Blood was already everywhere, and I had just begun.

It took a long time, but I managed to cut Braddy-boy up into manageable pieces. I put his cock in the sink with his head. That poor little piece of flesh seemed so ridiculous by itself that I ended up throwing it into the garbage bag with other parts.

There were a few times I thought I was going to toss my cookies. I made the mistake of trying to cut his torso in half. His guts spilled out everywhere, and I realized that they were going to be a bitch to clean up. For some reason, I didn't factor in how messy they would be with him propped up. Of course, he wasn't propped up for long after that. Still, the sight of intestines and blood and other gunk pooling and slopping made me nauseous. The toilet called to me and I dry-heaved a few times. I wanted to get a glass of water, but he was staring at me from the sink.

That was one of the times I checked on Vicki. She was out like a light. I even heard her snoring a bit. So it was fine to continue. I walked past the living room and thought about what a bitch it was going to be to clean up all that blood.

Brad was bundled up and off he went. I returned to the task of cleaning everything up before Vicki awoke.

She never saw any blood. Every single drop was accounted for. I even checked the light fixtures for any evidence at all. One little drop could spill the beans, especially if it was in a weird place. There have been enough forensic shows on TV for any normal person to know that.

So that she wouldn't be suspicious of all the cleaning smells, I boiled a pot of water with cinnamon and cloves in it. Soon the whole apartment smelled of delicious spices, although I could still detect an undercurrent of rotting meat. That was just my own imagination, though, because Brad hadn't been dead long enough to rot. The smell was my own guilt.

What's done is done.

There's nothing I can do about it.

I was wasted the same as everyone else. Maybe I didn't handle things as someone else might have, but I did what I did when I did it. I'm only human, and that's what humans do.

So I had to consider what to do next. What were my options?

Moving seemed so tedious, and it's not easy in New York. I was lucky to find this strange little apartment, and even that is not cheap. My landlord never bothers me, and my neighbors keep to themselves. In fact, if I ever saw one of my neighbors walking down the street, I wouldn't even recognize him.

There was no point in moving unless I went somewhere really far away. Over the rainbow.

I was in Oz already, and I sure as hell didn't want to go back to Kansas.

My job at Ooolala is a good job, especially for someone like me. I've got a few bucks in the bank. Maybe close to three grand saved up since I've been here. All that overtime is paying off, and since I have no life, no love, no hope, I might as well work as much as I can.

Work is my social life now too. Though I had Vicki and Brad for a while, now I'm back to square one. Of course, Vicki is still my friend, and I intend to see her as I always did. Maybe one day we can find another guy and share a life together.

But that won't be for a while.

So what do I do?

Should I be worried about police?

How do we explain Brad's disappearance after more time goes by? How do we explain to his job that he walked out and never came back?

I guess people do it all the time. It was Brad's turn now.

If I disappear during the early stages of Brad's disappearance, then people will either think we took off together or that I'm guilty of something having to do with him.

People disappear in big cities all the time. Some aren't discovered for months. Some are never found.

Brad could be one of those people that just suddenly snapped and wanted to be lost.

I knew how that felt. That was what brought me to this place to begin with. To feel lost.

Friday, November 11

Despite my seasonal melancholy, I've decided to continue with my fitness regime. Since I was unable to come up with a good life plan, I figured I should make my goals more realistic. Smaller and doable.

A new exercise program is in order. Now each day I must stretch from head to toe. I may sit or stand or lie on the floor, whatever my body tells me to do.

Sometimes my body wants to work hard, while other times it seems like it wants nothing more than a break. I can't always let my body decide for me what I may or may not do. Usually the problem happens when I have my morning routine. My body cries and whines, sluggish from dreaming and reluctant to fuel itself with pumping blood and the rigorous task of life. Sometimes I just have to accept the fact that I'm just not a morning person.

After work is when I fare best. I'm tired from working, but know that if I do something for my body, it will reward me by perking up later. On some days I need every breath to get started, but once I'm through the warm-up, I'm pretty good. I make sure each part of my body gets a good workout, especially my back and shoulders. Waitressing can make you really achy if you don't watch it.

My favorite part of the workout is choosing my three songs. Every day I give myself three songs to pick for my cardio. Today I picked random songs from Jay-Z and Linkin Park's *Collision Course*, Ludicris's *Red Light District* and Eminem's hit song "Lose Yourself".

Today's workout made me feel strong.

Sunday, November 13

She is getting on my nerves, I tell you. As I sit here, I would rather be somewhere else. Nearly anywhere else in the world right now.

Vicki has decided not to leave well enough alone. She bitches and moans constantly about Brad. Now that a bit of time has gone by, she's remembered some sensations.

At any rate, I thought the whole thing should have been put to rest days ago. We did a bad, bad thing and now have to pretend it didn't happen at all.

Vicki was horrified when I reminded her that she was just as guilty.

"What do you mean, I'm guilty?" she asked.

"Exactly what I said. You did nothing to help him. You didn't save him. You didn't call an ambulance. You don't even know where he went. So what are you going to tell to who?"

I had Vicki by the neck and pressed her against the

wall. Her trembling pulse was pumping rapidly, and I felt it cycle the adrenaline of fear and excitement through her.

"You are guilty. If any one finds out that we killed someone, then we are up shit creek."

"I saw you do it."

"And you did nothing. That's a crime too, Vicki."

Actually, I'm not sure what kind of crime it is to be being fucked and strangled while chained up, albeit willingly, and someone kills the guy doing it to you.

Maybe it would hold up in court. Maybe not. But I sure as shit had no intention of finding out.

"Maybe he's not dead," I said. "Maybe he was just wounded and eventually felt better and is walking around as we speak."

"If that's a fact, then why hasn't he come by to see us?"

"Would you?"

She hesitated and sighed. "Maybe not. Maybe he had enough of our petty little ways."

"Petty little ways?"

"Face it, Abby. You are major high-maintenance. One only has to look at you wrong and you will swoop in as if you could kill them."

"I was protecting you. He was too rough. He was always hurting you."

"Maybe I like it rough. Maybe I wanted to be hurt."

I squeezed her throat and she jerked her head. Her eyes were wide.

"Do you remember that? Do you remember how hard he was squeezing your throat? You dumb bitch, if you looked in the mirror once in a while instead of at your tits all the time, you would see there are still bruises there. I saved your life. Next time you could have been dead."

"I doubt it."

"How do you know? How do you know he doesn't make a habit of shacking up with women and strangling them to death? He could have been a serial killer."

"I hardly think so."

"We didn't know anything about him. All I know is that he kept getting rougher with you. Every time we played, he'd have a new idea or gimmick for us to try. He'd push and push. He wanted the ultimate sensation. Well, baby, he got it."

"What exactly happened again?" Vicki asked. I let go of her throat, and she leaned forward, gasping for air.

I forcefully shoved her to the couch. My lips were on hers as I roughly pinched and pulled at her tits. She kept asking what happened but soon stopped asking as I slid my fingers into her hot wetness. She cooed and sighed, her moods changing so dramatically that I thought I was in a summer storm.

I couldn't tell her what happened, and there was no way in hell I ever would.

I seduced her, shutting that inquisitive mouth of hers with mine. After I made her come a couple of times, I pulled out my cigarettes.

"Let's have a smoke, and then I have to go," I told her. I smoked her up, and while I did so, I weaved the fabric of a new tale. As the weed took hold, she began to believe our new fable. How we had an argument with Brad on Halloween night, and he stomped off, never to be seen again. Did he meet with foul play? Was it preplanned? We had no idea.

Of course, there would be matters such as unused bank accounts and missed work.

It wouldn't be hard at all to find his bank card information.

I realized that I had to stop carrying the wallet in my purse. I could use his money to buy time, a ticket to Greece or some faraway place. I could use his bank card to purchase such a ticket. Maybe I'd bring Vicki too, depending on how much savings he'd managed to amass.

There was the whole tricky business of not knowing his PIN number.

When I got back to my apartment, I punched in his banking information. It wasn't hard to get, since I had looked over his shoulders a few times and realized his password was something like "orgy." I printed it out. He didn't have his own computer and usually used mine. He had other stuff on my computer too.

That magical PIN number was going to be a bitch. It's moments like this that I wish I was psychic.

However, in cracking open his computer file, I was able to get an idea of what he might have used for a PIN number.

There were lists of dates, days, ideas. . . .

Maybe it was sheer luck on my part, or maybe it was fate, but I managed to figure out his password and get into his online bank account.

I wondered if they could trace the computer, and I immediately signed out.

Now that I knew his password, I could have access to his money, maybe make it look like he was living somewhere else.

Monday, November 14

Mavis invited me to a little soiree at her apartment. I'm not sure why the drag queens have taken a liking to me, but it bridges the gap of loneliness I've been feeling since Vicki and I don't talk much anymore. Or at least we sure don't talk like we used to. And I guess we won't be picking up men together anytime soon either. . . .

Wednesday, November 16

It's a good thing I've been sticking to my exercise routine, because Jimmie came in today and sat in my section. He looked sad and disheveled, and he wasn't in the mood to talk. Our exchange was short. He ordered and asked me how I was. I said I was fine, and that was the extent of our meaningful dialogue for the day.

That's OK. I know that sometimes someone can have a bad day and just needs someone to listen to him. He will have to talk to somebody someday, and when he thinks about who he should talk to, he'll realize that it should be me. I'm the one who's always there for him. I'm the one that knows what he likes to ingest. I know how to shut up when he's scribbling in his notepad and how to anticipate his refill needs.

It will take some time, but I'll coax him to me yet.

Later

Sometimes I wonder what I'm here for. What is the meaning of life? What is the meaning of me? Am I supposed to just live day to day, or was I meant for something bigger? I yearn to do something important, but I don't know what that is.

Since I wander alone, vacillating in emptiness, I've been trying to make my apartment more interesting. I've set up quite a display. It is good enough to be a museum.

Monica, my skeleton, sits in the rocking chair, with a jaunty hat. Brad's head sits in her lap. I got tired of staring at his open, rotting eyes, so I closed them a while back. He smells pretty bad these days, but it won't be long before he mummifies or something, I'm sure. To keep the smell from getting too bad, I constantly boil cinnamon-and-clove water. I also have a few of those plug-in air freshener things with that holiday smell as well.

Overlooking it all is my Angel. She's not smelling too good, either, and is getting pretty bloated and gross. I think that I'm going to have to do something about all the rotting flesh. I wish I was a witch or something and could just magically make them mummified. It seems to me that I may have to strip the flesh off and just have skeletons.

However, that isn't today's worry.

Today, I'm thinking about my life. I'm a bit depressed and I guess it has to do with the weather too. Sometimes it feels as if the world is closing in on me.

CHAPTER EIGHT

Thursday, November 17

Earlier today, I found myself walking by Jimmie's building. It's like there's a magnet pulling me there. He is such an enigma—one minute friendly and outgoing, the next silent and sullen. But isn't that just like a man? If only I could get close to him, he'd realize that I'm not like other girls. I'm especially not like that woman he keeps hanging out with.

I sat on his steps for a while, not really caring if he came by or not.

I've upped my exercise routine to push-ups and hand weights to build up my biceps and triceps.

Later

They were at Boingo's again. They didn't see me, I don't think. I watched them sitting around having drinks. They seemed to be arguing about something.

At one point, Shrew Lady looked like she was going to burst into tears. Wouldn't it be great if they broke up?

He looked so hot tonight. He wore tight leather pants and a blousy shirt. Those pants made his ass even more delicious then usual. Maybe he doesn't realize he can do better then her.

Friday, November 18

Vicki is making me crazy. Again there was a message on the answering machine from her. She was all hysterical, saying that Brad's family keeps calling her wanting to know where he is. I decided I'd better go over to see her.

She had just come home from working the afternoon shift when I got there. I hadn't seen her in a while, and she didn't look so hot. There were big bags under her eyes, and she seemed jumpy. Maybe she was taking new types of drugs.

As always, I had come over prepared to sedate her. She spoke of crazy things, like saying we had to go to the police before it's too late. I told her that there's no way we're going to do that. We need to stick with our story. It's a good story. He's disappeared. Finito. It's not our problem.

"But his mother has been calling here nearly every day to see if I've heard anything from him."

"And what do you say?"

"I say that I haven't, of course. Because I haven't."

"Good. That's all you need to say. That's all you can say."

"But I feel so guilty."

130

"Why?"

" 'Cause I'm lying."

"Don't feel guilty. You had nothing to do with anything. It was self-defense, plain and simple."

She stared at me with bloodshot eyes. "It wasn't self-defense. You killed him. He wasn't hurting you."

"He was hurting you. Remember?"

Vicki took a haul from the joint. "I don't even know anymore. It's all just a bad dream. I can't even imagine what life we had. It was fun, and now it's a nightmare."

"Life doesn't have to be a nightmare. So we had a lover that disappeared. It happens all the time. Especially in a big city like this."

"But Brad's mother said he was a good boy. He always e-mailed or called her. He always told her everything. She knew he was living with both of us."

"There's nothing you can do. Nothing at all." I leaned towards her and kissed her. She pulled back.

"Don't."

"Why not?"

"I don't want to."

"You don't like me anymore?"

She took my hand. "I'm very confused and sad. I don't know what to do about anything or anyone anymore. I mean, really, what should I do? What am I meant to do?"

"I told you, do nothing."

"It's hard to do nothing when this eats at me every waking minute."

"Push it away. You have to, Vicki. It will drive you mad if you don't."

"I am going mad."

Seeing that I was getting nowhere with the woman, I left.

I wandered the streets, alone and lonely. I stared longingly at all the happy couples. I needed a vacation.

Tuesday, November 23

On the spur of the moment, I took a leave of absence from work. It was time to get my head together. The ocean was calling to me, so I took a train and then rented a car until I found myself in a small town in Massachusetts.

Everything is so different in New England. I spent the money I had been saving for school on a little bed-and-breakfast in a cove. Well, I didn't spend *all* the money, but it wasn't a cheap deal, either.

Winter was quickly approaching. I was amazed that there hadn't already been lots of snow. That's global warming for you. The sky was turbulent and dark, as if warning of impending danger. The air was damp with a misty fog that clung to your skin. At random moments, the sun would peek through the clouds, illuminating the swelling waters of the ocean as if a show were about to begin. As nature danced her seasonal rituals, my mind slipped and shuffled through thoughts that spit images of things that had happened and things that could.

Walking along the beach gave me a sense of peace I sorely needed. Despite the cold, I took off my shoes and let the ice-cold water undulate back and forth along my toes.

It reminded me of a time when I was a child and saw

the ocean for the first time. It was a chilly November day much like this one. My eyes filled with tears as an elation swelled through me like nothing I had felt before. My mother was cracking open a beer with her sister as my cousins ran ahead into the water with their clothes on. They laughed and splashed, daring me to follow. I looked at my mother and she laughed too, waving me to follow them.

"Go on, Abby. Feel the ocean. It's like nothing else."

"Come with me," I pleaded, watching how the waves crashed, bigger and bigger with every push forward. It seemed to me that my cousins were bobbing out to sea as they floated and swam in the waves.

My mother took my hand and we waded out. It was freezing, but the sensation of the rhythmic water pulsing against me gave me the feeling that this was where I wanted to go.

When I went down a couple days ago, I had the same feelings. It was as if a dream I once had was real again. My cousins have grown up and I believe almost all of them have kids. I'm not sure. I don't keep track of anyone, just like they don't keep track of me.

The water called to me, but I didn't go in except for my feet. It was enough to gaze in wonderment at it. I remember reading *Papillon* and how he counted the rhythm of the waves for his escape. That first day I went to the beach, the tide was coming in. That is why the waves grew bigger and closer, as if to eat you, my dear.

Listening to the unending roar of the tide was soothing at first, but then it started to get on my nerves. After about an hour I went back to my room.

It's agitating sitting here in this little room. It's very small and it's all I have. There's a dining area for meals, but I seldom go. They leave me snacks, which I take with me on my walks.

Even though I had already done my exercise routine that day, I figured I may as well do it again. It passed the time and I liked rocking out to the tunes. Since I came here, I hunted down *Quadrophenia* and added some of the ocean songs to my routine.

After I was finished, I was still bored.

Gazing at my body in the mirror wasn't as traumatizing as it usually was. The results of my workouts were starting to show. I turned sideways, marveling at how if I looked just right, I could see the beginning of muscle tone along my belly. My arms were more defined too. I had to increase my hand weights to thirty pounds each.

My boobs were starting to shrink, though, and that was a bit depressing. I had hoped they would get firmer and fuller, but no such luck.

The cheeks of my ass were taking that apple shape I always loved on other women. It was amazing how just lying on the floor and lifting your ass in the air really worked if you did it long enough.

It wouldn't be long before I could pull out all stops and offer myself fully and completely to Mr. Johnny Depp Look-Alike. When that time came, I would be more then ready. It wouldn't be long before I could afford laser eye surgery and totally seduce him.

I guess if I hadn't taken this trip, I could have gotten my eyes done. But, really, I'm kind of scared. I have no one to go with me, and what if I go blind? Sure, they say no one has ever gone blind. And they say that if they do it wrong, they can do it another way and keep tinkering until they get it right. But what if I'm the exception? Even rich and famous people have horrible experiences with cosmetic surgery. Look at that novelist who died getting a face-lift. Or that musician who went too far with his nose. Actors and actresses looking worse then they ever could have if they had left well enough alone. Messing with my eyes was the same. If I was happy wearing glasses, that should be enough.

But I wonder what it must be like to actually see the clock in the middle of the night, or to fall asleep watching TV without waking up with dents on your face, or going swimming and seeing the seaweed waving, or even seeing the face of your lover as he comes?

What must that be like?

Part of me craved to see all that and more. The other part was terrified. It probably hurts too. The literature all says mild discomfort. Stories from people posting on Web sites vary from light pressure to sharp, cutting pain. Which way would it go for me?

I decided to walk away from the ocean and see where it got me. The roads were gravelly, and between the crunching under my feet and the waves in my ears, my nerve endings were throbbing. It wouldn't be long before I got a headache, and I didn't want to ruin my vacation with that.

After about forty-five minutes, I came to the main road. There were a couple of pubs, a few stores and some other stuff. The whole main drag was probably three blocks, if that. I walked up and down looking into places, trying to get a feel for the people. At last I decided to get a beer.

The Floundering Fisherman seemed like as good a place as any. The outside was paneled like a rustic little shack. Inside there were horseshoe crabs, lobsters and starfish stuck into nets that hung from the ceiling. The walls had seafaring stuff like boats and life preservers on them. Thank God there was a bar with lots of stools. There were a few tables and chairs for people that wanted to chow down. I picked a stool away from anyone.

There were quite a few people in the place. Couples sat at a few tables. There were rowdy people. Some men and women sat at the bar. I didn't feel too strange.

I saw with amazement that someone was lighting a cigarette. When the bartender came over, I asked him if there was smoking in here.

"Ayup." I had no idea what the smoking laws in Massachusetts were, so I got out my pack of smokes while he brought me a draft.

On my left was a couple probably on a first or second date. It was fun to watch their preening and cocking of heads as they sized each other up. On my other side were four guys razzing each other. I didn't know if they had all come together or if they had arrived separately. It didn't really matter; it was just curiosity.

A band was setting up. I saw guitars and a drum kit, and I smiled. I hoped they would play rock and roll and not some bluesy crap. At the end of the bar was a young-looking guy with scraggly blond hair and a baseball cap. He was wire-thin and looked nervous. He was young. I thought he must be about nineteen,

GET UP TO 4 FREE BOOKS!

You can have the best fiction delivered to your door for less than what you'd pay in a bookstore or online—only $4.25 a book! Sign up for our book clubs today, and we'll send you **FREE* BOOKS** just for trying it out...**with no obligation to buy, ever!**

LEISURE HORROR BOOK CLUB

With more award-winning horror authors than any other publisher, it's easy to see why CNN.com says "Leisure Books has been leading the way in paperback horror novels." Your shipments will include authors such as RICHARD LAYMON, DOUGLAS CLEGG, JACK KETCHUM, MARY ANN MITCHELL, and many more.

LEISURE THRILLER BOOK CLUB

If you love fast-paced page-turners, you won't want to miss any of the books in Leisure's thriller line. Filled with gripping tension and edge-of-your-seat excitement, these titles feature everything from psychological suspense to legal thrillers to police procedurals and more!

As a book club member you also receive the following special benefits:

- **30% OFF all orders through our website & telecenter!**
- **Exclusive access to special discounts!**
- **Convenient home delivery and 10 days to return any books you don't want to keep.**

There is no minimum number of books to buy, and you may cancel membership at any time. See back to sign up!

YES! ☐

Sign me up for the Leisure Horror Book Club and send my TWO FREE BOOKS! If I choose to stay in the club, I will pay only $8.50* each month, a savings of $5.48!

YES! ☐

Sign me up for the Leisure Thriller Book Club and send my TWO FREE BOOKS! If I choose to stay in the club, I will pay only $8.50* each month, a savings of $5.48!

NAME: _____

ADDRESS: _____

_____

TELEPHONE: _____

E-MAIL: _____

☐ **I WANT TO PAY BY CREDIT CARD.**

☐ VISA   ☐ MasterCard   ☐ DISCOVER

ACCOUNT #: _____

EXPIRATION DATE: _____

SIGNATURE: _____

Send this card along with $2.00 shipping & handling for each club you wish to join, to:

**Horror/Thriller Book Clubs
20 Academy Street
Norwalk, CT 06850-4032**

Or fax (must include credit card information!) to: 610.995.9274.
You can also sign up online at www.dorchesterpub.com.

*Plus $2.00 for shipping. Offer open to residents of the U.S. and Canada only.
Canadian residents please call 1.800.481.9191 for pricing information.
If under 18, a parent or guardian must sign. Terms, prices and conditions subject to change. Subscription subject to acceptance. Dorchester Publishing reserves the right to reject any order or cancel any subscription.

JOIN NOW!

even though you have to be twenty-one to drink. Maybe he just looked young, wearing a jean jacket and a plaid shirt. AC/DC's "Highway to Hell" came over the system and I bobbed my head along to it. Even though Young Buns looked pretty depressed, he nodded his head along to the music too. Somewhere someone screamed with laughter as a table full of young rowdies sang along, power-pumping the air with their fists.

Young Buns kept catching my eye, and soon he was mouthing the words.

After "Highway to Hell," they played "Hotel California," and Young Buns started to look sad again. I made my move.

I scooped up my beer and walked over. I perched myself on the empty stool next to him.

"Is this seat taken?" I asked. He stared at me with pretty blue eyes, looking both like he was caught playing with himself and carrying a hurt of enormous magnitude.

"Uh, no. No, it's not. Well, I guess it is now," he stammered and looked into his beer.

"Reading the future?" I asked.

He blushed.

"Gosh, no. No. Not at all. You can't read the future in beer."

"Sure you can. It's called scrying. It works better with water in a black bowl, but you can do it in a pint of beer."

I leaned over my beer and stared into it. I could feel the heat of his gaze upon me.

"Can you see anything?" he asked. It was hard not to laugh at his naivete.

"Oh, yes. Things are coming very clearly into focus." I squinted my eyes to add a bit of drama.

"What do you see? Is it about me?"

"It's about you all right. It's about both you and me."

"What do you mean?"

I took off my glasses and paused. I looked him right in the eyes as best as I could considering I can't see past the tip of my nose without my glasses.

"I don't think I should tell you what I saw. It's too embarrassing." I tossed my head, pretending to be flustered as I took a sip from my glass.

"Oh, now you've gone and messed it up," he said. "I wanted to see it too."

"If it's meant to be, you'll see it too." I pointed to his beer glass. "Now look at the froth and then at the amber liquid. Examine how they bleed into each other. Each swirl and texture melts together to create pictures. Open your mind and see what pictures are there."

"I don't see nothing." He pouted.

I pushed him aside and stared into the beer. "That's just 'cause you are new at it. I can see it here too. Plain as day. You and me. Take another look."

He came back to the glass and peered in. I coached him until he too saw the two of us lying tangled in bedsheets, grinning like we had tasted the pleasures of the devil himself.

"Oh my. What does it mean?" he asked.

"It's the future," I said to him, letting my hand brush against his thigh as I reached back to pull my bar stool closer.

"We saw the future?"

"We saw what we could have," I said.

"We can?"

"Why not?" I asked him, breathing in his ear.

The band broke into a smashing chorus of an old Stones song. Suddenly it was too loud to talk, so we turned and watched the performers. By the time the set was done, we had nearly finished a pitcher of beer. My new buddy, Simon, waved for another one.

In the silence of the break, I discovered that he was newly broken up with his girlfriend. He was living with a buddy who was away for a bit visiting his girlfriend at a faraway college. He worked for a construction company and was feeling lonely.

Of course, in the web of beer and music, everyone dances to his or her own agenda. When we got into the car, he broke down and confessed something else. He still lived with his mother and he was saving for college. We couldn't go to his place. There was no way I could take him to the bed-and-breakfast.

We hit the highway and drove until we found a little motel. It was perfect. Small and seedy and cheap. All I cared about was a bed and a bathroom. Nothing else mattered at all.

By the time we went through the check-in procedures, my heart was crashing wildly. I was so horny, so excited. This young guy was so eager and easy. The thought crossed my mind that he might be a hooker, but he had said nothing at all to indicate such a thing. Even if he was, who the hell cared?

We entered the room and shut the door. He stared at me nervously. I grabbed him and planted my lips on his. No point in being coy; we both knew why we were here. We kissed and he was trembling. His hands shook as he touched my arms. Poor kid was nervous.

"I'm going to freshen up," I told him as I went into the tiny, scuzzy bathroom. There was a sink and a shower stall. The walls were paper-thin. I could hear the couple next door going at it. The bed banged against the wall as the couple talked dirty to each other. I quickly went to the bathroom and washed up with one of the cloths hanging on the rack. I looked at myself naked and thought I looked pretty damn hot. I touched my pussy and felt my swollen lips, ready for some excitement.

When I returned, he was sitting naked in the bed. I had to resist the urge to laugh at the poor thing. He was even scrawnier naked. His thin, narrow chest had tiny little tits. He barely had underarm hair. His head almost looked too heavy to perch on that frail little body. He still looked pensive.

I stood at the foot of the bed and shook my tits at him. I thought he was going to come on the spot as he grabbed the bulge perking up the sheet that was wrapped around his waist. I sashayed over to the TV set and turned it on. "We don't want the neighbors to hear us." In that instant before I clicked the dial, I think the neighbor shot his load, because he cried out loudly and she ooh-oohed right along with him.

Young Buns blushed.

I fiddled with the crappy TV until I found some semblance of a station, which was playing crappy country music. At least it was something.

I crawled towards him on the bed like a panther

stalking her prey. His hands eagerly pushed on my head as I took him into my mouth. He seemed like he was getting too excited, so I stopped and worked my way up his body until I was kissing him. Just as I was about to straddle him, he pushed weakly at me.

"Wait," he said.

"What's wrong?" I was impatient to feel him inside me. It took all my strength not to just snap and sit on him.

"I . . . shouldn't . . . shouldn't we use protection?"

I grinned. "Oh, that's all. Sure, if you want to." I hopped off the bed and got a condom from my purse. I threw it over to him and crawled up the bed again.

I watched him stare at the package.

"What's wrong?"

"I, uh . . . I've never used one of these before," he said, blushing about fifty shades of red.

"Here, I'll help you." I opened the packet and started rolling it on.

"Why do you want to use one on me if you never use one?" I asked.

"Well . . . I don't know you . . . and, well . . ."

"That's OK. I use them all the time."

I jerked him with my hand to get him going again, but he was wilting.

"Is there something wrong?" I asked.

"I . . ." He looked over at the TV. "I've never, you know . . . done it."

"Oh . . ." I didn't know what to say to that. The thought of deflowering a virgin seemed like a delicious idea to me. He was here. He wanted it.

"Well, why don't I suck you again, and we'll see what's what," I said. I pulled off the condom and sucked him. He lay back, his eyes closed.

"You know what is really exciting?" I asked him.

"What?"

"If I handcuff you to the bed."

"Really? I've seen that on the Internet. You'll handcuff me and blow me?"

"Oh yes, I'll blow you."

I went back to my purse and got out the handcuffs and more condoms.

"Just in case . . ." I grinned.

"OK . . ." he said.

It was easy to slip the handcuffs on him. In fact, he was so skinny that I thought he might be able to get away. Thank goodness he had large hands. Well, you know what they say about large hands. He sure had what it took.

After I had him handcuffed and going good, it wasn't hard to blindfold and gag him either. Seeing him helpless made me shiver with delight.

When he was restored to full glory once more, I took another condom and put it on him. If he protested, I have no idea. I just knew that I rode him like the headless horseman rode that horse through Sleepy Hollow. Every time I thought he wasn't going to last, I shifted rhythm or stopped entirely.

Finally I had my fill and climbed off of him. He was still hard. Still unfulfilled. I chuckled as I went into the bathroom and took a shower. The water trickled out, but it didn't matter. Even the rusty sulfur smell of well water didn't gross me out as it usually did.

I crawled into bed, still half drunk, and watched some stupid country comedy show. The people next door were at it again. Simon struggled against his cuffs now and again, but I couldn't hear him complaining. Before I allowed myself to sleep, I made certain I tied his feet to the bottom posts of the bed.

When I woke, he was either sleeping or tired of struggling. I sucked on his dick, bringing it back to life. Still horny, he was unable to resist me, and I climbed back on top of him.

He lasted in this way for the better part of a day. Then he started to get tired or worried or just plain unresponsive. I wondered if anyone ever died from blue balls.

"You see, Simon, if you don't come, you are still a virgin," I said.

I was hungry, so I went to a donut shop that I had spotted on our way in. I came back armed with coffee and sandwiches.

I took his gag off and fed him. He ate like a man who hadn't eaten in forever.

"Do you like this?" I asked him.

"I don't know."

"Have you heard of bondage? Of S/M?"

"Yeah, I've seen pictures on the Internet."

"Well, in the pictures, you don't really have a sense of what people go through. Some people like to be tied up for days and put through tortures.

"All sorts of things. Clothespins. Floggers. You name it."

He seemed curious enough that I went into town and bought a few items. By the end of the day, he was covered in clothespins. I bet they hurt like a son of a bitch, especially on his scrotum and cock, but he was bound and gagged so he had no say in any of it.

By the time I had used up all the clothespins, I was exhausted. I munched on a candy bar and realized that I hadn't exercised for over a day and a half. The TV was a mess, but after fiddling with the rabbit ears, I found a sitcom. For half an hour, I did crunches and push-ups on the floor.

The exercise sent a new flood of adrenaline coursing through me. As I did my relaxation stretch on my back, my feet behind my head and my knees at my ears, I daydreamed about a big hard cock pounding at me. Brad was good at doing that. He wasn't afraid to twist me up like a pretzel, penetrating me from so many different angles that he hit pleasure spots I didn't even know existed.

Well, where there was Brad, there had to be other men that could do such a good job. If I had the time and patience, I could even train little Simon to do such things.

I stretched out on the floor, running my hands along my tits, fiddling with my nipples. Time was running out. My hand reached between my legs and I closed my eyes. The emptiness was there, a black hole gaping wider as turbulence swirled around it. Would I ever find a way to fill that hole?

Getting rid of Brad seemed logical at the time. I thought maybe without his irritating patter my nerves would get better. My job was going well. The drag queens loved me. I was going to more and more parties with them. I missed Vicki. I missed what I used to have with Vicki, when she was just an elusive enigma that I yearned to penetrate. Now she was worried and scared and she didn't seem to like me much anymore.

I wondered if she actually hated me at times. And did she love Brad?

If she had loved Brad, she never admitted it. I guess because she knew that, if she did, I would be hurt. It was supposed to be three people adoring one another equally. Of course, I didn't keep my end of it either, did I, fancying Vicki over Brad? And Brad fancied Vicki over me. It was doomed to failure no matter how you looked at it. I just hurried it along accidentally.

Out of curiosity, I riffled through Simon's things. In his wallet were his fake ID and his driver's license. Well, he got what he wanted; who was I to care at this point how old he was?

I chuckled.

There was coffee to be had as I mused over the best way to do what came next. In the end, I thought I'd try old Braddy-boy's technique. Give the boy his first fuck-orgasm with a twist.

After I drank two large cups of coffee with cream and sugar, and chowed down on a couple of donuts, I felt fresh energy surging through me. I debated doing some push-ups but decided on a more pleasurable way to do them. I climbed on Mr. Limpdick and tried to bring him to life. He shook his head weakly. I knew he must be hungry, and lying there all blindfolded and gagged while I drank coffee must have bugged the shit out of him.

"C'mon, baby, one more time and then I'll untie you." I licked his neck along the clothespins. As I unsnapped each pin, he flinched. At last I had cleared away enough pins from his groin and thighs that I could climb on top unencumbered. There were angry red pinch marks where the clothespins had been, and I could only imagine how much it must have hurt.

As blood throbbed back to his penis, it grew even bigger than it had been yet. This boy was gonna blow big-time.

I took the rope and got ready to wrap it around his neck as I climbed on board.

I'm pretty sure he enjoyed his last few minutes of ecstasy. Foam spilled out around his ball gag as he shuddered and tried to gasp for air. At last his twitching stopped and I continued on for a while, grabbing what last twinges of pleasure I could from him.

The next part would be easy. I'd pay the bill, and then when night came, we'd leave.

I went over to the deserted part of the beach I had gotten to know over the past few days, where the tide would eventually come up and cover the sand, and started to work on reducing him to a more manageable and unrecognizable size. As with Brad, I saved his head. The rest I managed to stuff into a couple of heavy-duty garbage bags. Simon was pretty much stew by the time I was done with him. I dragged him out as far as I could and hoped the tide would eventually pull him out far enough for sharks to smell.

It wasn't unreasonable to think that he could be shark food. There were sharks all over these waters. I didn't know if they still hung around in November, but even other fish might enjoy a snack. I can imagine him covered in little crabs and barnacles. Tiny sea creatures delighted at the feast they were going to have over the next few days or weeks or however long it took. I was certain that before that, some larger predator would scoop him up.

I tossed the head into a garbage bag and put it in the trunk. The chain saw is clean: I waded into the water, and the blood would be washed from the beach by the tide. I hope I thought of everything.

If I couldn't bring myself to be part of the earth just yet, I had to give a sacrifice. This sacrifice to the ocean would allow me to return to my beloved city awhile longer to taste what future delights might be in store with Mr. J.D.

CHAPTER NINE

Thursday, November 24

I've been sick as a dog for a couple of days. It's really sucked, because I had to work. You can't come back from taking time off and then take more time off because you got sick where you went. The staff thought that I had just been partying too hard, but I knew better. My stupid cold is the direct result of wading into the freezing cold ocean. When will I ever learn that I get sick so easily?

Time for more of that codeine cough syrup. Damn, that shit's good.

Friday, November 25

I've finally kicked my cold. I feel like a whole new woman. Today I managed to get through half of my exercise routine without coughing up a lung. It was just awful how crappy I felt. I don't even know what I was coughing up. It's funny how days pass when you're sick and you feel like you're trapped in some fever dream forever.

It's exhausting being sick, and now I'm pale and weak. I figure maybe I should get some meat in the place.

I should also pick up some juice. And cinnamon. And cloves.

Sunday, November 27

It was Thanksgiving on top of everything else, and even though I've been eating nonstop for two days due to celebratory functions, I can't forget to give thanks in my humble home.

I'm building a nice little family now, and caring for them sometimes takes my mind off Jimmie. However, if I had Jimmie, my hole of emptiness would be filled.

I can tell that he's the one by the ache that throbs through my body. When I don't see him, my body yearns for him. When I do see him, it's all I can do to keep from touching him.

I haven't seen him for ages now. Between my vacation and my cold, and how he comes in so sporadically, time has really marched on by.

No wonder I crave him.

If I wish hard enough, he will come in tomorrow. I made my sacrifice to the ocean gods. I will get my Johnny Depp Look-Alike if it's the last thing I do.

Monday, November 28

Wishes do come true. Jimmie came in and had a coffee. He sat scribbling in his little notepad. I pretended not to notice or care. I didn't even know if he was drawing or writing. I polished silverware, as it was a lazy late afternoon.

"What have you been up to lately?" he asked me, putting down his pen.

"Me?" I asked, my hand ceasing to polish in mid-stroke.

"Well, there's no one else in here. Of course, you."

"Oh." I put down the knife and rag and approached him. "Nothing much. Why?"

"Just making conversation. That's all."

He stared at me. "Christ, you have bags under your eyes that could hold a small city."

"Excuse me?"

"Partying too hard again?" he asked.

"No. Not at all. I've been sick. Real sick."

"Eew."

"Yeah. The snotty, sneezying, coughing-shit-up-that-you-don't-know-what-it-is kind."

"Too much information, Abigail. I haven't seen your buddy around."

"Which buddy? Mavis?"

"No, the other one. The tall Adonis guy."

"Brad?"

"Yeah, him. That guy. He doesn't come in much, does he?"

"No, I think that time you saw him was the only time."

"But you live with him."

"Not anymore. He was just a roommate anyway."

"I bet. I saw the way he was shooting daggers my way."

"You're imagining things."

151

"On the contrary, he was jealous as hell that you were sitting with me."

"So what's your point?"

"Nothing, I guess." He looked at his watch. "Shit, gotta go. Here ya are."

He gave me a twenty for the coffee and left. Who the hell was he? He always grossly overtipped me, yet he wouldn't ask me out? He came in alone and scribbled or drew in a book. An artist of some sort. A crazy one? A rich one? Maybe he was some sort of billionaire eccentric.

I'm burning with curiosity. I wish there was some way to find out more about him. Googling him did nothing. There are a million Jimmies in the world and I don't know his last name. I couldn't find anything at all about him. I didn't know what he really did for a living. Maybe that apartment was one of many. Maybe he owned it?

Wouldn't that be cool to be married to a billionaire in New York City?

Tuesday, November 29

Seeing Jimmie again inspired me to crank up my exercise program a notch. The time would be coming soon when he would ask me out, and I wanted to be ready. I wanted to look like a goddess naked, and my lord, isn't it starting to pay off? I'm finding melba toast and cheese or sometimes liverwurst is a somewhat satisfying and cheap diet. Of course, I have my coffee, and I often order one of the yummy salads at work. Chocolate is a must as well. A small bit every day can be heart-healthy. I've managed to get my willpower to a point where I can have half a regular-sized chocolate bar for the day and that is my dessert.

All the pigging out at Thanksgiving nearly did me in. I must have gained five pounds, and my gut was starting to hang out again. The sensation of bloated, gurgly guts was nauseating, and I never want to overeat like that again.

But I had those three feasts.

A very strained and strange one with Vicki and some of her friends from work. It was fun hanging out with a bunch of strippers of both sexes, and of course, as the night heated up, so did we all. At one point someone asked if we didn't have a roommate, but we stuck to our story about how he disappeared on Halloween night, never to be seen again.

"His mother said he's been using his bank account. So she's hoping he's not dead," Brenda said.

"That would be good news," I said. "I miss having him around."

Luckily someone handed me a joint right then, and the conversation shifted to other subjects.

Vicki looked like a nervous wreck, and I was afraid she would blow our cover. She twitched and trembled on the couch all night, alternately crying and laughing hysterically. Luckily some poor soul took pity on her at one point and included her in the orgy that was unfolding. Later on she had that look of ecstasy we all know so well.

I figure things will be fine for a while.

The second feast was with the drag queens at Mavis's apartment. It was a classy affair with formal attire and a big turkey.

My third feast was with my little family. I didn't prepare much since they don't really eat. But it was important to give thanks for having them in my life.

Wednesday, November 30

E-mails from Mom.

Now she's using Christmas as an excuse to get together. Well, I'm not going to respond. I really don't want to see the woman. I know Monica agrees with me.

Friday, December 2

It's always something. Or, I should say, it's always the same old shit.

Another e-mail from Mom.

Another hysterical phone call from Vicki.

Stop the world and let me off already.

Saturday, December 3

The first snow.

I always have mixed feelings about the first snow. I love the sense of excitement in the air when it first flutters down. I love to hear kids point and laugh and try to catch the flakes. However, I always know that after the first snow, there will be more and more snow. Soon it will be hard to muster up the energy to do anything at all. I won't want to go to work. I won't want to go partying. I just want to curl up in a ball and hold my breath until spring.

Today I'm not going to let the snow bother me. I

ought a new scale and am pleased to see that I'm
down to 110 pounds.

I went out and bought some new clothes to celebrate. I look pretty hip in the new fashions. Too bad
it's bundle-up time; I'd like to show myself off.

Winter always brings challenges. It will be hard not
to stuff my face. But if I keep up my exercise, keep my
goal in sight, I should be able to get through it OK.

Later

So I found my winter coat and faced my first snow in
New York. It didn't last long, and shortly after that, the
sun came out. Just when I was enjoying its brightness, it
grew gloomy and a slushy rain began to fall. It was cool
when it landed on your skin but soon warmed up. When
I ducked into a store, I realized my face was drenched. I
was glad I brought my winter coat from good old snowy
Buttfuck. It even had a little visor on the hood so my
glasses were safe from the snow. However, once that
rainy hail stuff started pummeling down, my glasses
were stored in my pocket. I couldn't clean them fast
enough to make it worth my while to keep them on.
Blindly, I weaved my way through the grumpy throngs.
Heads were huddled: a few smart cookies had thought
to bring umbrellas. I ended up buying one myself for
five bucks from a streetcorner stall.

Once I had the protection of the umbrella, I put my
glasses back on. Drops of rain still spattered against
them, but I could see well enough.

It was in this wretched drowned-rat state that I

bumped smack dab into Mr. Johnny Depp Look-Alike himself, also barreling down the road, sporting an umbrella. We didn't see each other over the buffeting umbrellas and smashed together. I laughed when I saw who it was. With a clumsy swoop, he retrieved his umbrella from the ground. He tried to shake it out, but it was so crowded that he couldn't find a space.

"Here," I said, gabbing him by the umbrella handle. He stumbled as I led him towards a doorway.

"Now you can shake it off."

Until that moment, he hadn't recognized me. He stammered as he tried to regain his composure.

"Excuse me. I must have been daydreaming."

"It was the umbrellas. No, it was the rain's fault," I said.

"It doesn't matter."

He didn't seem in the mood to say much more. Who could blame him? The weather was disgusting.

So our exchange was brief, but it made me think. Why had I bumped into him of all people? It must be the universe's way of putting us together.

Monday, December 5

Today is cold and gloomy. It matches my mood. Even my collection doesn't cheer me up. It was an effort just to get ready for work.

But I did go to work. And I did my job courteously and politely. I had a couple of nice customers, but for the most part, people just treat me like a faceless entity. Like I don't matter.

That's the problem sometimes with being a waitress.

You are just part of the fixtures. Just a slave there to fulfill people's whims. It can make you feel like you don't matter.

Once in a while you get people who understand what you are going through. But not always. They are few and far between. For the most part, people just want to come in, grab a bite, gawk at the stuff on the walls and get the hell out to do whatever they are doing next.

That's why when someone nice comes in, you really notice. When people treat you with respect, you can feel better about yourself.

However, that doesn't happen every day.

Seeing another e-mail from my mother didn't make me feel any better. She just goes on and on about the past, as if I can do anything about it. As if she can do anything about it.

I had a weird dream last night.

I was trapped in an aquarium. Somehow I could breathe. Maybe I was a mermaid or something, because I had human features and thought like a human. However, it seemed like part of my brain was foggy. Like it was missing. It was sort of like how a computer looks for a file that isn't there.

I could see shapes on the outside of the glass wall of the aquarium. People were looking in at me like I was some kind of freak in a circus. Maybe I was.

As I struggled to find my way out, there was applause from the outside. The sound rumbled through the tank, interfering with my homing devices for sensing where up might be. I swam around in circles, fearful of not ever getting out.

The top of the tank grew dark, and something was added. I saw in horror a huge fish with rows upon rows of teeth. It wasn't a shark, more like an eel or a catfish. Whatever it was, it was ugly as hell and I couldn't see past its gaping mouth, so I had no idea how it was propelling itself.

It snatched my tail with its long, sharp teeth, and I burbled in fear as I swam away.

As I leaped from the tank, I sailed through the air, looking back at the lurching fish, which was much larger and heavier. That hideous creature flopped to the earth with a thump and split open. I flew until I landed in a clearing. I must have passed out in my dream, because when I woke, I had legs. I used them too as I ran like hell away from the wild dogs or wolves or whatever was surrounding me.

When I finally woke, I was exhausted.

Tuesday, December 6

I am staring at the white wall, as if it will split open any minute like an eggshell. In a way, I wish it would. I wish that the walls would crack, that lights would flash and something creepy and strange would come out of there, offering me an opportunity, maybe madness, maybe an escape.

If I stare long enough at the wall, maybe I can will it to happen. I could call some wish-granting demon or god to fulfill my deepest darkest desires.

Wednesday, December 7

The snow was coming down pretty hard by the time my shift was over. It actually wasn't too bad out there save for the icy, sharp wind that wanted to reach down my throat with cold nails to tickle my lungs. My lungs weren't laughing, though. They craved the warmth of more comforting times. My chest hurt by the time I had walked a few blocks, so there was nothing really left to do but walk up the stairs in front of me. My feet had already led the way before I knew what I was doing. My hands had pushed and pulled through several doorways, my face lying to strangers about where I was going and why.

I was panting as I walked along the dimly lit hallway. Swirling wallpaper made me dizzy, and suddenly it was very hot. Now the air was so thick that I needed to inhale deeply to get even a little. The smells here were pretty rancid: a mix of stale cooking, roach spray and rotting garbage. There's nothing like the stench of a dirty old apartment building.

As if I was waking up from a dream, I realized that I was sitting on his couch. I don't remember how I got in, or even how I knew which door to open. But here I was, sitting on Mr. Johnny Depp Look-Alike's couch.

With growing interest, I looked around his modest apartment. He had books from floor to ceiling. Later on I was to discover he had a wide range of tastes when it came to his reading material, and even had a few textbooks from his college years.

There were knickknacks and a big television. In front of me was a large wooden coffee table with several mugs on it. Some of them had been there quite a while. I gathered that he was a chronic coffee drinker. Not only did he go out for coffee, but he drank quite a bit of it at home.

My hands were shaky and I didn't know why. In a way, it seemed like my body had gone on strike. It was limp and cold and seemed not inclined in the least to leave the couch. However, I forced my hands to reach over and pick up one of the coffee cups. I imagined Mr. J.D. lifting the cup to his delicate lips and taking small, tentative sips of the steaming brew inside. I held the cup to my lips. His dark eyes staring far away, his hair slightly tousled and unkempt. The idea of him filled me with longing. I put the cup down, and as I did so, my heat seemed to stop. There were lipstick stains on the mug.

Her lipstick stains.

That evil person with the big lips and the phony voice.

The idea of her made me pick up the cup and hurl it across the room. It smashed into a thousand little pieces.

Now look at what you've done.

You'd better pick that up right now, young lady.

My feet made it across the room before I knew where I was going. Hands picked at the bigger chunks and then feet took us back over to the garbage can. Back and forth feet and hands went, puttering and cleaning up the silly little mess. A quick wipe around the floor with a paper towel ensured that the spot looked just the same as it did before I was there.

Satisfied that my job was done, I retook my spot on the couch. My eyes were looking for something. They were looking and looking, but they couldn't quite focus on anything.

I removed my glasses, hoping that maybe an idea would come to me.

In the dark recesses of my mind, there were two figures approaching me. One was my beloved J.D. and the other was—who else? That woman.

In my mind, she faded away to nothing. The daydream I entertained about her would have brought her great pain and great pleasure, though I wasn't certain that I wanted to share my secrets with her ever in a million years.

I wondered if it would make a difference. If I were the girl he was dating, if I were the second shadow in the image, would he be happier? Would I be happier?

My feet led me into his bedroom. I looked at the piles of clothes on the floor, the clothes hanging off of a chair. Some of it belonged to a woman. I saw a pair of panties, and jeans that were too small to belong to him. There were a couple of thongs too. The sight of them made me sick.

She must be living there. Or at least staying over enough to have clothes there.

I wanted to take those clothes and rip them up. Going through the drawers, I didn't see any more of her clothes, so I could at least take a small bit of solace knowing that she wasn't really living there yet.

I lay in the bed smelling their smells, wondering how they looked tangled up in each other's limbs. My mind flipped over to how I would look riding on top of Mr. Johnny D while Screechy Queen of the Banshees watched. My fingers undid my pants and I slid my hands under my panties. I was going to do my business quickly, but found myself wanting to relish the time. I rolled around on his bed, finding the spots that smelled the most like him, riding my hand and imaging it was him. My other hand slipped under my bra and tweaked my nipple. Although my nipple knew it was just me, it pleased me by playing along with the fantasy. My man took me strong and forcefully. As I rolled in the covers, little moans escaped from my lips. It wouldn't do to be too noisy, yet I couldn't help myself.

When I was finished with my little game, I stood up and felt a bit dizzy. My eyes saw his dressing gown and my hands reached for it. With a little giggle, I donned his robe and studied myself in the mirror. I tried to imagine his trim figure all tied up in that gown. The idea excited me all over again, but I left the bedroom and returned to the other room.

All this thinking and snooping made me thirsty, so I poured myself a nice big glass of wine from a bottle on the counter. As I sat sipping it, I wondered what he would do if he came in and found me there. The wine went down easily and it made me sleepy. I realized that I should leave before I fell asleep. Sadly, my hands followed my advice on taking the bathrobe off and returning it to the chair.

I looked at his bedroom and then walked into the living room. My lips twitched into a grin as a little voice in my head said that I could go back anytime I wanted.

CHAPTER TEN

Friday, December 9

My dreams were full of angels and devils. I didn't know what to make of any of it. First I was swimming through a dark, dank liquid. It was more like jelly than water and it was hard to get any momentum. For some reason, I didn't have to come up for air. Maybe I was a baby in some strange womb. Maybe I was in the middle of an ocean. I don't know where I was; I just know that it was black and murky.

As I swam, I came to a lighter area. I crawled out of the water and lay on a rock. Above me, vultures were screaming and circling. Their shadows cast a darkness over me that was disturbing, and I yearned to go back into the water.

But when I looked at the water, I saw the dorsal fins of many sharks circling. Once in a while, one would cut to the surface, mouth open wide, flesh-filled teeth snapping into the air. They smelled me, but I was safe on the rock.

For the moment, at least.

Above me, above the vultures, the heavens parted and a bright glow of light filled the skies. I saw the sweet face of an angel looking down on me. Although the face alone was bigger than any shark, she didn't scare me. In fact, I wanted to be with her. I wanted to go with her to where she lived. I wanted to be an angel too.

My heart ached as the clouds closed up again.

I saw that the rock had floated to shore, and I got up and walked along a beach until I came to a cross in the sand. I knelt down before it. A voice from behind me spoke in whispers, but I couldn't understand what it was saying. When I turned to look to see who was there, there was nothing.

The sky was gloomy and dark, and a chilly wind stirred up. My feet sank into the damp sand with every step as I walked towards a wooded area.

My, what big eyes you have.

I looked around, but no one was there. I heard the distant snap of a twig and realized that I had been here before.

I stumbled across something, and this time it was Brad lying in repose. I felt pity for him as I saw his eyes staring up at nothing. The whispering was stronger, and I wouldn't have been surprised to see a huddle of gargoyles behind me, enjoying my sadness.

My body felt empty. The hole of my unhappiness ached excruciatingly. Despair and loss swelled through me, but not about Brad. About me. About my life. About where I was going to go.

The woods seemed to stretch around me forever, and I couldn't even see the path I had been on. I knelt down beside Brad and ran my fingers along his naked body. He was cold. Cold, yet still handsome. His penis was hard and erect and even more impressive then it had been in life. Without hesitation, I straddled him, wondering if he could fill the void.

I rode him for a while, my mind racing in a thousand directions. The whispering grew louder, and I dismounted him. Agitation swelled through me, and I continued on my journey.

There weren't the usual wood noises around me.

What big teeth you have.

No birds chirping, no woodpeckers chipping at trees with their beaks, no squirrels arguing over lairs or nuts. Just whispering from trees, from the wind, from whatever else might be in the woods.

My footsteps were even louder as I crunched through the forest. Every twig snapping sounded like cannon fire. Every crunching step was another mark towards my destiny.

With my tired, aching body, I trampled through the gloomy woods until I came to a clearing. My first instinct was to look up to the sky. My angel smiled down from above among the swirling purple clouds. The sky itself was dark and dangerous, and the air had a mossy smell to it.

Only after taking in the sky and the smells did my eyes alight on the spectacle unfolding in the clearing. There was a little fortune-teller tent set up. Out in front of it, a child played a recorder.

Upon closer inspection, I realized that it was an instrument like a recorder, but not a recorder. It was hard to determine if the child was a boy or girl. His hair was long and shaggy and his face unremarkable. His clothes were simple denim and dirty.

The child didn't seem to care that I was there and continued to play as I lifted the curtain to the tent. I figured this was a dream, and I might as well see what's going on. That's the weird thing about some types of dreams. You know you're dreaming, yet you are frightened just the same. And I was pretty nervous about what I might find in that tent.

When I entered the tent, my first impression was one of awe. There were hundreds of candles lit around the room. There was a small table with a couple of chairs. More candles were on the table, and a deck of tarot cards lay facedown on it.

At first glance, I thought I was alone in the room. Then I realized there was something else on the table.

It was flesh-colored and twitching, as if smelling me. Words cannot describe what that thing was, and that's the other strange thing about dreams. I can see that thing right now clear as day, but I can't begin to describe it.

About two feet long.

Fleshy.

Flesh-colored.

Moved erratically.

Seemed to have folds or openings.

I approached the table. The thing shifted, and one of the long slats of flesh widened and an eye was there staring at me. The thing mutated again to form a mouth.

"The angel sent you," it told me.

I nodded.

"What is it you need to ask?"

I stared at the cards. "I don't like those things. They freak me out."

The thing on the table laughed. "Don't worry about it. This is just a dream."

"Who are you, then? My dreams usually involve someone I know. Sometimes I think about that theory that everyone in your dream is really just a facet of yourself. I really wonder if that's true sometimes?"

"Then you would be me, 'cause I'm dreaming too?"

"A crossover dream?" I asked.

"Never mind. You're digressing. What is it you want to know? I can see it trembling on your lips."

The eye blinked slowly, as if it took great effort. In the dim light it was hard to say what color it was. Maybe a blue or something like that.

I knew what I wanted. I also suspected that whatever I picked would be meaningless anyway since this was just a dream. And as such, any card that I picked would have already been preordained by my just thinking about it. It's all so convoluted sometimes.

I told her that I wanted to marry Mr. Johnny Depp Look-Alike.

"Ah, love it is." The eye shut and the mouth closed up. Soon it was just a blob of flesh on the table.

"I will guide you," she said in my head.

I looked around to see if there were any hidden microphones, but the flesh blob just sat there as if she were all-knowing. Maybe she was. Which means that I am, if I am that flesh ball in my dream.

I didn't know how many cards I was supposed to pick or even how to go about picking them.

She guided me through the process, and soon I was

staring at three cards that meant nothing to me.

I got the Tower, the Five of Wands and the Page of Pentacles.

When the cards were laid out, she morphed back into the eye and mouth.

"You are going through rough times," she said. "You feel like people aren't working as a team. Yet at the end of it all, you see Jimmie waiting for you. He holds a coin in his hand, a gift for you. Maybe the marriage you desire."

The thing laughed loud and longly. I thought it was going to have a heart attack.

"You will never entice Jimmie. It's all just a dream. Wake up and smell the coffee, Abby. He doesn't want you."

"No. He has a gift for me. Even I can see it. There is a problem right now, sure, but I can take care of it."

My hands were shaking as I stood up from the table. I staggered over to the exit and walked past flute-playing boy.

The woods were gone, and there were just fields and fields on all sides. There was now an entire carnival set up and I wandered among the unwashed staff as I tried to figure out what to do next.

My dream had it all set out for me. I saw a figure on a swing in the distance. As I approached, I saw it was Jimmie. He swung slowly back and forth.

"Jimmie?" I asked. I could recognize that slouch anywhere.

As I drew closer, I saw he was holding something in his lap. It was Brad's head. Brad blinked at me and tried to say something, but he had no body.

"Brad wants to thank you for sending him into a life of damnation," Jimmie said with that sarcastic tone of his.

"He should be damned for trying to kill my Vicki."

"He was only having fun and you know it. You were just waiting for an excuse. Though I don't know why, when it's me you want."

"When will you realize that I'm the one for you?"

"Maybe tomorrow. Maybe the next day. Maybe never."

"Why do you torment me so?"

He laughed. "You only torment yourself."

With those sharp, bitter words still ringing in my ears, I burst awake and stared into the darkness for a long time.

Sunday, December 11

Vicki has been leaving her usual cheerful messages. Not. Now she is babbling about Brad's parents and how they suspect foul play and the police are trying to follow a few leads. They figure his bank card was stolen and froze the account. I had already figured that out when I tried to access it the other day.

Vicki is terrified of being caught. I keep telling her that if she keeps her cool, that we will be fine.

I'm going to go over after I do my exercises.

Later

I went to Vicki's place. Same old, same old.

Monday, December 12

When I woke today, I was hot and clammy. I was stricken with a fever or something. This won't do at all. I took a bunch of aspirin and I'm going to try to get to work today. I hope that I'm going to be able to make it.

My apartment has been getting a bit messy. I just haven't been motivated to clean much. My bedroom is a disaster, although in looking around my living room, it's not too bad. Just some clutter here and there. I could probably get it cleaned up before I go to work. But not the bedroom. That will take an excavation of several hours, which I don't have the time for today. Or the energy.

It is difficult just to hold my pen. But that's OK. As long as I can write, I'm OK. I hope I don't get sick again. That always sucks when that happens.

I think what I'll do is make some tea, take a hot shower and sweat it out. Maybe I'll pick up the living room first and get sweating. God, but my forehead is hot.

Tuesday, December 13

The computer both annoys and intrigues me. On the one hand, I enjoy surfing the Internet, looking for things I wouldn't normally see. Yet on the other hand, I find myself sucked into its clutches far too often. I can start noodling around for one thing, and then next thing I know, I'm clicking and clicking until I end up reading about something that had nothing to do with what I started looking for.

It always ends in porn.

I guess because it's been so long since I've been laid. Sure, Vicki and I fooled around a bit, but it hasn't been the same since Brad left. Her joie de vivre has flown the coop. She walks around looking like a wilted peacock. She puts on the garish makeup and stripper clothes, but her eyes hold a great sadness. The bags under her eyes don't help. She told me last time I talked to her that she barely sees anyone after work anymore. She says she's haunted.

She doesn't know anything about being haunted.

Last night, as I sat watching TV in the living room, I could have sworn I felt someone sit next to me on the couch. There was no one there, but there was a shift in the air or some kind of presence. I'm not sure what it was. Shortly after that, something in the kitchen smashed to the floor. When I ran in to check, one of the plates that had been precariously stacked had finally relinquished its hold and fallen to its death.

After I swept up the pieces, I ran a paper towel along the floor to pick up any tiny shards that I couldn't see. I didn't want to cut my feet; I need them for my job.

Whatever my fever had been the other day, it seems to have passed. I never actually got sick; it was more like a few hours of being really hot. If I were older, I'd swear it was a hot flash. But I'm not older. I'm not close to menopause.

The presence was gone from the couch upon my return, but for the rest of the night, I felt as if someone was standing behind me. So much so that I kept turning around to look. But there was nothing there. Nothing there at all.

But to get back to that damn computer.

It's all my mother's fault.

She e-mailed again, wondering where I am, what I'm doing. She is using the holidays again as an excuse to get together. Why can't she just leave me alone? I haven't answered her, yet she keeps e-mailing as if I will. As if I'm reading her e-mails.

I can feel her frustration, and I know it won't be long before she finds some other way to track me down.

I can't have her ending up on my doorstep.

I can't have anyone ending up on my doorstep.

I cruised the rentals for a new place, but they are so expensive. I won't be able to move to another apartment in New York. I'll either have to stay where I am or move to a different town.

Outside my window, the city bustled on. A light snow covered everything, and the cabs crawled along with lights glowing and wipers slapping. Although I detested the cold, I couldn't bear the thought of being alone with whatever was in my apartment and that damn computer.

I turned off the computer and unplugged it. Maybe it would leave me in peace if I did. There were too many disturbing things on it. Things I didn't want to see.

Things I didn't have to see anymore if I could keep that computer off.

I was lured out into the blinking lights and found myself at the nightclub, where I bought a couple of drinks and hit the dance floor. Becoming one with the music, I didn't have to think about anything. There was no one to answer to, no one to worry about. It was just one beat flowing into another, an endless collage of sound.

As the night went on, a drunk young man started to dance with me. Once I realized that he was there, I started to dance closer, batting my eyes and wiggling my hips. He danced closer to me as well.

As a rocking thrash song melded into something more mellow and tuneful, he screamed at me over the music. I couldn't understand him at first and realized he had an English accent. He wanted to buy me a drink.

We went into a quieter room and drank our drinks. His name was Scott, and he was here on some sort of exchange program. He had nice blue eyes and big teeth.

What big teeth you have.

I didn't know what to think and so chose not to think anything at all. He was eager to dance some more, and so we did. By the time the night wound down, we were laughing giddily at silly things and poking fun at others behind their backs.

I was a little shocked when he suddenly leaned over and kissed me. My lips weren't shocked, and they kissed him back hungrily, as if they had known him forever. My body was on automatic pilot, and I let his drunken fingers toy with my breasts. At last we left the club and stumbled along the streets. I showed him this and that as we walked by. I asked him if he'd been up the Empire State Building yet, and he said no. He was so busy with school that he had no time to himself.

He led me to the seedy hotel where he was staying.

"Are you over here by yourself?" I asked.

"Yes and no. I know people who are in the same program, but we're spread out all over town. I'm not rooming with anyone."

When we entered the tiny room, I was shocked at how tiny it was and how dismal. The bed wasn't more than a cot. The walls were stained with thick yellow splotches, and in many places the paper was peeling. I didn't even want to look at the ceiling when he turned the lights on.

"I hate these fucking roaches," he said as we watched several bugs skitter away from the light. Bolder ones hung around, searching for stray crumbs.

"The first night I was here, I found some fucked-up insect in my bed. I nearly had a stroke," he said.

"I know. I wasn't used to all these bugs either when I first got here."

"You're not from around here?"

"No. I've only been living in New York a few months. I love it, though. I wouldn't trade it for the world."

"I like it here too." He grinned. He kissed me awkwardly. We made out for a little while, sitting on the edge of the bed. He was suddenly shy and flustered, and it was sweet.

"Do you think there are any bugs in the bed now?" I asked him when we finally pulled our lips away from each other.

Wednesday, December 14

The darkness sets in, and when it does, the world is like an underwater dome. Nothing makes sense. Around me, everything moves in shadow. The universe seems so vast and powerful, and I start to wonder about it all.

Where did it all start?

Did we come from the big bang?

What was before the big bang?

What was before God?

Even if we came from nothing, we had to come from something. Where did something begin? Where did nothing begin?

It all makes me feel so crazy. My mind hurts when I think too much about it all. And then I think of the end. What is the end? When we die, where do we go? Why do people want to bury their dead bodies? Why are people so much more eager to be worm food then to give organs and flesh so that others might live?

Why was I so empty?

Was the nothingness I felt ever capable of being filled? How much further did I have to search before I found the other half of me?

My heart aches with a hollow thumping. I breathe. I live. I eat. But for what? We live and die, and in between, many procreate. The human race keeps multiplying, but why? What is the end result?

Are humans getting smarter or dumber? We are in such a technological age. Everything is computers and communication. Sometimes I wonder if people a hundred years ago were smarter. Maybe the Native Americans were smartest of all, keeping nature's rhythm and taking only what was used.

I realized that I didn't use what I took as efficiently as I could. Maybe I had to absorb more to stop the emptiness. Maybe there were other ways to fill the hole inside of me.

I know that many people feel aching and meaningless. I see it day after day as I bring them food and drinks. They are so caught up in their own miasma that they don't see the human being in front of them. All they know is that some robotic creature pampers them for an hour. Their bellies are full, their consciousness is altered and off they go into the night.

Most people don't even know they have a hole in their soul. If you asked them if they are happy, they may think and wonder and usually say yes with some sort of qualifier, usually relating to love or money.

Love has been rumored to fill the hole. When two souls meet as one, the hole may be filled.

Unrequited love can make the hole even bigger. This is why it's such a tricky business. When do you allow yourself to fall in love? For a moment? For a day?

Later

Moonlight washes over me
As pale strong fingers stroke my flesh
In the darkness of the night
He takes me with great relish

Ah but I can dream a million dreams
And none of them come true
For when I see Mr. Johnny D.
My thoughts are only for you

Well, I never said I was a poet. In fact, I never liked poetry much in school. I tried to get into the chic women poets. Plath, Dickinson, Sexton. Even though I got what they were saying, I wanted to read more words. I want to feel the lushness of sentences and paragraphs, to roll around in senses and touch new textures. Short phrases have that, but I like length.

Maybe that's why I like hip-hop. Rap is like a whole lot of babbling compressed into little sentences. Like tap dancing with words. You can have your ballet, like poetry. Or jazz, like short stories. Modern is like those esoteric plays by Pinter. And then you have your hip-hop. Tap dancing.

I always wanted to be a tap dancer. When I was a kid, I used to put tacks on my sneakers, hoping they'd click like a tap shoe. It never really worked that well.

My mom signed me up for classes once when I was little. I remember wearing secondhand shoes that didn't fit quite right. I'd do the *tapa tapa tapa* thing like Lisa Simpson, and unfortunately, like her, I was hopeless. My feet just didn't want to do what I told them to do. It's typical, though, since my body seldom does what it's supposed to.

Between my insatiable hunger to fill the hole and the reluctance of my body to follow my instructions, I'm not behaving like I should.

I had another weird dream last night.

I was walking down a dark hallway in some old wooden house. In the dream, I knew where I was. I had been there before. There was a low growling coming from behind the walls. Wherever I went, I could hear it. The sound was like a dog or a wolf, low in the throat like a warning. The walls curved and twisted. The damp, musty smell was overwhelming and familiar. Beneath the thick woody musk lay a scent of rot combining in the nose like a fine scotch. I wondered if the smell was the rot of unfinished meals for the wolf.

Sèphera Girón

The better to eat you with, my dear.

My feet were smart enough to figure out that they should speed up to escape the impending danger. However, danger loomed all around me. I was in a tiny hallway with only forward and backward to go. All four sides of me were walled in with wood paneling. A paneling where planks splintered and I could see glowing red eyes gleaming in the cracks.

Wherever I went, it was a death trap. No sooner had I considered the thought than the floor beneath my feet gave way. As I scrambled over to the next section, I was aware that all the floor must be rotten. There was little light and so I ran as fast as I could while keeping my feet light.

tapa tapa
tapa tapa

I hop-skipped along as the flooring collapsed behind me. My heart pounded wildly, and I thought I would have to run for the rest of my life. Which wasn't going to be long, since I never ran anywhere.

Breathing was a bitch as I tried to gulp in rancid pockets of air while maintaining my leaps. At last I arrived at a door and managed to claw open the lock before the last of the floor fell away.

As I fell into the doorway, I realized that I was now in a den of wolves. Several circled me as more clambered in from other tunnels. They stared at me with glowing red eyes. Growls rumbled low in their chests.

One of them started to yelp, like an aborted bark. It held my gaze for a moment and slunk away. In its place stood a larger wolf. The new wolf looked a bit different from the others. It was almost doglike, with a more refined stature and fur that was less mangy. While the other wolves were more ghostly, or maybe dream illusion–type creatures, this wolf king or queen was golden. Her fur was shining like the finest gold and I had to look around to see if there was some sort of spotlight on her. It was a her, I decided. She was far too beautiful, even though I know male wolves or dogs are supposed to be the pretty ones. There was something delicate about her structure, and I suspected she wasn't even a wolf at all.

She stared at me and then decided I wasn't worth the bother. Or maybe I wasn't to be destroyed just yet. It was with great relief that I saw her turn and pad lightly out of the room. The other wolves looked from her to me as if trying to decide what to do. A couple of them gave snarling warnings to me before they slunk off after their queen. One of them actually yawned, and it reminded me of how tired I am. Or was. Or still am.

Once the wolves were gone, I was left in the room, where there were a couple of torches in the wall. It was with little effort that I managed to disengage one and hold it out as I decided which tunnel to take.

Well, I knew I wasn't going after the wolves. Who knew when they would turn on me? There were already disgruntled soldiers in the ranks.

So that left four other choices. They surround me and I couldn't decide. The first one had an earthen wall and mossy floor. I thought about the insects that must be lurking in that dampness and decided not to take it. The last thing I wanted to encounter was a tribe of giant beetles. The next tunnel had a fire at the end of it. I could smell burning wood and it was enticing. It reminded me of roasting marshmallows. In a way, I was drawn to it. But I figured in a dream it was probably the fiery pits of hell. The next tunnel felt a bit windy to me. I couldn't see anything; it was terribly dark. I went down a little ways, but the wind grew stronger and more bitter. I figured it would probably start snowing or something, and I could get enough of that in real life. God, it's cold out these days. So in the end I picked a tunnel that sounded like there was a stream at the end of it.

Boy, was I glad. And I was right.

The tunnel led out to a meadow. The stream was right there, trickling along. On the other side there were people having a picnic. I blinked in the bright sunlight for a moment and recognized them all.

They waved me over, and I went.

Angel made me feel right at home, pouring me wine and feeding me cookies. Brad and Scott chattered on about something while Simon played with a pair of handcuffs. Monica the skeleton watched over it all.

Before long, my old lovers were all over me, as if each was trying to prove to the other that he or she had been my best, most attentive lover.

Though I relished the attention, I wished they would all relax and enjoy the moment.

It wasn't to be. Brad reached over to Scott and gripped him by the throat. His other hand pushed through the flesh of Scott's skull until he had his fingers firmly wrapped around the bone. Blood streamed down Scott's face as he whimpered in surprise. With a flick of his wrist, Brad shucked Scott like an ear of corn. Scott's bloody skeleton dangled briefly in Brad's hand for a moment until he tossed it aside. Scott's flesh kept form for a moment before collapsing into a heap upon the ground. Brad then turned to my Angel, who had been playing celestial music between my legs. He tore off her wings and proceeded to debone her as well. I shook my head sadly as his gaze fell upon Simon. Simon was pale with fear and weakly held out the handcuffs. Brad slapped them away, and the boy scrambled from his grasp. Simon gave Brad a good run for his money, but in the end he met the same fate as the others. With everyone out of the way, Brad turned to me.

"I was the only one that was good enough for you."

"Nonsense. There is only one I want, and you aren't him."

"You live in a fantasy world if you think that artsy-fartsy is going anywhere with you."

"So what if I do? I'm allowed to dream, aren't I? Everyone is allowed to dream."

"Maybe. Maybe not." His face changed and he touched my cheek. "Can I help you dream for a little while?"

"Do it like you used to."

He took me then and there, filling me with pleasure for a little while. We writhed against each other's bodies, coaxing each little nerve ending of pleasure from each other.

I rode him; he rode me. It was a wonderful blending of two familiar bodies.

The sky shifted. It went from the familiar blue to a strange purple. The brook was noisier too, as if it were suddenly being funneled more water from somewhere upstream. I looked over and saw that it was rising by the second.

"We gotta get out of here. The creek is overflowing," I said as I gathered up my clothes.

I started to run as a wind picked up. In my haste, I dropped my clothes and ran naked away from the raging waters.

It began to hail big chunks of ice, and I was fearful that I would be hit. I put my hands over my head and looked frantically for shelter. An image came into view. It was a little cabin.

With another great burst of energy, I ran to the cabin, dodging flailing hail and hoping the creek would stop rising.

When I slammed into the room, I saw there was someone else already in there.

The cabin was tiny and old. It was made out of pine—all you could smell was pine. My nose tickled and I sneezed.

"Bless you," a male voice said. The person was sitting on a chair. A candle glowed in the darkness beside him. It gave his angular face a creepy facade.

It was Jimmie.

"What are you doing here?" he asked me. His teeth glowed white.

"What big teeth you have," I said.

"The better to eat you with, my dear."

"Promises, promises," I laughed. He didn't laugh, and I stopped immediately. He was strangely calm, as if he were in trance. I could see the deep darkness of his eyes as the candle flickered.

"Sit down, Abby."

"There's a big storm out there. Hail stones the size of . . ."

"Yes. The hail. It comes now and again. You have to expect hail here."

"I don't want to spend all night running around dodging hail. I need to get some sleep."

"Then go lie down," he said. "The bed is right there."

I staggered over to the bed and lay down heavily on it. The springs squeaked beneath my weight. As I dozed off to sleep, I heard the faint growl of a wolf.

Then I realized my stupid alarm clock was going off.

I was wondering if I could get Mr. Johnny D. to lie down with me, but now I'll never know.

Dreams. What good are they, anyway? Why do we have them? It's like some vague landscape we stumble into. Sometimes it's familiar. Sometimes it's strange. Sometimes there's a sense of déjà vu, though you know you haven't had that dream before.

All I know is that was one exhausting dream. I was sleepwalking all day because I never really woke up from it.

Work just went on as it always does. After work, I tried to nap on the couch, but just had a bunch of disjointed dreams, dreams about all sorts of weird images that aren't even worth writing down because they didn't make sense to me at all. There was a sense of dread woven between the scenes, and that was enough to keep me from having a restful sleep. I finally got up in disgust and stared at the mess in my room.

Instead of cleaning it, I went into the kitchen to boil

some cinnamon and cloves. The smell was getting bad in there, even though I kept the heat down.

I wondered how much longer it would be before the maggots left.

I grabbed a can of Raid and sprayed a few flies. Between roaches and flies, I was keeping the insect-spray companies in business. There must be twelve different cans of the stuff in the cupboard. Nothing seems to work on roaches. And the fly population has to be monitored constantly

I found a sale on fly killer last week and bought a bunch of cans. But you know you've run out of things to say when you are babbling on about flies.

Friday, December 15

Speaking of flies, I must have killed about seventy-five of the damn things today. It took forever to clean their corpses off the floor so that I could do my exercises.

Breathing all that fly spray can't be good for me. I sometimes light a bunch of incense and crack the window open a little at night.

Wouldn't want the neighbors complaining.

Later

I've decided I've had enough of flies and smells. It wasn't the most fun in the world, but I decided to boil off the flesh from the skulls. So much for hoping they'd dry up and mummify like in the movies. I wondered how you could shrink them, but I figured there was a whole ritual tied into that. Maybe I'll go look it up on the Internet or in the library sometime. At any rate, I know that it's too late to shrink these heads.

I had to do something about my Angel too, and that was a long, grisly process. It was depressing, remembering her in her former glory. Now she was reduced to chunks in a plastic bag.

The only thing that I seemed to have done right was to save Simon's dick in a jar of formaldehyde.

Some of the stuff I was able to flush down the toilet, but most of it was sloppy work tossed into bags.

I put some of the bags down the garbage disposal; others I knew I would have to take somewhere.

The whole process took on the edge of forever.

It all started when I woke up this morning. Flies were everywhere. It was like something out of *The Amityville Horror*. Flies coated the windows, clung to lightbulbs, buzzed around my head. I think it's the constant buzzing that gets on my nerves. I don't really mind sharing my apartment with flies, but it's the constant buzzing. The near and far swooping buzzing. The zooming by the head or bouncing off the chin buzzing that makes me crazy.

I knew that breathing all that fly spray wasn't good for me either. I like to get stoned as much as the next person, but getting stoned on bug killer probably isn't the brightest idea. And I was getting stoned on it. I could tell by how light-headed I was getting.

So I dragged my sorry ass out of bed and prepared a plan. It was not fun. It was not clean. It was not pretty.

But now I sit here reveling in the smells of bleach and Lysol, and can enjoy the fruits of my labor.

While I boiled the bones, I set to work cleaning my room. I was amazed that most of the disaster was laundry, and once that was stuffed into a few bags, the rest was pretty easy to deal with.

I dusted everything until it shone. I even got the cobwebs in the ceiling corners and the dust balls under the dresser.

Once I had filled the garbage bags and tied them securely, double- and triple-bagging them, I lined them up by the door. I knew I couldn't hold onto them for long, because the maggots were still wriggling around and it wouldn't be long before they all started to multiply again.

I sprayed the insides of the bags with bug spray and hoped that would keep them at bay. And then I had to set to work dealing with the kitchen and bathroom.

God, but it was long, tedious work. I even wore rubber gloves and a little face mask thing to keep from throwing up. I never thought it would get so disgusting, but I guess I'm just naive.

I had been lucky with Monica. I never had to go through all this.

The cleanup part was very important, I thought. After all, what if someone came over one day? What if someone came to visit or to see me?

One little drop of blood could give me away.

Of course, no one would think that the skulls and skeleton in the living room were real. Or even if they thought they were real, they'd think I got them at some Goth shop or something. Lots of people had skulls and such lying around their houses.

I scrubbed and scrubbed. I used sponges and cloths

and brushes and toothbrushes. I poured bleach on everything, and luckily it's such a shitty old apartment that it really didn't matter.

All traces of the fly parties were removed.

All cans of fly spray were flung out into the trash.

There was to be no evidence left behind.

I hoped that by the time anyone would come snooping around, everything would be long gone, long forgotten.

I decided that the best way to dispose of the bags was to play games.

I found my oldest, crappiest clothes and donned a few of my "fat" sweaters. I put on two hats and wrapped a couple of scarves around my neck. My hands had fingerless worn-out mitts and I wore an old pair of Doc Martens.

Luckily I had brought my trundle buggy with me to New York. It has proven useful on numerous occasions.

Bag one I trundled along the streets, my scarf pulled up over my nose as I pretended to be old and sickly. The buggy lurched and shifted behind me, getting stuck in chunks of snow and trash every now and again. Since I was pretending to be feeble, I would wrestle with the cart in what I hoped was a convincing manner.

At last I was able to find a Dumpster where no one could see me. Oh yes, there is always the threat of security cameras. You never know when there is going to be a security camera. But I would keep my face covered, and I dumped that first sloshy bag of crap into the Dumpster.

For the other two bags, I met with equal success at

different Dumpsters. However, the night was getting busy with the evening crew of street people, and combined with the cold it was growing hard to find abandoned alleys. In fact, a couple of times, some of the more aggressive ones tried to steal my buggy.

I still had one bag of crap left to dump, and I wasn't at all sure where I should be dumping it.

The idea of venturing back out into the night to masquerade with the homeless and helpless soured after I spent many minutes contemplating my next move.

The homeless were a dismal backdrop against the festive glare of holiday glitz that adorned the streets. The hustle and bustle of early shoppers marched along the slush-filled sidewalks, their goal of securing the perfect offering blazing before their eyes in tunnel vision.

Christmas is a joke. The whole idea of it seems so wretched and garish in light of the cultural melting pot that defines our land. Are we not a mixture of many religions? So why do we persist in celebrating this festival of lights when many of us just want to wallow in the darkness of the human condition?

Some families are close and snatch at any excuse to celebrate together. Whether these families pass their time in joyful festivities or emotional tear-filled drama, they yearn to share airspace with their bloodlines.

Other bloodlines drift away from each other. Some have good reason. Others have no reason at all except following new dreams and new loves and new ways of being.

Some drops of the bloodline wish to remain their own individual specks on this vast planet, a crimson splash of existence in an ever-changing world. They feel invisible yet omnipotent as they forge ahead, carving out unique lives, daring to risk adventures that previous generations were too meek to explore.

My blood, my bloodline.

Sometimes I wonder if it will end with me. There are days when I wonder if I should continue the bloodline of emptiness and confusion. What joy is there in bringing a new life into the world when Mommy can't find the meaning of existence?

Why would I continue the human race when I could barely qualify my own existence?

But I don't have to worry about having children tonight.

I use condoms and have the patch, so I'm covered. It would be cruel and unlikely that the universe would punish me by cursing me with a child. The universe has other plans for this poor soul.

At any rate, I decided that I needed a different plan to dispose of the next bag. Something that celebrated the irony of the season. Something to thumb my nose at the festival of lights.

I'll admit that it took me a few tokes and a martini to get my holiday cheer. I dressed up in a big overcoat and a perky red hat. Underneath my coat I wore a red minidress and thigh-high PVC boots with a heel. I slung the bag over my shoulder and marched down the streets of New York, my head held high this time. My plan was to leave my package at the foot of one of those fancy-ass towers. But then I came to my senses. When it was discovered that the bag contained maggoty bits of boiled human flesh, DNA or something might be taken, and missing people might be traced.

It wouldn't look good if any bits of anyone showed up anywhere. So I marched out in the bitterly cold night and eventually ended up at Ooolala. After taking a few deep breaths, I hefted my cargo into the Dumpster.

I went inside.

There was a band playing, and the place was packed. I checked my coat at the door and went inside. It didn't take long to spot my drag queen friends.

"Why, Abby! How long have you been here?" Mavis said as she came over. Storm was close behind.

"A while. Just dancing by myself as I always do," I said.

"You look simply divine," Storm said, looking me over. "My, but you've really slimmed down, girl."

"Yeah, if only I could lose the glasses," I said as I slipped them off and grabbed a napkin from the bar to wipe them. They were fogging up from the sudden change from cold to hot.

"You should wear contacts. Would save you all that hassle," Storm clucked.

"I know. But I hate contacts. They bug my eyes. And the whole idea of them grosses me out."

"She's saving for laser surgery, honey." Mavis patted Storm on the arm.

"That's right. Well, soon you won't have to worry about it anymore," Storm said. "Where's your drink?"

"I guess I need another one," I told her and raised my hand to catch the bartender's attention. I ordered drinks for all of us, and we had ourselves a little toast. The drinks went down really well, and the night continued on in a soft, hazy blur.

By the time I got home, the efforts of my day and night seemed a dream until I wrote them down.

But they still seem like a dream.

My life often feels like it belongs to someone else.

It doesn't matter.

I'm very tired and need to rest.

CHAPTER ELEVEN

Friday, December 16

'Tis the season to be bitter.

Yeah, well, so what? Who cares what I think or want? Work sucked. Everything sucked today. I don't know what is going on, but I do know that it's all just a big pile of shit.

Mr. Johnny D. actually came in today. He sat in a different section, no fault of his own. The new stupid hostess doesn't really take requests, so even if he asked to sit in my section, she wasn't listening. I hate idiots like her. She's one of those puffy-haired blond creatures with a hard face and snotty attitude who come into a place and try to take it over. You're only a hostess, honey; get over yourself.

Maybe once upon a time being a hostess was some kind of glamorous thing, but to me, this Twinkie only got the job because she was too hot to turn away yet too stupid to be a waitress. So she works at minimum wage and minimum tips seating people all night and day.

She thinks she's the Nazi Queen.

Sometimes I want to push her back against her hostess stand and squeeze her by her tiny little stupid squeaky throat until a bubble of blood leaks from her gaping mouth.

But she's not worth the effort.

I wouldn't want to waste my time and energy on an idiot like her.

So Miss High and Mighty was working today, all perfume and hairspray as she bustled around in her miniskirt and stilettos. Everyone knows you shouldn't wear stilettos at work no matter what job you have, unless you're in the drag queen show. You can't get anywhere fast.

She liked to believe she was fast and efficient, but by the time she clomped over to you in those stilts, the moment of urgency had passed and there would be a new crisis to confront.

It was by accident that I saw Mr. Johnny D. in the place at all. I had to pee really bad, and I don't like to use the restroom where my customers dine. So very quickly I darted over to the next room, and stopped still in my tracks.

At first, I was hurt to see him there. My Mr. J.D. sitting in someone else's section. I wondered how many times he had come in and not sat where I could see him. Then I remembered who was working the floor and shook my head sadly. As quickly as possible, I ran into the bathroom and did my business. My hair and makeup were fine, and I returned out to talk to him

But even in that quick burst of an instant, he was gone.

The stars had it in for me all day.

Grumpy customers. E-mails from Mom. Phone calls from Vicki. It was endless.

By the time I made it home after work, I was exhausted and depressed. Feeling sorry for myself, I lit a couple of candles and put my feet up on the coffee table. Tears flowed down my face as I idly clicked through the TV stations.

"No one understands me," I told Monica. "No one at all."

There were some music videos on, and I watched beautiful bodies strut and gyrate to upbeat tempos.

What would it be like to spend a day inside one of those party-on rock videos?

I don't mean making the video.

I'm well aware of how boring making anything visual can be.

I mean being part of the fantasy that has been created. Being part of the story unfolding. Or the story hidden, yet to be unfolded.

How I would love to be jumping around with those glistening bodies, rubbing against man or woman. Iron pecs and six-pack abs. Big thick lips touching me from head to toe.

Watching a young big-assed girl shake her booty or a muscular tight-butted man strutting, up close and personal, would give me a rush like nothing else.

Later, night

Had the weirdest dream. I was walking through the Central Park Zoo when I heard a growling noise. Upon turning around, I beheld wolves. Wolves that had escaped from their cages. In the dream, I recognized their growling not only as warnings but also as pleas for hunger. These poor wolves were starving to death, and I was the only one who could feed them.

I hoisted the garbage bag from my back and slid it to the ground, where the contents spilled open. The wolves hungrily attacked the rotting flesh, savaging it with hungry, sharp, pointed teeth. As they feasted, I saw the big wolf, the wolf that was not a wolf, take her place above the other wolves. She turned to me, her eyes a golden hue, her paws sharp with claws already in position.

"What do you want?" I asked the wolf.

She growled, her teeth drawing back from her lips.

The better to eat you with, my dear.

Although I live still, in the dream she ate me alive. It was both humiliating and paradoxical that I would be consumed by a wolf. Me, the hunter. Me, the predator. Hunted and stalked like an animal.

But I realized then that no wolf was going to make or break who I was as a person.

I wanted to know, really know, what it was that would make a man love a woman.

Saturday, December 17

Vicki invited me over for dinner, because Brad's parents were coming and we were all supposed to put our heads together to see what happened with Brad.

The idea of hanging out with Brad's parents unnerved me, but I knew I had to go and face the music. Vicki suggested I make my trademark meatloaf to help grease the wheels. Little did she know what I had saved in the freezer for just such an occasion.

Brad's parents were strange. His father was a tall sharp-looking man whose eyes kept welling up with tears. It was easy to see where Brad obtained his good looks. His father's face was red, as if he were a heavy drinker. Brad's mom was a short little thing with curly blond hair and a classic taste in fashion. She held her wineglass nervously and let Brad's father stammer through questions. Her eyes too welled up with tears as her husband pried us with questions about when we had last seen Brad.

Vicki was clearly nervous, but managed to keep to her story. We had spent all afternoon rehearsing our lines and were prepared for anything.

When Vicki served dinner, I made an excuse about not feeling well and passed on everything except another glass of wine. I watched with great interest as the three consumed my meatloaf, commenting on the spices and different blends of meat I had used. The slightly gamy taste was probably the buffalo meat, I had assured them with a sly smile.

After dinner, my pretend gastrointestinal distress was accelerating, and I excused myself from the party. As I made my way back to my apartment, I realized my heart was pounding a mile a minute and I was sweating profusely.

Vicki chided me later on the phone for leaving her stuck with the parents, but she claimed that they were none the wiser about Brad's disappearance then when they had come. Part of me believed her. The other part wondered if she had confessed and that any minute the cops would be pounding in my door. However, the call display showed her number, and she sounded like she was puffing a doobie while she spoke, so chances were good that there was no one tracing us, and her voice surely would have sounded even more neurotic then usual.

Vicki was getting on my nerves, though. She wouldn't leave things alone. She couldn't let things rest. I had to keep reminding her that we were on a phone and shouldn't be talking about anything at all in case we were being bugged. She understood that for a while, then would get freaked out all over again as something would remind her.

It ended with me having to hang up on her by saying that I still wasn't feeling well and had to run to the toilet.

She called later to check on me, but I let the machine get it.

Sometimes after a hard day, you just want to kick back and not think about anything at all.

This is one of those days.

Later

My collection is desperately missing a couple of items. But on the other hand, it's starting to take form in a nice way. My Angel looks down upon my two gleaming skulls. Monica relaxes nearby in her rocking chair.

I think my Angel should have something in her hand. An object that signifies her omnipotent compassion and ruthlessness.

In a moment of boredom, I plugged in my computer and booted it up. There was an idea that had been niggling at me for a while, and finally it was time to explore it in more detail. Although I knew a trek to the library was in order, I decided to do some preliminary research on the Internet.

Among Halloween trinkets and bizarre animations, I found sites on shrunken heads. When I read the Web sites, the ideas that I had held about shrunken heads evolved into clearer understanding. The practice was not nearly as widespread as I had believed. In fact, it was seldom practiced at all.

There were a couple of sites that went into detail about how the tribe prepared the shrunken heads. They were trophies of battles well won.

The ritual of preparing a shrunken head appeared tedious and time-consuming. It requires days of execution and sewing.

I hate sewing. Sewing is one of those necessary evil things.

When I sew, you know the world is caving in or something. It is a rare sight indeed to see me pulling needled thread through fabric in sloppy, uneven stitches. It's not like I don't do it at all. In fact, I sew far more often then I like to admit. But to do justice to my display, sometimes I have to sew a little something here and there.

Then there are items to sew such as my uniform or favorite undies or a split seam. Pretty much everyone has to sew at one time or another. I guess that's why I was forced to take home ec. Even in Scouts you have to learn how to sew, although it's usually cleverly disguised as decorating your uniform.

To prepare a shrunken head, I had to sew. And devote a couple days to the ritual.

I didn't doubt there were quicker modern ways to shrink a head. The use of an oven or microwave could possibly shave hours off the process, but I didn't want to screw around. The Jivaros had it down to an art, and maybe I would experience some sort of spiritual insight as I prepared my head.

I didn't have a head yet, but it wasn't going to be hard to find one.

Sunday, December 18

That stupid-ass hostess nearly became part of my collection today as she hobbled along on her stilts, shaking her apple butt at every table with a man that she passed in her travels. Don't think they all don't look. That's what she's paid for. If they could have her parade around in underwear, they would do it.

She wasn't thinking today, not that she thought any other day of the week, for that matter. Her lips would flap away while random words spilled out. The clippity-clop of how she formed her sentences was like crunching ice on sensitive teeth.

Her whole existence got under my skin. Yet I knew why she existed. The men loved her. The management had guessed well in placing this bubblehead. No one but the waitstaff gave a shit about her screwups. No one, but Mr. Johnny D.

I heard a raised voice coming from the front and then her squeaky squawk countering it. The man was being more then firm about his seating request. Curious, I walked over to check out the hubbub, and there was Mr. Johnny D. demanding to be seated where he wanted to be seated.

The idiot hostess didn't even recognize him as a regular. I stormed over to the booth and tried to set her straight.

"We have a policy in place now to keep the workload even between the staff."

"But he's a regular customer. He likes the room where I work."

"Policy. If he makes a reservation, then he can choose."

"Bullshit," Jimmie said. "I come in here all the time and I always sit at the same place."

"Company policy," she said firmly.

"Company policy is that the customer is always right. You should realize that a happy customer is a repeat customer," I said, hating the robotic way it came out.

Twinkiehead sighed and acquiesced, and I showed Jimmie to his seat. He didn't feel like talking and in fact seemed embarrassed by his outburst. I thought it was great and still do. But of course, heaven forbid he take pride in his assertion.

I don't understand men; I really don't. Or at least I don't understand that man. He's one of those enigmas. He makes no sense whatsoever. Why was he so vehement about sitting in my section, yet he ignores me when he does?

Why does he come in and sit in my section?

He must like me. He must be paralyzed with fear to ask me out.

Yet he's had plenty of opportunity.

Maybe he's just getting his ducks in a row for when sanity hits and he realizes who he could be stuck with for the rest of his life.

I hoped he was waiting for me.

How could he not be?

Why else would he come in?

Yet why doesn't he talk to me?

I don't get it.

Later

This is the third time I've done it, and I've got to stop.

But I can't.

It's addictive.

Well, it didn't happen today, but still . . .

After watching carefully to make certain he had gone off to work, I snuck into his apartment again.

I tore off my clothes and slipped on his dressing gown. I poured myself a glass of wine and watched his porn videos. When I had my fill of the videos and self-pleasure, I snooped around his apartment some more.

I couldn't find that notebook that he wrote in, nor could I find any recent sketchpads. It seemed obvious on these visits that he was a dabbler. A few drawings here and there, unfinished poems, a half-written manuscript lay by his computer. His sketches were of women's underwear. At least I sort of knew the answer about what had brought him to Ooolala in the first place. He was a big ol' pervert, just like the rest of us.

Reading didn't interest me, yet I was curious to see what was in his head.

However, both times, I had watched TV far too long and had to put my clothes back on quickly and leave in case he popped home for lunch or errands or any other number of reasons.

His work hours were the same in the morning, as in he went to work at nine, but he could come home and be home the rest of the day or work late. You never knew with him, and I had yet to figure out his schedule.

The magazine where he worked was in a tall, glassy office building. The lobby was lush, but the actual office where he worked, though modern, didn't boast of opulence in any way, shape or form.

I wondered what his job was.

I didn't want to call and ask, for word might get to him that someone was inquiring about him. Chances were good that he'd never suspect me in a million years, but I couldn't take that chance.

After I left, I bought a coffee at the little bakery across the street. At first I stood inside the bakery, watching out the window, but I could tell I was getting on the owner's nerves. When I deemed my coffee cool enough to travel with, I stepped outside. The wind had picked up and it was bitterly cold. The parka hood did well both to cut the wind and hide my face.

Many minutes passed, and I was about to leave when my persistence paid off. Coming down the street, her impractical boots tapping on the ice, Ms. Annoying Bitch was making her way to his apartment. Without missing a beat, she picked her way up the stairs and entered the building. I expected her to come back out when she saw that he wasn't home. But after fifteen minutes, she never did. I didn't see her waiting in the lobby. I would have seen her shape through the glass of the door.

A slow anger rose in me. She must have a key.

It irked me to no end that she could just go waltzing over to Jimmie's house whenever she wanted. What was he thinking? She probably was going through his stuff right now.

Then I grinned a little grin. If she went through his things, then she probably wasn't too bright about putting them back. If he found something disturbed, he would think she did it.

Yes, I have a new plan, and it is a good one.

Monday, December 19

My heart is still pounding from my little escapade earlier today.

My collection is now growing in an interesting fashion. My Johnny D.'s pen and underwear are lying on a little table in front of Monica. She stares forlornly at the objects, as if something is missing.

Something *is* missing.

There is a lot missing.

My goal is to amass my own little Ooolala dedicated to Mr. Johnny Depp Look-Alike.

It will be a ton of fun collecting my objects.

I just missed Miss Screechyface by seconds today. It was a good thing I had my hat pulled down and my parka hood up when I came down the stairs.

I wonder what would happen if she caught me.

Tuesday, December 20

The collection grows. I even have a bedsheet that I found in the back of the linen closet. It is draped along the back wall, giving the room a circus-tent feel. I think I'm going to get two more, maybe even three to do behind the couch. I've started acquiring underwear too. His underwear and those that he sketches. Might as well display his deepest fantasies.

I bet I could charge admission.

Later

The last couple of times that Mr. Johnny D. has come in, the bubblehead has dutifully sat him in my section. I wonder if management had ended up getting involved. It didn't really matter to me; I just was glad to see him.

He seemed distant and sad.

I couldn't coax much information out of him. Both times he brought busywork—reading the paper and clicking away on a laptop. Even Mavis couldn't coax a grin from him as she flitted through the room on a break.

Poor guy was probably regretting letting that bitch have his key. He no doubt had little rest, always coming home to that. No wonder he was coming in more often.

I had prepared a list of conversation topics in order to pep him up or pry out more information. But there was no opportunity for the slightest bit of repartee, as he clearly desired no eye contact and minimal conversation.

With great sadness, I watched him leave. The other day when it happened, Mavis saw me staring after him.

"Don't worry, honey. He's just moody."

"I'm not worried," I said.

Maybe he was depressed because he was noticing things missing. Who else to blame but his new roommate?

As she moved in slowly, I made certain not to touch them or look at them lest she could point to her own property being rummaged through.

Boy, wouldn't it be a shame if he discovered that his sweetheart was nothing more then a petty thief?

I wondered how long it would be before he cracked.

Wednesday, December 21

I was flouncing around the apartment of Mr. Johnny D. when the door flew open. It was her. She saw me instantly. There was no way to run or hide.

Instead of screaming like a normal person, her mouth opened but no sound came out. I realized that it was because I was wearing his bathrobe. For all she knew, he had come home for a quickie and I was to let myself out.

"Who are you?" she asked, her hand still resting on the doorknob.

"I could ask the same of you," I said, crossing my arms.

She shut the door as a wave of recognition swam over her.

"Of course, you're that waitress from Ooolala. I recognize you."

"Me?" I laughed. "Whatever."

"Why are you wearing Jimmie's bathrobe?"

"Why do you think?"

She sighed. "I don't really want to hear that."

"Well, I'm sorry, but I guess you don't know everything about your handsome Prince Charming."

Her actions puzzled me. She flopped down on the couch.

"It's always the same. Eventually they all cheat on me. To think he denied it when I accused him."

"Men . . . who can trust them?" I said. "How did you get in?"

"I have a key."

"He gave you a key even though he's been seeing me?" I asked, batting my eyelashes in fake indignation.

"I guess it was too good to be true. Why can't I find a nice, hot, faithful man?" Her eyes welled up with tears. I was shocked; I had fully expected a bigger outburst.

"Well, I guess it's better you found out now instead of later. It would be a sad thing if you had moved in with him."

"And to think I was thinking about it too," she said as she punched the pillow.

I sat down on the couch next to her.

"It always sucks to find out you've been played for a fool. I guess you'll break up with him."

She stared at me, her eyes blazing. "I'm not going to break up with him."

"Why not?"

"I love him, of course. Why else?"

"But he's cheating on you."

"Not for long. I'm going to tell him I saw you here

today and make him choose. I know what he will choose. He loves me too," she said.

"He can't love you that much if he's cheating on you."

The idea of her telling Jimmie that I had been in his apartment, naked in his bathrobe, was troubling. There was no way in hell that I would let that happen.

I knew then who the shrunken head for my Angel would be.

There wasn't much time before Jimmie came home, if he was keeping to his usual routine. It wasn't hard to shut her up for good. But then I had to figure out how to move her. It wouldn't be fair for Jimmie to come home to a corpse. My DNA was all over the place.

I rolled her in one of the king-size bedsheets from the back of the linen closet. I had wanted another one anyway, so I was killing two birds with one stone, as it were.

My strength from all those push-ups paid off. She was very light, and I slung her over my shoulder with ease. If questioned, as if I would be questioned on the streets of New York, I would just say it was a bolster of cloth.

It was hard to believe, but I was sweating in that frigid wind by the time I trudged home. Around me, people carried all sorts of gifts and bags and toys and even Christmas trees. I with my odd baggage wouldn't stand out at all.

There were only two times I had to stop and take a breath. One time I collapsed on a set of stairs. For a moment I had forgotten what I was really carrying, since my thoughts were swimming with how I was going to make the best shrunken head in the world.

She rolled down the stairs with a heavy thump. A

couple who were walking by paused midconversation to stare. I giggled and acted like I was drunk.

"My mom loves pretty cloth. So I got her a whole bunch of it," I said as I moved her around so she lay in repose beneath her royal sheets along the stoop.

They continued on, no doubt cattily sharing comments on crazy people at Christmastime.

She is sitting on my couch right now. Or at least part of her is. I shoved a towel down her neck hole to stop the bleeding. The smell of her head bubbling on the stove is rather nauseating, so I'm burning a whole bunch of vanilla incense.

After my excursion, I took a much-needed pee and then went back out before my overheated body got chilled again. One of the shops nearby had exactly what I needed. I bought a large kettle and many sizes of tongs. At the last minute, I bought a miniature Christmas tree. It was easy to carry home. It fit nicely in the kettle.

The tree sat perfectly on the coffee table. I started the kettle boiling before I decorated the tree.

Once the tree was finished and I had arranged Jimmie's cigarette case, a disposable razor and a comb under the cute little limbs, I set to work getting my tsantsa.

It will take a few days to do it right, but I figure if I work on it a little at a time, I should be able to do it.

.

CHAPTER TWELVE

Thursday, December 22

It's kind of cool how it doesn't really matter how well you sew when you make your very own tsantsa. It was really coming along already.

I had already shrunk it quite a bit and it was kind of cool to turn it inside out to scrape off the excess skin. It was like turning a Halloween mask inside out. It wasn't that hard to do a good job on the inside with my trusty Swiss Army Knife.

I was eager for the next phase, where you roll around the stones inside. I thought that would be fun and thought it fitting for someone who had rocks in her head all along.

I still laugh when I think about her on the couch. How she cried when she thought I was screwing around with her lover boy. She had met her fate quite easily, almost as if she considered herself a sacrifice. Maybe she figured if she couldn't have him, she didn't want to live anymore.

That's no fun to think about, though. I prefer thinking that she was too much in shock to realize that I wasn't kissing her, but was sucking the life right out of her. My fingers went from soft caresses along her hair and cheeks to deadly weapons punching out the useless parts of her face. I wanted my tsantsa to be perfect.

She is perfect. Or she will be at least when she's done.

Don't worry, my Angel. Soon you shall have your playmate.

I know sometimes my Angel, my poor fleshless Angel, gets lonely up there by herself.

If she had someone to play with, her time would go much faster. They would be good for each other, the spirit trapped in the tsantsa and the Angel. They could share secrets beyond any dream.

Friday, December 23

Rolling, rolling, rolling my tsantsa!

Now I'm at the sand-and-pebble phase.

This thing should be ready soon.

The only problem now is Mr. Johnny D.

He came in tonight looking all sad and dejected. And no wonder: His girlfriend was missing.

"How do you know she's missing?"

"She's pretty punctual. I can't imagine her just disappearing without leaving a note of some sort."

"How do you know she's disappeared?" I asked.

"She hasn't been to work, she hasn't been home, she hasn't been to see me or call or e-mail."

"Maybe she went visiting."

"She would have said something."

"Maybe she just wanted to disappear. Without a trace."

Jimmie stared at me.

"Why would she want to do that? Especially just before Christmas."

"Maybe she was sick of everything. With the holidays coming, people do strange things."

"She was so happy, though. Especially with the holidays coming. For me, they are a grim reminder of all that I'm not. But for her, well, she had a source of joy and innocence that I found quite inspiring."

Gag me with a spoon, as the Valley girls used to say. Her expounding joy and innocence, my ass. She was the last epitome of the holiday spirit that could ever exist. If I didn't know better, I would swear he was mocking me or her or something.

"What's there to be happy about? There's war. There's poverty. There's broken homes." I sighed as I cleared away his cake plate.

"She was teaching me about the joy in the little things. The joy in the moment. It was refreshing, you know?"

Again a knife cut through my heart. He probably didn't like my natural gloominess. He wanted something that I wasn't. Sudden tears sprang to my eyes.

I hurried off with the cake plate and caught my breath in the back room. The cook looked at me funny, but I didn't care. How dare she be so damn perky?

Then I chuckled a bit. She wasn't so perky now, her mouth tied shut with wooden pegs, her head drying on a wooden spoon in the kitchen so I could put my finishing touches on her later.

I wasn't so careless this time with the rest of her. I

processed what I could and distributed the remainder around town. A couple of dogs followed me; I guess the hunger of winter gave them more courage then usual, and I wouldn't have been surprised if they jumped into the bin after her.

I returned to the dining room elated but he was gone. In his place was money for his meal and a tip.

Saturday, December 24

How fitting that on Christmas Eve I was able to give my Angel a present. I tied the tsantsa to her hand, and she seemed to smile as she flew into the skies with her new toy. Monica looked on happily, and even Brad and Simon seemed to take joy in this season of giving.

I put on some rock-and-roll Christmas carols and did two hours of dancing and exercise. Tomorrow was Christmas, and I had plans.

Sunday, December 25

Christmas didn't go so well.

Well, it wasn't that it didn't go so well; it was just depressing. Everything is depressing.

Monday, December 26

The streets are madness with people rushing around for after-Christmas sales. You'd think Christmas was coming all over again with all the people clutching bags and gifts. I couldn't believe the sheer decadence of the spending. Then again, I can play spot-the-tourist pretty well, and I swear the streets were swarming with them.

I finally plugged my phone back in and checked my messages. About forty from Vicki, wondering where I was and how I was going to spend Christmas and New Year's. I could hear the growing frustration in her voice as she left message after message. By the end of it all, she was begging me to call her.

The whole idea of it made me laugh, and I drank some more Grand Marnier before giving her a call.

This time I got her voice mail and I left a caustic message about how she's not there when I call back.

She'll call again eventually.

She's probably out banging a new guy. Or maybe she was even working. Lord knows work was just as busy as ever for me.

It was a good thing I had work to pass the time. I enjoyed looking over my collection, but I wanted more.

I still feel empty and incomplete. I have all the trimmings, but I'm still missing the centerpiece of it all.

My body aches for my missing soul mate.

Sometimes I dream of finding a soul mate who is just like me. Well, not just like me, but who understands me. Someone who can put up with my mood swings and who wants to smell my pillow when I'm gone. Is there really someone for everyone?

I wasn't so sure about it.

I've been feeling agitated of late and really want to go find someone to love.

Only for the night, though.

I know who my true love is, and one day he'll realize it too. Once he realizes that Miss Squawkyhead up and left him, he'll see who has been standing there for him all along.

It won't be long now. He'll know all there is to know about me, and he will crave my touch.

In the meantime, I will just take solace in the fact that I'm looking pretty damn good in the mirror. My hard work has been paying off more then I ever dreamed. My arms have little biceps and I have muscles in my abs. It's amazing how when you really want something, you can get it.

If I was able to change the shape of my stubborn, soft body, I could surely reach my goal of landing Mr. Johnny D.

Tuesday, December 27

Vicki returned my call while I was getting ready to go out, so we decided to meet for a post-Christmas drink. She never asked what I did on Christmas, so I never had to tell her.

We drank and danced, and as the evening spun on, it felt like old times. I was glad to see her smile and flirt, and it wasn't long before we had two handsome men bending over backwards to fix us drinks.

I don't know if Vicki said something to them when I wasn't looking, but they went from friendly to downright lascivious. I was so randy myself that talk of sports and other blustery blather didn't even faze me. I kept my goal in sight, and soon I had Paul begging for mercy in the darkness of the night.

He reveled in the way I played his body, and soon he was trembling. I looked over at the other bed where Vicki and her lover were fucking like rabbits.

Seeing Vicki on her back, her legs over her head and her pussy getting reamed out by a tall, handsome man, gave me another surge of pleasure. I made my young buck get it up again and rode him further into the night. I must have fucked that poor boy awfully hard, for he seemed to be screaming in pain instead of pleasure by the end of it all.

As long as someone had a good time, that's all that counts.

And I had a fantastic time playing with that young, hard body's eager cock.

The only downer to the whole evening is that we were never left alone.

It was understandable, since they were out-of-town tourists, only here for the weekend.

I'd have to make sure they didn't lose their way or fall in with an unsavory crowd.

I left while Vicki was waking up her partner with a blow job. If there was anyone hornier then me in the world, it was Vicki. The difference was, Vicki knew how to coax a sleeping cock and I didn't. I felt pretty satisfied with what my guy had to offer earlier, so I wasn't complaining in the least.

Wednesday, December 28

I couldn't get any post-Christmas artifacts from Jimmie's place because his schedule was so erratic that I never knew when he was coming or going. I guess he was off for the holidays. I wonder if he's planning to go away.

Today I watched him leave his place and I ran

around the block so that I would accidentally run into him. He was a bit surprised to see me, but then snapped out of it. I made him stop when I spoke.

"Happy holidays," I said cheerily.

"Same to you," he said, his voice low and quiet.

"You don't look like you're having happy holidays," I said.

"No, I'm not."

"What's wrong?"

"She's still missing," he said. "Vanished. Without a trace."

"Oh." I was quiet, as if I was sympathetic to his woes.

"I thought for sure she'd call on Christmas. Or even sometime after that. Even if she suddenly grew bored and left, she should send me an e-mail. Or send someone somewhere an e-mail."

"That would be the polite thing to do," I said.

"That's why I think there's something wrong. She would have contacted me at some point, even if it was to tell me to fuck off."

"Some people just walk away and forget about it. No rhyme or reason. Maybe an ex-husband came back and she ran off with him."

"She didn't have any ex-husbands."

"Maybe she did and didn't tell you."

Jimmie frowned, his eyebrows knitting together as he pondered the idea.

"That would make nearly everything she ever told me a lie. She said she'd never been married. Had never lived with anyone. She enjoyed her work. I thought she enjoyed me."

His eyes were wounded, and I wanted to slap him as

I saw them fill with tears. Wouldn't you know, the waterworks started pumping and his lips quivered, just like some damn soap opera star.

I put my arm around him as he sobbed like a baby.

"I'm so lonely, Abby. Do you know what it's like to feel so lonely and alone in the city?"

"You don't have to be lonely, a nice, handsome man like you."

"You don't understand. I'm thirty-four years old and life is passing me by. I've never met the one. I've never felt as close to falling in love as I did for her." He wiped his tears from his eyes as I watched, trying to keep my face from betraying any of the rampaging emotions surging through me. I was crushed he adored her so much, yet elated that he said he had been close to falling in love with her but wasn't in love with her.

I take great comfort in that thought.

That means that he's waiting for fate to intercede. And how coincidental in fate that I kept running into him.

"Maybe you are looking too hard—for a soul mate, that is," I said.

"I'm not looking at all. I'm afraid that I'll find her and not even realize it."

"It happens."

"Have you ever been in love, Abby?" he asked me.

I blinked a few times and pushed my glasses up on my nose. "At the time, I thought I was in love. But I'd always end up with a great disappointment. Someone cheating on me or lying about something or maybe just doesn't live life how I want to live it. I would love to live a life that I want to live and be able to share it."

"I wish I could find someone who truly understood

me. Yes, she did in many ways, yet in others, there was a spark that was lacking. It seems to always be that way. Someone has almost everything, yet there are things that aren't quite right."

"It's human nature to always be searching, to never be satisfied. I think it's more true for men, 'cause they are biologically created to spread their seed."

"Do you think love is a myth, then? Or that people who claim to have true love are liars?"

"No. I think that when it comes along, it's often ignored. And those that don't ignore it are blessed. They take giant leaps of faith. They trust another fallible human being to share in the life they have worked hard to create."

"You're quite interesting, Abby. I have to get going now, though. I have to get to work and do a bit of research for an article due in the morning."

"Are you a writer?"

"I do a lot of things. I like to think I'm a writer. I write little fiction tales for fun, but my day job is journalism. Pays the bills, you know."

"I find writers fascinating. Do you do other art?"

"I dabble in art, some music. I've done a bit of theatre and modeling, but not for a few years. When I was in my twenties, people liked to use me because they thought I bore a resemblance to a certain movie star."

"I can't imagine who that would be," I said with a grin.

"It's all moot, though. It's fucking cold out here, and I have to go."

"See you, Jimmie," I said.

"Yep." Mr. Johnny D. disappeared along the sidewalk, enveloped by the throngs of people rushing to get somewhere five minutes ago.

It warms my heart to think that Jimmie doesn't know whether to believe in love or not. That's because he is on the cusp of falling in love. Now that she's out of the way, I can make a move.

I figure I'll let a couple more days pass to see how he is. Then I'll invite him out for New Year's Eve. I'll take him to the Ooolala party. He'll love it.

Friday, December 30

When Jimmie came into Ooolala today for his afternoon coffee, I took the chance and invited him to the New Year's Eve party tomorrow. He really had no choice but to accept my invitation, because he had already admitted he had no plans that night.

The only bummer about the whole thing was that he wanted to meet here.

I said I could meet him somewhere else first if he liked, but he said meeting here would be fine.

I thought it was a strange way to begin a New Year's Eve date, but I figured he had his reasons. Maybe he had to work late, or maybe he was coming from another party first.

It was a bit of a drag, because I was hoping to get some time alone with him before he gets lost in the throng of the party.

I bought a red dress with a plunging neckline. If that doesn't get his attention, then he'd better switch teams.

These days I was wearing a size five. The whole idea

of it thrilled me and spurred me to exercise even more.

I've grown addicted to fruit shakes. They are delicious and fill me up quite nicely. Sometimes I'll throw some rum in for good measure. It seems like my metabolism has sped up, and booze doesn't go to my gut like it used to. When I drink rum, I do a few extra situps to compensate.

The CD player is cranking *Collision Course*. That music has so much energy, it gets me going even when I feel totally unmotivated. The rapping and yelling and angst in that noise vibrates deep within me.

I put my headphones on so that the neighbors won't complain. Sometimes I'll catch myself singing along and have to stop.

It's really bad when I'm playing *The Eminem Show*. That's one of my favorite CDs and I love to yell along to his raps.

Well, whatever floats your boat, I always say.

Music is so subjective. Even within yourself. It depends on your moment, your mood, your activity. Sometimes I need dead quiet to think. Other times a light classical station on the radio can help me unwind. But nothing gets into your soul like rock-and-roll or rap or that delicious combination of the two.

Later

Where the colors go, nobody knows. When you are waiting forever in the bathroom for some bimbo to fluff her beehive, you notice how weird people are. That girl over there had little tiny thorns growing out of her head instead of hair. I looked closely to see if she had purposely spiked her hair that way, but it wasn't true. The tiny points mock me.

Sitting on cold porcelain makes your thighs feel like they don't belong to you.

Where the walls get sharp, the stones will grow.

Stones . . .

Little pebbles smoothing out coarse bits of skin.

Molding and shaping. A tool derived from nature.

Trees sway in the wind, but the tornado clouds hide them.

Bamboo flies in the air, careening in a single point towards me. My feet run before I can figure the best course of action.

Run.

Run away.

Run before it is too late.

But he is there waiting, pulling me back. His longing envelops me like soft, fine calf leather against my flesh, and I yearn to be in his arms.

No tornado will stop me.

Heavy wind and pelting hailstones.

My eyes sting; my glasses get blown away.

Blindly I reach for him. The trees slap me with angry branches.

Wrinkled tree stumps glare and call me names.

I can't hear them because the cat fell off the shelf and the wine spilled. Carpet Fresh will get that out.

Saturday, December 31

I barely slept a wink; I was so excited for my first date with Johnny D. Look-Alike. While I tossed and turned in anticipation, I dozed off now and again. It took a really big joint to knock me out for about two hours. That was a mistake because I had terrible dreams.

Some of my dreams were repeats of other dreams I've had before. Then there were new dreams. A stupid dream of going to the party and everyone making fun of me because of something stupid. Maybe I forgot to wear my clothes, or I was blind because I didn't have my glasses on.

The dreams twisted and turned and always ended up with me crying on the toilet in some bathroom stall somewhere, while dingy water circled my ankles.

Waves of humiliation and despair swept over me, and even when I woke, it was hard to shake. So I had to have another joint to get rid of the thoughts.

That joint just made me more wakeful.

However, I forced myself to stay in bed. No diary. No music. Just stare at the blackened walls and watch the shadows form into little demons with clawed hands and tiny red eyes.

The wolves were in my dream.

The Central Park wolves. Or maybe they were wolves from other places.

White wolves.

And that big golden wolf who lorded it over them all. That was so weird. Even now, I can almost see her sitting in the corner behind Monica, tongue lolling, panting as she watches me.

We watch each other.

But not really, because she's not there.

In the dream, we always watch each other. I can be battling a grizzly or waving off diving bats, but if she is watching me, you can be sure as shit I'm watching her.

She controls all the wolves. If she tells them I'm pissing her off, I'd be lunch faster than one of those big-ass roller coasters can whip around a corner.

Man, I haven't been on a roller coaster in years. It's hard to find them in Buttfuck, Nowhere, and there aren't any major amusement parks that I've seen in New York.

There are some places that have great coasters. But I wouldn't even know what they are. My coaster experience is limited, though in my dreams I'm always riding those rails. I love the thrill of the car reaching higher and higher as it climbs the hill. That pause on the tiptop as the car shifts balance. It's like hovering on the brink of an orgasm. And then the rush. A good coaster can get the ol' adrenaline pumping like no tomorrow.

Coasters are like sex, now that I think about it. Sometimes the ride is scary and thrilling, and when you get off, you want to jump back on and experience those highs and lows all over again.

Sometimes the ride is disappointing. The hills weren't as high as you thought; the speed just wasn't there.

Yup, sex, roller coasters—it's all the same thing.

Man, I shouldn't be sitting here writing about roller coasters. I've got to start the excavation for my date tonight. New Year's Eve means that it's going to be an all-day event. First stop, the bathtub. Lots of oils and pleasant scents. I read somewhere that men love fragrances that remind them of food. Cinnamon, lemon, vanilla.

I was tired of cinnamon myself, so I thought of a

vanilla bath: vanilla shower scrub, and after my bath, vanilla body crème and then a dash of vanilla powder. I would be the vanilla lady today.

Later

Bath is complete. I soaked myself good for an hour, making sure that oil sank in and moisturized my skin like a fancy-ass movie star. I put cucumbers on my eyes to try to get the circles down.

It was astonishing, when I looked in the mirror, to see the puffy dark circles under my eyes. There was a sunken hole, like I had been worrying too much, and then the eyes puffed up because I hadn't slept properly.

In fact, it's been a long time since I had a really good night's sleep. One where I didn't have strange dreams, or burst awake, or have to pee fifty times, or be sleeping with someone who wants more sex. There's always something keeping you awake at night.

I remembered that I had a cucumber in the fridge. I buy one now and again, imagining that I'll get the urge to eat it one day, or if nothing else, see what it feels like inside of me. But I never get around to doing either one. This last cucumber is only about five days old, so it's still good. I cut a couple of hunks from it and placed them over my eyes when I had my bath. They were cool and soothing, especially in contrast to my hot, oily bath. I could imagine now what the expression "cool as a cucumber" meant.

After my bath, I had a shower and washed my hair. It was getting long and took more time then usual to wash. It was falling out in fistfuls. I didn't know if it was because I always had it up in a ponytail, or maybe I wasn't getting enough vitamins, or maybe it was stress. I don't know and really don't care. I just hope that it stops. Maybe if I brush it more, but I don't know. It comes out quite a bit when I brush it too. At least I have lots, so I'm not going bald or anything like that.

I have an oil conditioner on my hair right now, and it's kind of dripping and getting on my nerves. However, I can do my nails while it penetrates the shaft.

Later

I hate doing my nails. They are always a pain in the ass. I got one hand done and then did a number on the other hand. I guess it's because it's hard to do all that finger dexterity with the hand you never use.

It's not that I don't use it; I just don't use it as much. I can do a lot of things with both hands. But painting nails isn't one of them.

They look OK, but you can tell that I did them myself. Maybe if I stick those little jewel things on them.

I have some in my drawer somewhere: I bought them when I first moved here and never found a reason to sit and do them.

Later

Makeup is done. I still have two hours to go. I realized that I didn't incorporate working out into my schedule, but what the hell, it's New Year's Eve.

And I have a date!

Later

I'm almost ready to go. I look great, if I do say so myself. I played with my hair forever, but at last I got it to look good in a Veronica Lake kind of way. It swirls and curls around my face.

If I didn't wear glasses, I'd look even better.

The darkness of my latest hair color contrasts nicely with my dress. My breasts have shrunk quite a bit, but they are still there, and give me a nice hourglass shape. I'll wear my practical boots and parka to brave the elements, but underneath the parka I'll have my white fur stole. It will be warm, and I don't feel guilty having it since I got it at Goodwill. My theory on buying fur at Goodwill is that you aren't increasing the demand. You are just buying what someone threw out anyway, and if it wasn't there, you probably wouldn't go looking for it in a regular store.

So I have this nice warm fur wrap and I look like a snow queen or something.

That *Snow Queen* cartoon scared me as a kid. There was something just awful about how the boy changed and the queen was omnipotent. As an adult, I can laugh at my fears, at the writers' manipulations of the story line. But as a child I was scared to death.

What if I got trapped in a world of hate and snow? Maybe I was already trapped there.

I'm not trapped tonight.

In about half an hour, I can go and be there right on time.

He said around eight, and that's when it will be.

CHAPTER THIRTEEN

Sunday, January 1

I can't believe it. I can't believe what an asshole he is
to me.

It makes my heart ache to think about it at all.

What can I do but be patient? He doesn't see me
yet. That's all. I'm just invisible.

Later

Why are some women sluts and some aren't? Why do
men say they don't like or respect the sluts, but they go
out with them anyway?

Underneath there's a heart of gold.

A tale as old as time, yet it happened to me.

It always happens to me.

Well, sometimes it happens to me.

It happened on New Year's Eve of all times.

Later

Now that I've had a chance to calm down, I have to make a plan. This time I know I have to be smarter. I have to be cunning and strong. I have to set my eyes on my prey and go after it.

It's the only way to get by in this concrete jungle.

California may have sharks, but New York has cougars.

An older woman, dressed in classic fetish gear, took Mr. Johnny D. home last night.

Right in front of me.

I couldn't believe it.

Later

My hands are still shaking. I just want to cry forever. Happy fucking New Year's to me.

I barely got a New Year's kiss.

Men are all the same. A bunch of dogs.

No, dogs are too good of a creature for them.

I guess I should recap the dismal events of the night. I know that I'll never want to look back on them, but at least they'll be recorded. God forbid I ever have a good time.

I waited forever and a day for Mr. Johnny D. to show up. When he finally did, I forgave him my wait. He looked so delicious. He wore a white dress shirt, sort of a puffy piratey-type thing, and leather pants. He fit right into the glam fetish New Year's Eve atmosphere. His longish hair was tousled, as if he hadn't slept well either.

He wore knee-high leather boots with many buckles.

Men are so lucky they can wear boots all the time. They didn't have to bring a change of shoes. They didn't have to endure foot aches and other problems. Even the fact that his boots were sloppy with salt stains didn't matter, since he was a handsome man with long tousled hair. A renegade fantasy for any red-blooded woman.

My own toes ached already from my platform stilettos. In them, I was as tall as he was. I wondered if my being so tall bothered him. I yearned to put my boots back on.

At some point during the night he asked me to take my glasses off. He stared at me, as if he could make love to me right then and there.

"You really should. . . ." he started to say, but I finished the sentence for him.

"I know, I know. Wear contacts or whatever. But I can't wear contacts, as I've told you a thousand times. I'm saving up for laser eye surgery, though."

"So you keep saying."

"I am. It's not easy saving for anything in New York City."

"True. She used to say that all the time. How hard it is to get ahead." He sighed and stared into space for a moment. Then he abruptly turned away from me, as if I didn't even exist.

He went to the bar and ordered himself a drink. By the way he ordered from the bartender, I realized that he had been drinking quite a bit before his arrival here. He grabbed the glass of booze when it arrived and swilled it back in nearly record time.

After he slammed it down, he ordered another one. As he did this several times in a row, it was obvious he was becoming enamored with the nearly exposed breasts of an older woman across the bar from him.

I had to admit she was rather spectacular and on another night would have been eyeing her for myself. However, since I was on a date with Mr. Johnny D., I was not impressed in the least to see him ogling the lady with the splendiferous cleavage. Hugged together with straps of leather, it went on for miles and miles.

She was a shapely woman; I'll give her that. She had the classic hourglass figure with a meaty butt and slender waist, yet even with her tight leather merry widow, she had a bit of a belly.

Her face more than anything belied her age. Sure, her eyes were blue and engaging, especially with the ring of black painted around them, but she had the face of someone who has had multiple worries and disappointments along the way.

So there he was, staring at her. Ordering drink after drink after drink.

The whole scene made me sick.

How I wished it was one of the drag queens he had set his sights on if I wasn't woman enough for him.

As the booze flowed, he started to share his sick, sordid thoughts with me.

"Do you know that woman?" he asked me.

"No, not at all," I replied. It was the truth. I'd never seen her before, and if her tits hadn't been hanging out, I'd swear she was a drag queen of some sort.

"Why do you want to know that woman?" I finally

questioned him after I'd had five or six drinks. He laughed long and loud and even cupped my face in his hands. His words made no sense to me at the time, nor do they now as I try to remember what he said.

Something about how some women are for cherishing, while others are for pleasure.

I'm pretty sure I asked him what pleasure meant to him, and why he thought that the present company couldn't provide it.

He babbled on about something or another. The whole song and dance is a bit of a blur. It always comes down to me not being the one desired in the end, so what difference does it make which production number carried the news?

I was abandoned on New Year's Fucking Eve by my dream date.

The worse part was, I was abandoned before it even started.

He hadn't seemed into the date at all.

And that hurt plenty.

But then I realized that it was too soon after her disappearance for him to realize what was going on and how to deal with it.

He probably knew he felt something somewhere, somehow, for me, but was unable to express it because he was sidetracked by what he thought was grief.

In typical man fashion, he had been on the prowl.

Yet I wasn't good enough.

He had to leave with that woman. That older, plump woman.

I couldn't understand it at all. I wasn't very plump anymore, and I was way younger.

I looked fantastic. I had spent hours pulling myself together for him.

And for what?

To be abandoned at the dawn of the new year, when not only my date went wrong, but the whole symbolic mess of the situation didn't bode well for things to come.

I should say it doesn't bode well.

There is nothing good about the coming year. This is something I can wrap my head around. I believe that if you have a shitty New Year's Eve, the rest of your year is going to suck.

My heart was aching and my body felt hollow as I watched them leave. Well, the feeling was more like everything had been yanked towards the center of my stomach, like there was a big rock sitting there. It reminded me of some grizzly fairy tale I read as a kid, where the fox has rocks sewn into his stomach while he sleeps and then for some reason he goes for a swim and drowns. That was the sensation. Heavy and sinking and doomed.

What was I supposed to do?

My thoughts ranged from pondering and being sad to sitting and being complacent. I also toyed with getting drunk and weepy or maybe loud and aggressive but in the end tried to be more Zenlike in my approach to the situation. I couldn't blame him for wanting to stick his dick into that woman with great advertising. He was lonely and single and probably wrestling with his mortality. He probably didn't know if he should screw someone else or not. He didn't know how much I loved him.

I sat and stewed over events until Mavis found me.

"Why are you sitting by yourself on New Year's?" she asked me, half scolding. "Did you come here alone?"

"Well, yes and no," I told her as I pieced together events. "Yes, in a way I came here on my own. And in the end I guess I'm definitely here alone. I'm not even sure where the middle part went."

"You weren't here long enough for there to be a middle part. I saw him leave around midnight."

Mavis reached over and wiped a tear from my eye. Sometimes she could be so caring. Mavis confused me—she was a man, yet also a woman. When Mavis was a woman, she had so much femininity, or at least the way a drag queen that looks like Judy Garland has. Classy I guess is what you would call it. Not like Liza, all brash and glitz. When I was with Mavis, I often felt like I was in the land of Oz. I wondered if she had seen me come in. Mavis didn't miss much, and if she didn't see it, one of the other drag queens would have.

At some point in the night, the manager staggered over and gave me a sloppy New Year's kiss. He praised my work and offered me a raise in the new year. After he left, I dabbed his spit from my mouth, but I did it carefully so as not to wreck my lipstick.

The girl staring out from the mirror glowered, her eyes ringed with tear-streaked liner, clumps of mascara gathering in her eyes. I took off my glasses and set about repairing my makeup. I didn't really care how I looked anymore, and I was pretty trashed.

Midnight had seemed exciting for a moment. Mr. Johnny D. and I and that woman were all dancing, as were many other people. The strobe lights stopped and the glitter ball spun as the new year was rung in. Mr. Johnny D. grabbed me first and tipped me backwards to plant a big romantic New Year's kiss on my lips. The touch of his flesh against my flesh sizzled to my toes, and the moment was suspended in time as I grew limp in his arms. I didn't have long to enjoy the moment: He flung me back up and planted an equally juicy kiss on our dance partner. As I watched in horror, someone else kissed me and then more people were kissing me. Everyone was joyous in the new year. Mavis kissed me long and hard, not caring if her lipstick got smeared. Which it did. Everyone's lipstick was smeared.

I returned to the dance floor to see Mr. Johnny D. still kissing that woman, and my blood boiled.

They continued their flirtations until they left. I kept reliving the moment over and over.

Mavis told me that Ooolala would be closing up soon. Can you believe it was a quarter to five when she told me that? I nearly shit my pants. That last call hit me like a ton of bricks. People blinked in the sudden white light. Management isn't totally cold. The light could have been way brighter, but it was bright enough after being in the darkened comfort of candles and strobe lights.

Mavis invited me to another party, and since I had nothing better to do, I decided to go. The sun was a warm glow in the sky while we organized our thoughts.

It was a bright crisp new morning. A bright crisp new day. Who was to question it?

I felt as though I was on the eve of adventure, and boy, did I find out that was the case.

I didn't make a habit of going to booze cans or after-hours places, namely out of fear of safety since I was single.

"If there's no one to bounce off of, then you're a pretty boring person in bed," Mavis said. I don't know if I heard her right or not; she was pretty trashed.

"You worry too much," I heard myself saying.

We found the secret entrance to the booze can and went in. The place was packed. New Year's Eve was far from over in this club. I bet most of the people were so trashed they didn't even know that it was morning.

I was so trashed and depressed that I didn't care.

More drugs and booze were consumed, and I ended up dancing. The place was a dive beyond all dives. Garbage was everywhere. It was really an old warehouse space, so there were giant cables all along the floor and hanging down everywhere. Tables were mostly pieces of plywood laid across boxes or piles of bricks.

There were tons of people there. A hundred, perhaps. Maybe more. Maybe less. I was in no position to really count.

It was expensive to get a beer, but it didn't matter. People were buying me drinks left and right. I was happy to take them. Most people just seemed to be in the mood to party. There were bikers and gangbangers and gay people. A whole mixture of people that normally wouldn't get along too well. But here we all were, happy to be here with one another.

I expect that most of the people there were like me: They had a disappointing night and didn't want to go home to emptiness.

I didn't want to go home to emptiness.

But there came a point when I did.

I'm going back tonight, though. I bet the party will still be going on, and no one will even know that I left.

Tuesday, January 3

I shouldn't have gone back to the booze can. What a bad idea. When will I ever learn that if you have a good time somewhere, it likely isn't going to be repeated? For someone like me, good times are rare, and I should be happy I get any at all.

I was hungover, angry and tired when I arrived at the booze can. The bouncer recognized me and let me in with no qualms. I didn't recognize many people there, but there were still quite a few.

I had a couple of drinks and tried to get rid of the hangover. They made me a bit jittery, and my nerves were snappy. Colors were bright and clear even in the dim light of the room.

For a moment, I thought I saw the large golden wolf watching me from a corner, but then I realized it was just the way the lights made shadows with some cables.

Tired, I sat in a corner and watched people talk and dance and pick fights.

Someone came over to me. She recognized me from Ooolala and wanted to smoke a joint. Never one to turn down a toke, I took her up on her offer.

We were toking, starting to get to know each other, when suddenly there was chaos in the room.

People were running, and we were pushed right out of our chairs in the wave of panic that swelled through the club like a tidal wave.

Before my new friend and I could comprehend what was going on, cops were forcing us onto the ground and slapping handcuffs on us.

It sucked mightily.

A headache started to grow behind my eyes as I was led to a cop car and roughly thrown inside. I guess I fared better then some of the others, who were thrown into paddy wagons.

I've never been busted before, and it was a huge downer.

Luckily for me, they found nothing on me. They didn't even catch me with the joint since it had been flung out of my hands in the stampede. For once, I didn't have any pot on me, and I was so grateful I started to cry, though no one knew why. They probably thought I was a big suck.

At the end of it all, there was nothing to hold me for, since they didn't care about pressing charges against people who were just hanging out. They were probably more interested in ganghangers and bikers than in a lowly waitress who was hanging around on New Year's Day.

The night in jail sucked, though. I was cold and shivery, not to mention terrified, all night. I was in a cage with a bunch of women, and not all were from the club. There were some mighty scary-looking women in there, and I was afraid one of them would hurt me.

My dreams were weirder then ever, and I guess mostly due to fear and the fact that it was hard to sleep anyway. Every couple of minutes, I would find myself dozing off, though I didn't want to doze off at all. Then the strange blurry dreams would take hold, and I would be sucked into some bizarreness that I can't even remember.

The next morning, a few of us were set free. Mostly girls like me, waitresses and bartenders and other such types that go to after-hours parties. None of us had been caught with drugs of any kind, though I'm sure if they had bothered testing us, they could have sold our urine to addicts somewhere.

I realize now that I can never go to jail. It's too fucked up in there. Even in the few hours I had to be in that cage, I realized that there was a whole other world, a whole other hierarchy that was followed by the girls behind bars.

Being locked up in a cage with murderers and violent offenders would be a one-way ticket to death for someone like me.

It makes me realize that I have to figure out what I'm going to do and how I'm going to get out of this mess that I've created for myself.

What will I do, though?

My options are pretty limited.

In the can, there was some chick who was prattling on about nonsense. As she babbled on, I realized that she was either strung out on some drug or she was crazy. Either way, her nervousness at being locked up made her natural babblings into full-blown verbal diarrhea. She went on and on about this and that. At some point she was telling me how to make homemade piccalilli. She went on at length about vegetables and cutting, but I began to listen more intently as she explained the pickling process.

The idea of pickling appeals to me, so I made mental notes as she got on and off track repeatedly. Even though the woman was clearly fucked up, I hoped that there was some truth in her pickling expertise.

Before I started writing, I looked up some pickling recipes on the Internet. It doesn't look so hard, especially after making a shrunken head. Been there, done that, never want to smell that smell again.

Pickling, on the other hand, might be fun.

Thursday, January 5

While I was watching TV, I thought about an old *Daily Show* that I saw once. I always thought that show was pretty good, but I don't watch TV much except for music videos. Who knows if the show's even on anymore?

Anyway, I was thinking about a crack Jon Stewart made, implying that if we were being nuked, we'd have a big fuck-fest. I wonder if that's true. If North America is really so decadent, so free, that we would make love and not war.

It doesn't seem like a feasible idea to me. It's like something some old hippy would say, but I guess that's what he is, that Jon Stewart. Some old hippy.

If I knew the world was coming to an end, I'd probably stuff my face with whatever I had been denying myself. Lots of chocolate and ice cream. Maybe a big chocolate chip cookie dough ice cream sundae with hot fudge cappuccino sauce and mounds of real whip cream. Of course, I'd like to fuck myself to death like anyone else, but how do you do that? Do you say, "Oh shit, a bomb is coming and we're all going to die. Can I suck your cock?"

Somehow I can't see it happening even if you were with your lover.

The chaos of knowing death is imminent would cause mass panic and people would kill each other trying to escape the inevitable.

The chances of people whipping off their clothes for the last orgy on earth would be pretty remote.

But wouldn't it be cool if it happened? Wouldn't that be the greatest show on earth?

It would also be tragic. It would show the true stupidity of man, that we can't get along in our day-to-day lives yet we can put aside our differences when we think we're going to die.

It's to be expected. Man is a fickle creature.

I still can't believe I went to jail. Every now and again, the idea of it hits me, and I start to shake. My hands take on a mind of their own and they fiddle with things. At one point today I realized I had been flicking Jimmie's lighter for almost an hour. The only reason I clued in to that much was because it ran out of fluid and I realized what time it was.

Jimmie never even called me. But of course, why would he? I don't think he even knows my number.

Little Shrunken Shrew sways lazily, dangling from

the Angel's hand. I put a little fan up so that they'll look like they're flying through the universe.

Actually, it was my hands' idea. I had nothing to do with it. As I was thinking about something else, my hands decided that my little collection needed some movement. Art should never be stagnant. Your eye should always be moving.

It was funny that my hands knew such things before I even thought about it.

In fact I would never have thought about it at all, because it didn't occur to me until I looked at what they had done. Maybe my hands are smarter than me. They always act before I have a chance to think.

They seem to be particularly attached to the chain saw. Over the past few days, they've been repeatedly drawn to it. They fondle it, craving the buzz beneath their fingers. But I won't let them turn it on. It's too noisy. The chain saw can only be used on special occasions or the neighbors might get suspicious. I explain to them that I can get away with it once in a while, because maybe I'm making bookshelves or something. But I can't turn on the damn thing just to hear it sing. That's wasting valuable noise time.

I've even taken to training my ears to prefer the headphones. At least with the cordless ones, I can wander around and do my chores without blasting out the neighbors.

My exercises are back on track. I decided to stop drowning my sorrows in decadence. My New Year's resolution is to turn over a new leaf. Be the happy chipper girl that Mr. J.D. seems to want. And be a bitch too, cos that seems to be what he likes or desires.

That woman he went home with looked pretty rough. If he got involved with her, he'd be getting a shiner in no time.

But maybe not.

Maybe she was just a domme and found a little play-mate to quench her loneliness on New Year's Eve.

I had to give her the benefit of the doubt.

It was him I was upset with in this scenario. How could he go on a date with me and leave with some-one else? I wasn't so terribly hideous, I don't think. Sure I still had glasses, but the rest of me was looking pretty good.

Well, all I can do is wait for him to show his face around again. He's probably embarrassed at what he did and won't dare to come around again.

Saturday, January 7

Well, I was wrong about Mr. J.D. He came in today and acted the same as he always does. He didn't seem remorseful or embarrassed. He seemed like the same old guy. He didn't even acknowledge our date until I brought it up.

"So, you have a good time New Year's Eve?"

A small grin flashed across his face.

"New Year's Eve? Oh, yeah. Man, was I trashed."

"I guess."

"I ended up going to an all night coffee shop with some woman. She was really depressed about spending her first New Year's Eve alone in many years. Her hus-band died in the summer."

"Oh, that's too bad," I said.

"I could commiserate with her since there's still been no word. She thinks there's been foul play too."

"What does she know about it?"

"Only what I told her, I have to admit."

"Well, then, she probably doesn't realize that your girlfriend might have just left town."

"You're so sure about that."

"Just a gut feeling I have."

"I don't know . . ." He stared into his coffee cup.

"So, back to work?" I asked.

"Yep. Back to the old grind, though it's hard to concentrate."

"I'm sure it'll get better."

I had to go tend to some other customers. The place was suddenly busy and so I never got a chance to ask him out again. By the time he wanted his bill, I was flying around like a chicken with my head cut off, my hands knowing what to grab, my feet knowing which table to deliver items to. My mouth and brain were not engaging very well, so I mutely handed him his bill and he paid, leaving a big tip as always.

The rest of my shift was a blur and now I'm tired. I'm working a split shift today and I have to be back at nine.

At least I'll have time for a shower, and even a bit more time to putter.

CHAPTER FOURTEEN

Sunday, January 8

While I was out for a walk, I saw ahead of me two people in garish fur coats holding the leashes to trotting rats. They weren't really rats, they were small dogs. Since the couple was moving slowly, because they were stopping and talking every five feet, I caught up to them with ease. It was Steve and that Club Owner. I followed them til they reached the club and watched them enter. I wondered if the dogs would be let loose in the back like they sometimes were.

Sure enough, as I picked my way through back alleys, I saw a bored cook in a chef's hat let the dogs out. He looked around and didn't see anyone so he went back inside. I knew he didn't see me cos I was crouching behind a fence and watching him through a peephole. I hustled my ass through snow-covered fencing on the other side and broke off a piece of the wooden fence.

My mouth puckered into a whistle, enticing the

yappy little bastards towards me. My hands scooped them up, and as the dogs wriggled and snarled, they were silenced once and for all.

I took off my hat and scarf and wrapped them around my prizes until it looked like I had a bundle of clothes. The door opened again with a groan and back at my peephole I saw the cook light a cigarette. He looked out into the dingy yard/dump/parking spot and whistled for the dogs. When they didn't answer, I heard him sigh "shit," and carefully make his way down the stairs. He looked high and low for the damn dogs, but not good enough. Even though he ventured into the alley, he didn't brave the snowy lanes to look for the dogs. If he really cared, he would have followed what few tracks he could find, and I would have been up a creek without a paddle.

However, I was lucky he was not so adventurous. In fact, judging by his apathetic hunt, I figure I did the poor guy a favor. He was probably assigned to picking up their shit as well.

At last he returned to work, or maybe to tell the boys of their loss. It didn't matter. What mattered was getting the hell out of there before panicked pooch lovers launched an all out hunt for their pets.

My hands were happy to feel the buzz of the chain saw once more. They even didn't mind wiping up the mess afterwards. My eyes kept constant vigil for telltale splashes of scarlet along the door frames and ceiling. Nothing must betray the secrets that I kept. One stray drop will be my undoing and my eyes and hands know that.

My nose isn't too happy with the strong vapors of bleach, but there's nothing I can do about that.

Making piccalilli is fun. I'm not done yet, but the preparation was a breeze.

Monday, January 9

My new jars of piccadoggy are set up at the altar. Now I have something to offer my guests, should any drop in.

My e-mail held false "Happy New Year" greetings from my mother. My phone had several messages from Vicki. In fact, in one of them she said something about coming over tonight.

I sure hope she doesn't do that.

Tuesday, January 10

The stress continues.

Miss Vicki decided to pay me a visit. She knows she shouldn't do that, but she chose to anyway. So be it.

When there was pounding at the door, I ignored it. However, when I heard Vicki screaming to her in, I knew I had to act fast. I stared with disdain at my circus tent, and all my lovely artifacts. The walls had little shelves now and the fabric went behind them. My skull collection was displayed in its entirety. She had seen my skulls before, so I wondered what she would think of the rest of the room and the underwear collection.

She had seen Monica before and I had explained that she was a movie prop. My new additions seemed to fit right in. I would just have to tell her that I don't tell her every little thing, that I had been buying skeletons off the Internet.

My plan was short-lived. When I let Vicki in, she buzzed around the apartment like a fly trying to find a window.

"I can't take it anymore," she said. "The cops . . . the cops were questioning me all afternoon. It won't be long before they come to you."

"That's great," I said. "You didn't tell them where I lived?"

"I didn't have to. They had your address already."

I don't know if she was lying to me. It didn't matter.

"You gotta joint or something? I missed a shift 'cause of those fuckers, and now I may get fired."

"You can't get fired 'cause the cops were questioning you," I said.

"I've already had too much time off." She sighed. "They are just looking for an excuse to can my ass."

"They need you. You're good," I said.

"They don't like me doing stuff on the side. If they don't catch me, they don't care. But I've been caught. That and calling in sick a few times."

"Why are you calling in sick? You getting some?"

"Partly. And partly 'cause some days I just keep reliving that night. More and more is coming back to me. Sounds I heard in the night. What did you do with him?"

"Who?" I asked. I wondered if she was wearing a wire. She had spent all afternoon with the cops; who knew?

The only way to find out if she was wired would be to get her naked and check. I had to search her clothes and her body without her knowing that was what I was doing. I started my seduction by running my hands along her breasts, checking her pockets.

"Here, let me hang up your coat," I said, taking her damp fake fur jacket from her. She reclined on the couch, not seeing as I checked her coat for bugs. She wouldn't know if I hung up coats on a regular basis or not, since she had seldom been here.

It was a good thing I was on a neatness binge. My apartment wasn't messy, and it didn't look too weird if you didn't count the greatest show on earth. When my hands had finished patting down her coat, my feet returned me to her. On the coffee table there was a little wooden box, and I opened it to pluck out a joint. Again it was lucky that my hands had thought ahead in a moment of boredom to roll a few joints in advance for times like these.

I handed her the joint, and she took it gratefully. As she lit it, I resumed my stroking of her.

"You must be frightened," I said softly. "I think you need a nice massage."

"Oh, yes. I love your massages." She started to peel off her shirt. I helped her as much as I could, and as I folded up her clothes, my mouth had a great idea.

"Go into the bedroom and wait for me."

She skipped off to the bedroom while my hands resumed searching. There was nothing in her clothes, which was good. I went into the kitchen and found some olive oil. I also decided that more cinnamon should be added to my brew bubbling on the stove. I added more water too in case I didn't get back in time before it burned.

Naked on the bed, Vicki waited eagerly for me. Her back and ass were beautiful, and I knelt above her.

"Take off your clothes too," she said. "I like it when you are naked and massaging me."

I stripped off my clothes and resumed my position. I rubbed her all over with deep, rotating movements. She sighed and squirmed under my touch.

After a while she turned over, wanting me to do her front. That was as much fun as doing her back was, and I paid special attention to her pleasure zones. Soon she was thinking of anything but cops and Brad. I took her mind off her problems for quite some time, and then she returned the favor. Everything was going great until we returned to the living room and had a smoke.

She took notice of my collection, even though I tried to distract her with the television.

"When did you add all this?" she asked.

"Over the past month or two. Since I've been back."

"Where do you get this stuff?"

"Internet mostly. I've been collecting skulls since I was a kid."

"Is that a real shrunken head?"

"Who knows? It's supposed to be, but I have my doubts. I think it's plastic or leather myself."

"Kind of gross, don't you think?"

She sat and stared at Monica and at Brad's head in her lap.

"I don't like how that one is looking at me. It's like he's accusing me of something."

"Come on." I laughed at the absurdity of her comment.

"I do. It's almost like waves of something are coming from him. Like despair or anger. A whole bunch of stuff."

"It's probably not even real. Check it out." I handed her Brad's skull. She nearly dropped it when she touched it.

"God, it's even worse now. It's almost like screaming in my head."

"Oh, stop it." I sighed. "You're hallucinating. I tell you, that's some good pot there."

"It's not the pot. I know what it is. This head was real."

"You a psychic or something?"

"Not really. But now and again I get these flashes."

Her face went pale and her bug eyes bugged out even further. She stared at me in horror, her hand touching her lips.

"What did you do with Brad's head?"

"I disposed of him. I told you that." I took the skull from her. "You are getting all freaked out again."

"That's Brad, isn't it?" She stared at me as if I was some kind of monster.

"Why would I keep evidence around?" I said. "Am I stupid?"

"That's Brad. And who are these other people?"

"I told you, I bought these things."

Vicki put her hand to her forehead. "I don't feel well. I think I should go."

"No, you're just stressed. You're safe here," I said, pushing her back on the couch.

"How do I know I'm safe with you?" she asked.

The look of her made me feel wet and excited, and I

kissed her. "I love you, that's why. I'll always take care of you." I leaned back, admiring her. She blinked nervously, her eyes darting from one skull to another. After a moment I got up.

"I'll get us something to drink."

I went into the kitchen and took bottled water from the fridge. I opened it and poured it into a glass. I took a capsule from a container in the cupboard and broke it open. A splash of amaretto completed the cocktail. My hands were twitching with laughter as they handed her the glass.

"What's this?" she asked as she took it.

"Amaretto and water. Just how you like it," I told her. She took a sip and rolled her eyes.

"Mmm, it is too. I'm sorry I'm so jumpy. Of course that isn't Brad," she said. I wasn't sure I believed her; she had a quiver to her lips that happened when she lied. She had it the day I found out about her and Brad. It didn't matter: She was asleep in minutes from the sedative I put in her drink.

Before the drugs took effect, I offered her piccadoggy and toast, which she tried. I declined, saying that I was sick of it, having consumed mass quantities when it was first done. Of course, I didn't tell her what it really was, just said it was some old Italian recipe that called for all sorts of weird stuff, almost like calamari or something. She was too freaked out to question it, or even to look at what she was eating. It was rather gag-invoking to watch her chew and swallow, but I kept my Cheshire cat face intact.

I really didn't like the idea of Vicki having to be resigned to a fate of worrying about whether or not she'll ever be connected to Brad's disappearance, and I didn't like being at her mercy. So my hands set to work balancing the universe in my favor for a while.

They were quivering with excitement as the hum of the chain saw raced through them. My eyes spared me the gruesome sight of the best parts of Miss Vicki being compacted into little manageable piccavicki slices.

Thursday, January 12

Miss Vicki's skull is boiled nice and clean, so I won't have to worry about flies. She is perched in Monica's lap alongside Brad. The piccavicki is on display with the piccadoggy.

Work was slow for some reason. Maybe everyone overspent at the holidays. At any rate, if tips don't pick up soon, it's going to be hard to stay on top of the bills. Having only one rent is hard enough, what was I thinking paying one and a half?

In some ways I miss Vicki. Yet in others I know she is right here with me always. I talk to her more then I do to the others. Even more then I do to Monica.

Monica isn't too happy these days. She thinks this place is getting crowded, and we should move or get rid of some of the new people. I think that everything is just fine, but it's hard to convince her sometimes. We can argue about it tirelessly, but in the end it's my decision. The idea of trying to get first and last month together along with saving for laser eye surgery with work being slow isn't practical.

She doesn't care. She wants to keep moving. She's worried that I'll get caught.

My argument is, caught for what? Sure, the skulls would show DNA if they were tested, but why would anyone test then? Lots of people have skulls around their houses. Goths, artists, poets, props people, you name it. People have skulls.

What difference does it make if you got the skull yourself?

I guess it does, although it shouldn't.

I was making art as much as any artist.

People would pay good money to see such a collection.

I can see it now: I could be out front barking at everyone.

"Come see the greatest show on earth. Admire Abigail's Collection of Loathsome Lovers."

I bet I could make some money. But, of course, the questions would begin. To put on a proper show, I'd have to wait about fifty years and say I acquired skulls in my travels.

In the meantime, Monica nags, nags, nags.

Friday, January 13

At work today, I saw Mavis. She stared at me with a kind of weird look on her face, like she was in shock.

I asked her what her problem was.

"You look . . . terrible, my dear," she said to me. "Tell me, what is going on? You're not pining for Jimmie-boy, are you?"

I shook my head. "I didn't think I looked so bad. I'm not pining for Jimmie or anyone else. Who would be worth the bother?"

"Is it because you got picked up in the raid?" she whispered.

"Who told you that?"

"Please. I hope you aren't fretting about that. I've been picked up so many times, I couldn't even count them. When you walk down the streets as I sometimes do, the cops have a field day with you."

"Well, I'm not freaked out about being in jail. I didn't have charges laid against me or anything."

"I'm glad you're OK." She gave me a little hug. "Hey, I'm having a few people over for cocktails later. Would you like to come?"

"Sure," I said.

"Maybe you can bring a little something to munch on. I'm having everyone bring some sort of food. Like a potluck dinner kind of thing. I'm going to be too exhausted to cook when I get home."

"Sounds good," I said.

I was excited about going over to Mavis's apartment. She threw such wonderful parties, and everyone was always so nice to me.

Since the party would be mostly drag queens, I changed into a slinky dress and donned a bright red feather boa. It didn't take long for my hands to make my hair really high. They did a good job on overexaggerating my makeup as well.

As to what to bring, I didn't have a clue. My cupboards were pretty bare. I looked around, hoping to find crackers or tuna or anything I could make into party food. But I had been sadly neglecting my shopping since I mostly ate at the restaurant when I remembered to eat at all.

As I bustled around the kitchen, my eyes fell on the jars of piccadoggy on the display table. There were many there, so I could afford to take a couple with me. I could explain it was some sort of Italian recipe.

On my way to Mavis's house, I picked up a fresh loaf of bread. It would go well with the piccadoggy.

Imagine my joy and surprise to see Steve and that club owner whose name I can never remember at the party. It was hard to keep my mouth from giggling as my hands spooned out great chunks of piccadoggy into serving bowls.

My treat was a hit, though I never tried it myself. I told those who asked that it was a secret family recipe, some kind of antipasto delicacy handed down for generations.

It was hysterical to watch Steve and Club Owner Guy chew on the piccadoggy while lamenting the loss of their pets. I feigned interest in what had become of their beloved pooches while relishing the sight of said pooches being swished around their mouths.

Their mastication fascinated me so much that at one point Steve stopped chewing and asked me if there was something wrong.

"No, not at all."

"You're staring at me like you've never seen anyone eat before."

"I'm sorry. I'm just a little stoned and tired. Long day," I said, my mouth trying its damnedest to keep peals of laughter from slipping through it. "I don't mean anything by it. Surely you know what I'm talking about."

"Sure, honey. I just have a sense that you haven't

heard a word I've said the whole time I've been talking to you."

"Of course I've been listening. You were talking about how you miss your dog, and you are still pissed at the cook for letting him out of his sight."

"Two dogs he lost that day. How do you lose two dogs?" He sighed and ripped into another bite of piccadoggy and bread. "This is really good, though. What is it you said?"

"It's like a piccalilli but made with slightly different ingredients. I think the magic is in the garlic and the dill."

"I would have to agree. I love garlic. I could eat garlic for the rest of my life and not be tired of it. You can have garlic in so many ways."

"That's true. I especially like to broil up a clove of garlic with paprika and butter drizzled over it. That will clear up any cold."

"Broiled garlic is like butter. All soft and mushy. Perfect for spreading on fresh bread."

"Let's face it, anything is good spread on fresh bread."

"Fresh bread can make up for a lot of problems in the kitchen, that's for sure."

Mavis was clicking her glass and calling everyone's attention. "I want to thank everyone for coming here tonight. I know that I said I was having an impromptu potluck party, but there is method to my madness."

Everyone stopped talking and turned their attention to her.

"As everyone here knows, two of my dear friends have suffered a loss. I wanted to pull together this party so that I could give them a new start."

We all watched as Storm entered the room carrying two tiny puppies and placed them in the arms of the grieving ones. The room erupted into applause. Steve and Club Owner Guy were crying like little girls.

It was all quite nauseating. Steven and Club Owner Guy cradled those puppies like babies and fed them little bits of piccadoggy and other snacks while people admired them. I left shortly after that.

Despite Mavis thinking that I wasn't looking too good these days, I went to Boingo's to dance. In the bathroom, I studied my face and thought it didn't look too bad.

My eyes were dark as ever, though a little puffy even under the extreme makeup. I had dark circles beneath that the makeup wasn't doing a very good job of hiding. My body was growing smaller, and that pleased me a lot.

The night was uneventful, but I did feel better after dancing with myself.

CHAPTER FIFTEEN

Monday, January 16

Mr. J.D. thinks he's too good for me these days or something. He didn't come in for a few days, and then when he did, he didn't even sit in my section. The stupid airhead hostess wasn't even working today.

It took a couple of tries to get some conversation out of him on my pretend trips to the hostess desk. He was stewing over some deadline and still wondering where his shrew went.

Same old, same old.

That's OK, though. If he's back to his routine, I can go over to his house again. I haven't been there since the new year began.

Even though I was squeaky happy when I saw him, he didn't seem to care. He was locked into his melancholy and wallowing in it. I wanted to be melancholy too, but knew that he needed a woman to pull him out of it. My mouth was pretty good at finding perky things to say, even though I don't know where they came from.

I even got him to crack a smile for a moment.

But in the end I was just a waitress and he was a customer. He didn't yet see me as he needed to.

I went home to tell Monica all about it.

She didn't want to hear anything, though. She just wants to move. She feels like my time is running out.

No one is bothering me about anyone. The cops never came, that I know of, to question me. I wonder sometimes if Vicki just made that up to fuck with my head.

I doubt it, though. I can't imagine why she would bother lying about it. She already knew the truth of what happened that night.

It was weird, though, that the cops didn't call on me. I haven't changed my name or anything. I'm probably not that hard to find.

Abigail Barnum is hardly an unusual name.

Well, I wasn't going to let it worry me. If they wanted me, they knew where to find me. Here or work.

If they had searched my place while I was out, I would be in jail by now for sure.

So I wasn't going to let any of that bother me at all.

Wednesday, January 18

Sometimes I am startled by my own audacity. It seems funny to me how I can be so quiet and shy in some ways, yet in others I am as bold as bold can be.

I spent a pleasant morning at Jimmie's house.

He wasn't home, of course, but it was almost as good as if he were.

First thing I did was draw a long bubble bath. I didn't care if he noticed moisture or mildew or heat upon his return home. I didn't even really care if he found me in there, though I knew he wouldn't. I had watched him and saw that he was keeping his old work hours. In the office every morning, and at noon he would come home or continue to work in the office. Then there was his drink or snack at Ooolala a couple of times a week as well.

The bath was warm and relaxing. I poured some of his bath oil into it. At first I had found it strange that a man would have bath oil at all, but I knew too that many men these days wanted to smell as good for their women as women wanted to smell for their men. He wasn't a full blown metrosexual, and in fact most of the time he was grubby and dirty.

He cleaned up really well when he wanted to.

I lay in the bath dreaming of him. I imagined the day he realized that it was me he wanted, me he desired. He would kiss me hungrily and never let me go. He would chide himself for being so foolish as to not see that the girl who should be his was right here in his own backyard.

I lay back in the bath, letting the warm oily water caress me as I imagined his long gentle fingers would one day. My fingers stroked and cupped my breast, lamenting the drop in size, yet feeling there was still more flesh there than the average bear. My nipples hadn't lost size at all and in fact seemed to overtake my breast. They still ached to be fondled, and I tweaked them with one hand while the other hand snaked its way down to my pussy.

His lips would be velvet on mine. His lips would kiss me, licking and nipping at me from the ticklish crook of my neck to the trembling folds of my pussy.

My legs were in need of shaving, so I took the liberty of using his razor and shaving cream to lather up my legs, my underarms and even my pussy. I had to crouch half out of the tub to shave my bikini line or the shaving cream would be washed away.

When I was all smooth and feminine, I reimmersed myself into the water, half hoping for him to come waltzing in and be so taken with desire that he'd fuck me over and over again.

It wasn't happening, though, so I had to satisfy myself. It's never been a problem for me to satisfy myself; I just prefer the touch of another human being. No matter who you are with, man or woman, they add warmth and contact to the experience.

Everyone is so different that you learn different techniques and that you really do have to ask what someone likes. What works for one person may be torture for another.

I wonder what Jimmie is like when he fucks. I wonder if he's big or little. Does he like to take his time and make it last all night? Does he go quickly and fall asleep? Does he have several short sessions in one night?

For a while, I fell into a reverie where events unfolded like the unfurling of a flower. Impatiently I waited for the center, the heart of the matter, to be revealed. Patience is not my forte, and my dream seemed to unravel in slow motion, as if taunting and tormenting me in a most disdainful way.

The beginning was sweet adventure, exploring winding roads that led to lands beyond the fabric of reality. It was as though particles were parted in the air or in a void—I'm not sure which it was or even how to describe it. The vibrations leaking through teased my senses, coaxing me towards them in my explorations for the pure experience. I followed the faint tendrils, naming them Enthusiasm, Mystery, Curiosity and Orgasmic.

As I stepped upon the threshold linking the world as I knew it with the world I was about to experience, my body seemed to ripple as if it was a miniwave. For a moment I was in the void or some kind of emptiness. Any sensation of longing or grief I had before was multiplied manifold in that dark, dismal space. It wasn't like I was on a bridge, but in a way I guess I was. The threshold was a gap, a bridge, a footpath, a tiny doorway. . . . It was everything and nothing. But the vibrations that swirled around in that space-that-wasn't-space overwhelmed me. I wasn't equipped to experience the onslaught of all emotion from the beginning of time, so I let the tendrils embrace me and pull me with lightening speed towards their world.

Once I had arrived, they recoiled back into their plantlike bases. The world here was full of animations that bore no semblance to creatures or creations that I could name. The tendrils were only a part of a being. Each plant-type thing had a variety of tendrils. Some had many colorful ones, while others only sported one or two darker ones. You didn't know what the tendril contained until it touched you. When it wrapped around your flesh, its meaning rippled into you, forming into your very cells.

There was no need for talking. Even at bay, the whispering of tendrils followed me as I began to walk.

The plant-type things began to thin out. The whispering grew fainter, and soon I had left them behind. Now that I could see the sky, I marveled at its crimson and magenta shades. They swirled into each other like the most delicious ice cream.

Before me were stones and rocks and caves that looked like they held primitive dwellings.

Again I was faced with the choice of what to do.

The sky was swirling faster, and I thought a storm might be coming. The wind picked up, and there were shrieking sounds from all around. Normally I would say they were birds, but these noises weren't like any birds I've ever heard.

Unlike people in B movies, I decided to run away and not worry about what the hell was behind the sudden shift in barometer pressure.

I ran for the nearest shelter, a tall tree in front of one of the caves.

Then I realized that if there was lightening around here, I would surely be struck.

By the way strange-looking creatures raced past me, I wondered if something worse was coming along.

Images of a T. rex stomping my way set my heart racing, and I began the dream paralysis of running without getting anywhere.

No matter how I tried, my feet could not find purchase in the slippery ground. The grass or whatever it was that coated the ground turned into slick mulch whenever my feet touched it. Maybe my body warmth was too much for it, and it melted under my touch.

Anything was possible in a dream.

For the rest of the dream, I would move at a random speed. Sometimes I could run like hell, and other times it felt as though I were swimming in quicksand.

The petals unfurled a little more.

The cave was dark, and I actually did feel like a cheesy actress in some shitty B movie. Maybe there would be a handsome pirate king tucked away in the darkness. It's my dream; I can wish it if I want, can't I?

Apparently I can't. I bet I wouldn't have so many problems if my dream program would read my reality program and each do a bit of translation for the other. If I could get both tracks functioning at a parallel level, I might feel more balanced at the end of it all.

The cave didn't have the welcoming aura that the tendrils did. This cave had vibrations too, but they were dark and dusty. Not as chaotic as the pass had been, but an uncomfortable feeling just the same.

Outside it was nearly impossible to see, but a few feet in front of the cave there was an opening. The sky had either darkened or something big was covering it up. I kept coming back to the idea of a huge monster because of the way the ground was trembling. For the longest time I had thought that the shifting ground was my own fear quivering through my bones. It was both a blessed relief and a new desperation to realize that it wasn't.

I fled into the cave before I could feel jagged teeth snatching at my back. There were noises of vast proportions, scaling the higher range of discordant patterning. My ears tried to shut down in protest. My hands clumsily protected them as I ran through the tunnel.

In a way, I wish it had been pitch-black. There was no need to see the shadows of pointy-ended creatures hanging down from the low mossy ceiling as I raced through.

When I recognized the creatures as something between a scorpion and a bat, my legs went on strike and slowed right down. My hands were reluctant to let loose of my ears to help. Although I screamed at my legs to hurry up, they shifted gears into that stupid slow-as-molasses-in-January crawl.

A petal fell off.

The light that I had seen came from a brilliant stone in the center of a large cavern. Never had I seen such an amazingly luminescent rock. It may not even have been stone at all. It could have been a ray of light. It could have been the Holy Grail.

It doesn't matter.

What mattered was that I was walking like a retard, and if anyone of importance was to see me, I'd look like an idiot ripe for plucking.

There were many hallways leading from the cavern.

That stupid sense of déjà vu that I always get in dreams came back to me. Weird how that happened at the time.

I remembered that the last time I had to choose a path, I had picked water. This time I chose earth. I wanted my beloved earth back. I hadn't been in this new place long, but whatever it was that drove all the creatures into a mass panic was enough to get concerned about.

With the exception of bombs and terrorists, there was no threat like that in New York City. Tornados and hurricanes may abound, but everyone knew where those would happen. It sure as hell wasn't New York. Except in a couple of movies.

The earth plan wasn't so hot.

I found myself outside again. This must have been a different outside, because the sky was clear and blue. The trees looked like trees and the creek looked like a creek.

There was a brief moment when I felt that maybe things would be OK after all.

Then I heard it.

What big eyes you have.

Seemingly from through the grass, yet I knew there must have been a small hill, the wolves were suddenly there. The whole damn pack assembled as if attending a solemn ceremony. I've never sat and counted them, but I knew they were all there.

SHE was there too.

She stood with the tall golden wolf and stared at me with accusing eyes. I couldn't meet her gaze, and even though I knew at the time it was a dream, I couldn't figure out how to tell her to go away.

So I didn't.

My feet and legs were both being stubborn now. Maybe they were being pulled by her invisible force field that was rapidly winding around me like a spider-web. I was the hapless fly and she was the hungry predator.

She had always been a bitch. She was always the prettiest, the fastest, the cutest, the funniest. Damn her. Damn Kimberly. Damn them both to hell.

Even thoughts of Kimberly don't make me feel as

bad as thoughts of HER. That beautiful icon of hopes and dreams. Of how we used to talk long into the night. How her golden body would press against mine, teasing out the most delicate of sensations with a quick flick of her tongue or a gentle pursing of the lips.

No one understands the web of delight she wove for me night after night. I was ready to give it up, all of it up for her.

Oh Mistress of the Dark
How you deceived me
Teasing me with curling fingers
Yet taunting me with your mocking mouth

She feasted on my adoration for her. I was the perfect sycophant for her narcissism. She constantly primped and preened in the mirror while I tried to hold down a few jobs on the side.

We made an unlikely couple. She had her blond curling waves, and I was dark and plump and not a little foreboding.

She stood there with the golden beast, watching me. Daring me to do something, anything. But what was I to do?

All the wolves watched me.

A wrong move, a sudden move, might startle them.

I couldn't decide what to do.

They sat panting, watching me, watching her.

In a strange way, I wanted to go to her.

But the sky was growing dark once more, and I feared what was to come.

I ran away from them, half expecting them to take

up chase. But they didn't. They watched me go and went back to wherever it was they had come from.

And so another petal was loosened.

I had to be nearing the eye of the dream. The purpose. The soul. The reason for it all.

The ground rumbled, and the strange scratchy noises filled the air. I imagined giant claws bearing down on me as I ran, ready to scoop me up and consume me like a tasty morsel.

I fled into a clump of trees and stopped. There shouldn't be danger here. This was the real world again.

The trees whispered and shook. Snatches of words danced along my ears, but my ears ignored them. We didn't want to hear what was being said. It didn't matter anymore. What mattered was survival.

I wandered through the woods, not paying attention to what was directly in front of me, more worried about what might be following me from behind. I managed to walk right into a large sticky spiderweb.

It was no ordinary spiderweb as these things go. I was stuck in it, getting more stuck with every twitch I made. I hoped that whoever made the web was harmless and absent, but I was wrong. A large hairy spider, nearly four feet across, scuttled towards me.

"Now this won't hurt a bit," she told me in a low, seductive voice as she started to wrap me up.

"I don't want to be spider food," I said. "I really don't."

"You won't be spider food. You will be set aside for a special occasion. You are meant for better things." She was actually quite glamorous and interesting, especially for a spider. I'm glad I've never been very afraid of spiders, although anyone would be alarmed at one bigger then a toddler. Such a large spider had large multijointed legs and many eyes. She seemed to be covered in a sort of fur, like a tarantula. Many people I know would have passed out cold at the sight of her, but I didn't. Passing out was reserved for far scarier stuff then a giant talking spider. What she was doing to me was daunting, however. She continued to wrap her silky web around me like a mummy case, and it didn't matter how I tired to escape; the web just rendered me more helpless with each flail of my arms or legs.

"I don't think I'm meant to be someone's dinner." I was reminded of how Vicki had been wrapped in plastic that one night and hoped that was where the dream image was coming from.

"You are meant for what fate has in store for you. We all are. Some of us are just part of the food chain. We are lucky to survive as long as we can. The rest of us are destined for greatness, if we put what we have for good use."

Whispering grew louder from the trees, and it caused me to wonder how many creatures were in hiding. Why were they hiding? Surely one spider couldn't take on the multitude of these whisperers.

Maybe the spider was doing their bidding. Maybe the spider knew what it was doing and didn't care about the consequences.

All I knew was that the atmosphere had changed yet again and panic flooded my bones. I was Fay Wray tied to the stake for King Kong.

A giant gorilla would be welcome relief to the images I was conjuring up in my head about what I might be destined for. Some sort of familiar horror would be soothing to my shattered nerves.

The spider had me wound up tight. She admired her handiwork with her many beady eyes.

"Now you know what it is like to be all tied up with no place to go. To be waiting and waiting, as you have done to so many souls."

"I've done nothing to any souls," I said.

"You've deprived the souls of proper resting spots for their worldly vessels. Until they are buried or cremated, the souls wander around aimlessly."

"Like in this dream," I said.

"Exactly like in a dream. Only this is no dream, this is reality."

"That's the most commonly used dream euphemism there is. I won't fall for such clichés."

"You don't have to fall for anything at all. It will only get worse before it gets better."

"Why am I tied up? Who am I waiting for?"

"You'll know. You'll see."

The whispering shadows pressed closer. I could almost make out shapes in the bushes and behind trees. What did these dream demons have in store for me? I wanted to know, but was afraid to know. If I died in a dream, would I die in real life? There are all sorts of wives tales that support such a theory, but mostly it's been debunked over the years. The number of times the average person dies in a dream or hallucination is many, and who was the one that came back to tell people that if you dream you are dying, you are really dying? How do they know these things? And who are "they," anyway?

Wondering and worrying was a way of life for me. I could spend a dream suspended and spinning, or I could use the magic of dream power to escape my bindings.

These bindings were not so easy to escape.

I closed my eyes, wishing really hard that I wasn't there anymore, that the dream would flip into something else and I would be free of the woods, the spider, the shadows in the trees.

When I opened my eyes again, I was lying on a large rock, surrounded by ocean. I was still bound, but now I was exposed to all the elements and whatever birds of prey happened to be making the noises.

Maybe it was noises of birds or of something much more sinister. Even though I could open my eyes, they were obstructed by the layer of web the spider had wrapped around me. I'm sure it was just another form of torture. But you could never be too sure.

The long, sharp beaks on the circling seabirds frightened me, and in looking around the rock from my vantage point of being tied down flat, I knew that I was in big trouble when the tide came in.

And the tide would be coming in.

I could taste seawater in the air, in the damp mist that hung around me. As tied up as I was, I was also glad that I was adventurous, that I liked to try new things. At least once. Just like Miss Vicki used to like to do.

I wished Vicki was here with me in this dream. I wished that she would appear and talk to me. I could really use some sort of communication with someone who had a handle on what was going on.

But my wish wasn't to come true. The sky grew dark and violent. There was a cold wind, and drops of the rising tide were splashing my face.

The whispering now seemed to come from the water, as if the very waves themselves were speaking to me.

A dark shadow appeared in the air. It grew larger and larger as it approached.

My body was trembling, and I wondered if it would be better to fling myself into the ocean and die a quick tidy death than wait to be carried away.

As I tasted the salt and closed my eyes, flashes of other images came to mind. Images that I didn't want to remember or even see.

I thought about the little bed-and-breakfast I had stayed in a couple of months ago. It was a nice place, and I longed to live there again for a little while. Not for a long time. I missed the hustle and bustle of New York. There was too much whispering in this country-side for my liking.

It's not nice for people to talk behind your back, but they seem to go right ahead and do it anyway.

The snatches of whispering I caught had moved from one wave to another.

Louder. It was like the waves whispered, the clouds whispered, even the circling birds were whispering and muttering secrets within secrets.

The rock where I was trapped rumbled, and I wished I was in a train or running from a tidal wave.

But no matter which tactic I chose to veer the direction of the dream, my fate remained the same.

Through the film covering my eyes, I made out a giant shape. The shape filled the sky, as I had suspected before. There was movement and shifting, and I was lifted and tossed and fell, fell, fell down into darkness.

The darkness turned to water, and the acidy foam stripped away my bindings. I tried to swim, but realized that I had to escape from the churning acid-fest that I had fallen into.

My hands reached up blindly, grabbing at the sides. At first my hands were reluctant to take hold of the wall, which was fleshy and moist and breathing. I realized that I was in the stomach of the creature, being reduced to digested dinner.

I fought my nausea at grabbing onto the stomach and pulled myself with a groan from the swirling water. There was a loud thumping that banged through the walls, and I realized it must be the creature's heart.

With tears in my eyes, I climbed and climbed. My arms ached and I nearly screamed as I reached the top. There was no way to get out; there was no opening that I could find. I could vaguely see this. It was almost as if my eyes were giving me selective vision.

My fingers were sore and cramping, and I realized that I was losing my grip on the slippery flesh.

It was to no avail.

I fell.

I fell and fell, and this time it was different from when I fell before. The dark murkiness sprawled out below me and never seemed to end.

When I landed, it was on a bed.

I was back in the bed-and-breakfast in New England.

Around me sat my collection come to life. They watched me with great amusement as I got my bearings. In the center of it all sat Jimmie.

Jimmie beamed broadly as if he had a great secret and could hardly contain it.

"What?" I asked, seeing that SHE was in the room with her wolf pack.

"You have it all, don't you?"

"I don't have anything. I don't even have any clothes on," I whined.

"Don't worry, you don't need clothes," he said as he stood up. Beautiful in his own nakedness, he walked towards me. His hair was freshly washed and combed, and he gleamed as if a fine oil had been rubbed all over him. Around him, the other people started to kiss and touch each other.

Even the wolves were whining and pacing, torn between the desire to mate and the desire to satiate any whims of their mistress.

As Jimmie pressed his mouth over mine, blackness consumed me.

And again, just when I thought I was going to be able to have my way with him, I woke up.

I cried, wondering what the dream meant. I cried, wondering if I'll ever feel happy again.

Friday, January 20

The skulls look really cool with hot wax dripped over them. It wasn't my idea. I was just an onlooker as my hands took control of the situation. They were fidgety and wanted to do artistic things. So next thing I knew, candles were lit and skulls were lined up on the coffee table.

Some of the skulls were painted with different colors of wax. They looked like weirdly shaped Ukrainian Easter eggs. On one of them, I tried for a somewhat human-type effect, dripping on scarlet lips and green eyebrows. The skull looked garishly surprised.

With Brad's skull, I paid careful, close attention. I wanted his to be gleamingly perfect. Snatches of memory flittered through my mind as I carefully dripped the wax on him. Those nights Vicki and I dripped hot wax all along Brad's body came to mind. As I coated the skull, I remembered coating his dick.

It took a really long time, but at last he was done. He glimmered with a sheen in the candlelight.

As I looked around my living room, I realized I was becoming quite the artist.

The Angel had grown bored of her toy, so now my tsantsa hung around Monica's neck. The Angel flew freely, with nothing to bind her to this earthly coil. With her newfound freedom, she was able to come and go at will.

CHAPTER SIXTEEN

Saturday, January 21

I rearranged everything so that I can prepare for the next addition to my collection.

It won't be long now before it will be complete.

I will be complete.

The wolf is outside my door. Every now and again I can hear her whining and scratching and trying to get me to open the door.

Not by the hair on my chinny chin chin . . .

If I let one in, who knows if the rest are there lurking in the corridors.

If I let in the queen perchance, will the rest follow suit?

Why are they there?

Do they plan to eat me?

Monday, January 23

The phone keeps ringing. They are concerned that I haven't gone to my last three shifts. I don't have the energy to go to work.

My lethargy keeps me paralyzed, and sometimes it is all I can do to crawl from the bed to the couch.

I don't like being damp and sweaty, but I can't bear the thought of taking off my clothes and taking a shower. That would involve standing, and I don't want to stand. I just want to lie here with the curtains shut and watch the candles flicker.

Wednesday, January 25

If he only knew how much I cared. How I dream of him night and day. Does he miss me? Has he gone to Ooolala and asked where I am?

Thursday, January 26

There was frantic knocking on the door earlier. This time I knew it wasn't the wolf. I didn't think it was the wolf. The knocking sounded strong, and there was shouting from the other side.

My name was called several times.

"Abby . . . Abby . . ." the voice cried out.

Finally I summoned the energy to stagger to the door and look through the little peephole.

Mavis stood on the other side. Her face was red with exasperation.

"I see you, Abby. Come out and tell me what's going on."

I turned away from the door. Looking at Mavis through that tiny keyhole made my head swim.

At long last, she finally stopped slamming at the door. She pointed and said something that was probably caustic, but my ears squeezed tightly shut and refused to listen to her shouting. All I knew was that she was mercifully gone and the wolf resumed her post.

My hands decided that my ears should be protected from any other intrusions, so they found my headphones and cranked up some tunes. With my brain filled with explosive guitar and smashing drums, my ears couldn't stray to pick up other noises.

To pass the time, I did two hundred and fifty push-ups followed by two hundred and fifty sit-ups, and then a bunch of bicep curls with a large fabric softener bottle filled with water.

I was sweatier than ever, so I guess I should go wash, though I don't really want to.

Maybe if I wash, I can baptize myself into a new reality.

One where Jimmie and I can sit on the couch and watch TV. Where Jimmie and I can make dinner together in my little kitchen. Where Jimmie and I stay up all night fucking until it's time for work the next day.

Friday, January 27

When I was getting ready to take my shower, I accidentally knocked one of my pictures of Jimmie off the counter and it smashed onto the floor.

Stupid picture jumped when I was taking off my shirt.

There was no reason for it to jump. But that picture has never wanted to be there.

Even when I set up the pictures a few days ago, that pesky picture was trouble.

The stand for the frame didn't want to behave and kept snapping shut, causing the picture to fall open. At one point, I finally had the damn thing open, and then, as if to mock me, it leaned over, barely touching the picture beside it, and soon they all tumbled over onto the counter.

Every time I brushed my teeth that picture would torment me.

This time when it jumped, it was for good. Its suicidal glass guts were shattered all along the bathroom floor. My hands quickly set to work gingerly picking up the pieces and tossing them into the trash. Soon my fingers were bloody from tiny little cuts, but it didn't matter to them. They kept going until every little shard was accounted for. For the tiniest shards, they just set their warm fleshy pads onto the glass so that it would jump into the skin. Once the glassy bits were tricked into leaving the floor, they were brushed into the garbage. Sometimes they clung with their little teeth, and that's how the blood came.

It was all part of it, though. Wolves, renegade pictures, candle wax.

Everyone had shit to deal with in life, and this was mine. Luckily I had a team with me who could handle the stress of it all.

My hands decided they had enough of the picture

frame and tossed that out too. My eyes had deemed the picture of Jimmie too unworthy to keep. It didn't capture his beauty, and maybe that was why the frame was constantly rebelling.

The set of pictures in my bathroom was called the Field Trip Gallery. These were pictures of Jimmie taken with my little digital camera as I stood across the street from his apartment. Every once in a while, as he came and went, I'd discreetly take a shot of him.

One day my hands and eyes were so excited by how hot he looked that there were a hundred and fifty pictures taken. It took a long time to print them all, and in the end I only displayed a few.

In my bedroom were other pictures. Across my dresser and along my nightstand, my Boudoir pictures were displayed. These were taken one night when I was trapped in Jimmie's apartment. He had come home early, and I thought for sure I was fucked. But my hands and feet took care of me, moving me from closet to closet until he fell asleep in front of the TV in just his boxers. If he had taken a shower or something, I could have escaped. But the most he did was pee twice, and he didn't shut the door. He would have seen me had I chosen to flee.

So he had dozed off in front of the TV that night, looking so cute in his boxers. I took a pile of pictures then too. It was so hard not to plant a kiss on his cheek as I snuck out, but I resisted the urge. My feet were out the door before my lips could protest.

On one wall I had a collage of him. I had blown his picture up huge on my computer, and it took about fifty pieces of paper to make the mural. His eye took something like four or five sheets. It was like a giant jigsaw puzzle.

The picture was funny because it looked like he was looking right at me.

But he wasn't.

How could he be?

He didn't know I was there.

That huge picture isn't a Boudoir picture, though. It's a Walking Down the Street picture. I had a camera in my headband that day, so in a way I guess he was looking at me, because after I snapped the picture, he noticed me a few feet later as we approached each other.

That was back around Christmastime, when I still harbored hopes and dreams that he would come to me of his own accord.

But some people don't have common sense.

Some people need to be told what to do and how to do it, or they just can't cope with anything.

He didn't know how to cope now that she was gone.

He didn't know what to do with himself.

Even that night I was locked into his apartment, he randomly amused himself. It's fun to watch people when they don't know anyone is watching.

Of course, I bet someone would have a heyday with me.

Watching me. Wondering what I was going to get up to next. Watching how my hands and mouth were in cahoots with each other and not necessarily doing what was best for all of us.

No matter.

Everyone has their shit.

I have wolves and pictures and rebellious body parts.

Saturday, January 28

My hair is so clean it squeaks. It is actually squeaking too much, and it makes my teeth hurt. My fingers don't want to touch it at all, and I'm out of styling products. I was out of crème rinse too, which is what all the squeaking is about.

It's hard to do anything with squeaky hair that tangles up together. My hair won't let me put a comb or a brush through it. Even my niggling fingers can't coax the strands to separate.

Maybe my hair will stop making life so hard when it dries.

Later

I finally had to put a hat on to cover my stupid hair. Maybe it will dry faster because it's one of those little winter hats.

If I dry it with a hair dryer, I'll be in worse trouble.

My hands are being pretty good about putting on nail polish. I didn't realize that I hadn't filed my nails since New Year's Eve, and they were looking pretty ratty and torn. Especially the third one on my left hand that I'm always biting when I'm thinking about something.

I've been thinking a lot lately, that's for sure.

There are so many things to think about, and sometimes the images flash by too fast for me to digest what I'm supposed to be thinking.

But my nails look pretty good. Now I just have to

find some clothes and then cover them up with a stupid parka, because it looks pretty damn cold out there.

Later

It was cold out for sure. My stupid hair turned to icicles under the stupid hat. I should have seen Jimmie going into or leaving his apartment in the three hours I stood there, but his timing was off. He never showed up.

Sunday January 29

I went to Boingo's last night to get rid of my anger at not seeing Jimmie when I finally had it together to go out into that damn freezing cold weather.

When I walked in, the bouncers looked at me as if I was from another planet, but they didn't stop me. They probably recognized me even though I was all bundled up.

Many drinks into the night, I danced by myself. I lost myself in the haze of swirling lights and writhing bodies. A few times, I bumped into people, but no one seemed to mind. It felt at times that people were staring at me. And talking about me. Laughing at me.

Maybe they saw my angst on my face. Or maybe they caught me telling my hands to stop reaching for pretty girls' breasts.

My hands were terrible. They wouldn't leave well enough alone.

They flopped and flitted when I danced and groped asses while standing in line for drinks. My face was unaware of my hands' bad behavior, so when people would turn around to see who had touched them, my face was nonchalant.

What did it matter?

Everyone was here to get laid anyway. What difference did it make if someone was stroking them softly between their legs? My hands were just crying out to give pleasure where pleasure was due.

Somehow my hands found the large jutting breasts of a lonely brunette. She had a quirky smile and a thick accent. I didn't know who she was; I had never seen her around before. Not that I'd seen many people there before, but I also recognized the people that had always been there. Sometimes I wondered if people actually left Boingo's or if they just were there always.

Go-go dancers gyrated on the speakers and in a couple of cages that had been set up. I guess, with the new year, Boingo's was trying new things to attract the club kids.

My body sprang into ultraflirtation mode, and despite my brain's attempt to tell it that I didn't have time for such nonsense, my pussy was singing a song of its own. It pleaded for attention; it had been too long since it was last touched by a stranger.

So we went back to Lucy's apartment and spent the night quelling our hungry quims in mindless oblivion. Lucy was a practiced lesbian; she didn't hunt around my cunt with curiosity like most women do. She spread my lips, took one quick look and dove in like it was the tastiest buffet she had enjoyed in a long time.

I found out it had been a while for her too. She had left her lover, a teenager, in Mexico. Lucy had grown tired of the daily doldrums of her life at the market. She wanted to start a new life in America, but her lover was fearful of leaving the only life she knew. It had been a difficult decision, but one made nonetheless.

Lucy made beautiful jewelry and pottery. Her apartment was filled with the products of her crafts. In fact, she had enough to open a store and I told her so.

"It's a dream of mine to have a small boutique in New York. Maybe in the Village or something. But it'll take a long time to save up to be able to do it. Unless I had a partner."

"You mean to support you or to open a business with?"

"A business partner, silly. Someone who has an equal interest. A lover never cares like someone who has money invested does."

"You're right about that." I smiled and kissed her hand. We were sitting on her couch. We were wrapped together in a colorful cotton blanket that her grandmother had woven for the market. I thought about what it must be like to sit at a loom all day. Not just for a week, or long enough to make a rug or two, but to sit there hour after hour, day after day until the weeks melt into months and into years. Children are born and grow up. Grandchildren are born and still you sit at your loom, moving the thread in steady, rhythmic pacing.

Talk about neck ache. Or carpal tunnel.

I would go mad listening to the clacking and watching the colors evolve into long, straight lines. Red on the left, green on the right, three colors in between. It is your job to be certain that each color has the required number of rows. That each thread is hooked to the other one in a competent fashion.

There can be no snags, no loose ends to catch and destroy the formations.

At any rate, we sat under the blanket and it was late. Or maybe it was early. We had left the bar around one and spent a very long time fooling around, so it must have been three or four. I remember lighting a cigarette and her wrinkling her nose at me. She waved the smoke away from her face furiously.

"I'm sorry. Am I bothering you?"

"I wish you wouldn't smoke. It's annoying."

"I seem to recall you smoking earlier."

"I was drunk. And I was trying to pick you up. Of course I'm going to smoke. Now I've had what I wanted, so I don't need to smoke anymore."

I nodded my head in agreement. I didn't know about her, but I was still trashed. She probably wasn't drinking before she went out. She probably didn't have a wolf at her door and shattered glass hiding in her rugs.

The pictures are truly conspiring against me. I think it's because the hands are so bossy. They go around straightening and fixing, as if lining up one skull in exact precision to the candleholder, on a diagonal from another skull, is going to make any difference.

It's just me here.

It's always just me here.

Sometimes I get the urge to invite people over, but then I see the depressed look of my friends. They stare at me with their gaping eyes and mouths open in a cry of rejection, terrified that I'll leave them and never come back.

In fact, Monica is getting very stern. She has gone

past the idea of leaving. She can see that I'm in no shape in the middle of the worst winter storms to go apartment hunting. Anyone in their right mind hibernates like a good little bear.

So Monica has taken up hibernating as well. She sees no need for me to go out partying all night, although she does live vicariously through my many adventures.

She's not too pleased with me that I went out again. No one is pleased. The wolf barks now and again outside of my door and paws at it fruitlessly. Now and again I get the nerve to look out the peephole for it. But I'm always afraid I'll see a giant eye staring back at me. I'd rather pretend that I'm just imagining things.

Many pictures leaped from the wall in my absence, like fish fleeing from a tank. I remember when I was a little kid I had a tank of guppies. Man, there were so many stupid guppy incidents when I had that tank. One of them was when I went away for a few days one summer, or maybe it was weeks, who knows. When I came back, all the stupid guppies had jumped from the tank and died. They lay scattered on my bedroom floor like little dried leaves. Maybe they had been trying to follow me. They had never leaped out before.

Lucy found plenty wrong with me after a little bit of time. I was too quiet, yet I laughed too loudly. I seemed to have no ambition beyond working as a waitress. She started in on how I should go into business with her. We could set up a little store. I knew how to work with people in a friendly fashion, and she had the stuff.

The concept didn't sound too bad—if we lived in

Buttfuck, Nowhere. But we lived in New York. It was very expensive to get a store, and there were no stores we could afford as near as I could tell.

In Buttfuck, there were empty storefronts almost every five or six stores. A lot of people had fled from there. I was part of a mad exodus. Or maybe the exodus had already happened, which is why the stores were empty. Without stores, there are no jobs and no places to get cool stuff.

However, she was starting to get on my nerves in that Bossy Boots way she was talking. At first I tried to pretend it was just her accent getting to me. Maybe what I had found interesting about her was now a pain in the ass. That happens to people, doesn't it?

That's why there's divorce. When there's marriage, everyone is so lovey-dovey; when there's divorce, it's all ugly. And it's the same old shit. No one really ever changes, as much as they might try. So if someone is a stinky old alcoholic who bitches and moans all the time, he will be that way forever. The moaning and groaning may seem sweet and endearing at first, but there will come the time where you just want to reach over the table and smack him.

I bet Jimmie would never get on my nerves. At least he wouldn't be bossing me around. His biggest problem with me is that I wear glasses. Once I get the laser eye surgery, he'll see me for who I really am. I lost all this weight for him, I've built him a special shrine and if his only problem with me is that I wear glasses, well, I can fix that, can't I?

But not yet.

I checked my online bank account today and saw

that I don't have even half the amount squirreled away yet. That's because it's been so slow at work.

Oh yeah.

I haven't been to work.

I took myself a little seasonal affective disorder holiday.

When I pull myself together and go back there, they'll be glad to see me. After all, I'm a hard worker, and until the past few days—or is it more?—I never missed a shift. I've barely been late. And when I'm at work, I do my duties and I'm pleasant to the customers.

Everything should be working out just fine, or should have been.

But Lucy kept talking and talking.

Each suggestion grew more aggressive until it felt like she was screaming at me, physically knocking me over with her words.

In reality, she was just speaking loudly and firmly, and if I was falling over, it was because I was pretty wasted.

She had convinced herself that I was the perfect partner for her new business, and even took a drag of the joint that I offered out to her.

"I can see it all now. You would be so good with the customers. If you have two grand, we can be partners."

"I don't think so," I said.

"Come on, it would be fun."

"No. It might be for a little while, but I'd grow bored and unable to function."

"Don't say that."

"I know myself, man. I like waitressing. I meet people and can yak a lot. I may not make a king's ransom,

292

but I have my own place in Manhattan. That's pretty tough to do."

"Tell me about it," she said. "I can't believe what I pay here. And couple that with my place back home."

"You have a place back home?"

"Well, my girlfriend is still living there. What can I do? I promised to take care of her, and she's only seventeen. I can't send her out into the world: She'd get eaten alive by the wolves, both animal and human."

"I hear you on that."

Lucy sighed and took a haul of the joint. "Actually, I'm lying. Not about her—she really is seventeen. I'm not taking care of her. I wish I were."

"What happened?"

"She's gone. One minute she's there, the next minute she's walking straight out of my life like I don't exist."

The subject turned and twisted around relationships and love and money and back to the business idea again. She was a dog with a bone, that one.

When I finally became firm with her, she turned on me. "You just use me for sex but have no interest in anything about me?" she asked with a haughty tone as she sat up and glared at me.

"I have interest. But I'm not interested in running a store with you. I like my job. I like my life the way it is."

"So much so that you spend the night in the arms of a stranger?"

"I'm between relationships."

"So you used me for sex.

I wanted to say well, duh! You used me too. But I held my tongue. Shouldn't have bothered.

293

"Then for sexual favors, I charge one hundred dollars."

I'm sure my jaw hit the floor.

"Pardon me? You want me to pay for sex?" I asked, standing up from the couch.

"Yes, I want you to pay. You can't treat me like a piece of trash. I'm here to make money, and if you won't start my business, then pay me for sex. You know I'm good."

"No one's treating anyone like trash. I thought you liked me too. Spending a few hours together doesn't mean I'm going to change my whole life. Maybe it will change if we keep seeing each other. But I'm thinking I'm not too thrilled about the idea of seeing you anymore."

"Fuck you, then," Lucy snapped, and lunged at me. Luckily my hands saw it coming before my brain, and they were able to bat her off. In a flurry of flailing limbs, she fell back and hit her head on the coffee table. She was out like a light. I thought she was dead.

As she lay twisted half on and half off the couch, I studied her face. I did like her lips. They were full and plump, and when they weren't yap-yap-yapping about something, they were pretty nice.

I found an X-Acto knife in her artist's kit and started sawing at her lips. That's when I knew she wasn't dead. She reached up and grabbed my hair to pull me off of her. It had to be a battle now. A battle to the death.

As she lunged towards me again, I grabbed the nearest thing, one of her pottery vases, and flung it at her face. It exploded, and she grabbed at her eyes with a scream.

"Shut up," I said. "You'll wake the neighbors."

I flung vase after vase at her until she sank to her knees sobbing. At last I found one that wasn't fragile pottery but had a bit of weight to it. I threw it at her, and she was silenced once more.

My hands itched to pick up all the broken pieces, but I knew I had to act fast. We had been really noisy, and the cops might be on their way any minute. I set to work cutting away her lips and found some plastic wrap in the kitchen. After wrapping up my prize, I slipped it into my purse and got the hell out.

Not a moment too soon, too. The cops were on their way with shrieking sirens. Amazing to know that they still came for domestic abuse cases.

If I didn't get out of the building, I was fucked. I flew down the stairs and out a side door just as the cops were tappa-tappa-tapping up the front stairs. I checked to make sure my hands had remembered to bring everything. They had.

I hurried home, hoping against hope that I had left nothing behind.

CHAPTER SEVENTEEN

Monday, January 30

My collection is a shining glimpse into a better tomorrow. When I stare at my accomplishments, I know that I can do anything at all.

Sure, I'm lonely. No work. No friends.

My stomach is growling, so I guess it's out into the world for some grub.

Later

It was a strange and eerie walk. No longer did I have my daily ritual of waiting and following Jimmie. I had him right where I wanted him. If he wouldn't have me in the flesh, then I had to make sure no one else could have him, either. He was mine, is mine. Mine forever.

Why did I leave the house at all to walk in the bitter winter wind? The store was too much to bear. I walked into it several times, but each time the noises and the lights drove me to distraction.

It was the colors, so bright and vivid they melted and morphed around me, whispering words that I couldn't quite hear.

It happened in three stores, and finally I found a fast food joint where the bright lights positively hummed, but at least I could go on autopilot and not have to make any decisions. My mouth ordered my favorite cheeseburger and fries, and my hands found the money.

Money is not my friend lately.

But I can last a while longer before either going back to Ooolala's or finding a new job.

I could just pick up and leave.

But how would I pack up my collection?

My collection sits there, complete. But who will ever see it but me?

If I abandon it, the cops will find me eventually unless I totally change my identity. I will have to research that one for loopholes.

If I stay here, I might run out of money. This place isn't the cheapest apartment in town by any means. Rent will be coming up soon.

Wednesday, February 1

They stare at me. Day after day. No playful flirtatious glances. No joy at the candles I burn for them or the delight I find in playing with them.

They are angry.

Monica is very angry.

Brad and Simon and all the others. They glare at me

with hollow, empty eyes. They saw the whole thing go down, and they didn't like it one bit.

I lured him into my spider's lair with greater ease then I ever expected. I ran into him on the street.

No, I lie. My fingers are making my pen lie.

My mind is making my brain remember things that aren't true.

I lay in wait on his corner and bought coffee and magazines hourly until he came by. Despite the cold, there was time for chitchat.

"I'm a bit of an artist," my lips said. My hands wanted to slap them, but then they started to envision the meaning behind the lack of movement.

"Really?" Jimmie's face lit up. For a moment, he seemed almost happy.

"I do sculptures mostly."

"That must be hard."

"It takes a lot of work and patience. Would you like to see my latest pieces?"

"Where are they showing?"

"I'm afraid they aren't showing anywhere right now. I've been waiting for a second opinion to see if they are good enough."

"I'm sure they are good enough. If you think they are, they are. What do critics know?"

"I guess you're right. Still, I'd like you to come and take a look sometime."

Jimmie looked at his watch. "When do you get off?"

"In about an hour."

"Then I'll wait."

He actually did wait, my Jimmie. I was never so

happy in my life. That last hour took forever as I polished the silverware and prepared my station for the next day.

No, wait. . . . It didn't happen like that at all. He wasn't sitting at my table. I don't have a table anymore. He didn't wait for me to polish the silver, because I had no silver to polish.

We stood shivering on the street corner until my clever lips convinced him to follow me home.

My hands were shaking as they unlocked the door. Here he was on my doorstep, my Johnny Depp Look-Alike. I wanted to photograph the moment. It's freeze-framed into my mind forever, but I'd love to have a photograph. Johnny Depp standing right there on my doorstep. Me, little Abigail Barnum, and Johnny Depp. Don't we make a wonderful couple?

As he stepped across the threshold, Johnny's face fell.

"What the fuck?" he said slowly, as if the words were smashing through his teeth. He wasn't looking at my collection; his eyes were traveling around the room at lightning speed, staring with wide-eyed astonishment at the pictures of himself.

I shut the door behind him and leaned against it.

"Take a look around," I instructed. My fingers turned the lock quietly behind my back as he stepped into my little living room. The wolf whined and scratched from the other side, but he didn't hear her. He walked up to first one picture and then another. I had added collages of pictures inside the bigger pictures.

When he went into the bedroom, there was a moan as if he had been impaled.

He swore when he saw the giant mural of himself.

Eager to explain my photographic techniques, I proudly went in to stand beside him. I also was eager for him to check out my collection.

"When? How?" he asked, his face pale, his lips trembling. His lips were dancing back and forth, and I yearned to taste them. His dark eyes were so wide, so innocent, and my heart beat faster as my pussy mewed.

"I've loved you for a long time, Jimmie. I've been waiting for you." I held my arms out to him, as they do in the movies. But instead of rushing into them, he burst into anger.

First he ran over to the mural and tore it into shreds. He ran around throwing the pictures to the floor and smashing them in a fury. He ripped away the stapled pictures and I watched, frozen with despair.

This wasn't at all what I had imagined.

He turned to me with hatred in his eyes. "Who are you?"

"I-I . . . love you, Jimmie. Please know that."

"You are sick."

I rushed into Jimmie's arms. Tears flowed from my eyes against my will. Stupid leaky eyes. No ones likes it when a girl is boohooing all over the place. He tried to push me away at first, and then reluctantly wrapped his arms around me.

"Abigail . . . you need help. You don't even know me."

"But you love me too. You must. Why else would you sit in my section or be places that I am?"

"Fate . . . I guess. I sit in your section because you don't bother me like the other waitresses do. You let me work in peace."

"That's because I love you."

I was embarrassed at how I was sobbing into his shoulder. My makeup must have been a disaster.

"Abby, pull yourself together."

"Do you love me, Johnny? Do you love me too?"

"Jimmie. I'm Jimmie."

"I know. . . . I know. . . ."

"How can I love someone I barely know?"

I ran into the kitchen, my mind black with rage. I was crying, sure, but it was from anger, not from helplessness.

He came up behind me, trying to coax me to him like some kind of wounded animal. I clung to the counter with one hand, my knuckles clenching so hard they were white. I wasn't falling for his games. He didn't love me. My ears could barely hear anything else, they were ringing so hard. My mind was a fuzzy TV station that didn't come in. He didn't love me. He didn't appreciate my art. He didn't appreciate my shrine to his magnificence.

"Come on, Abigail. We can talk this out."

I spun rapidly and plunged the long thin knife under his rib cage, jutting up and up, pushing with all my might as if I was fucking him with my cold steel hardness. He didn't have time to move or run or hit at me.

"Tell me where your heart is?" I said coldly as I withdrew the knife. His eyes bulged with shock, and he looked down at himself where blood spilled like a newly opened waterfall.

"What are you doing?"

"You don't love me." The words were a statement as the realization of how he felt and what I had done hit me.

"I love you as much as a person can love a stranger." He gasped as he stumbled, then slid down the far wall. He had tried to get away, but his movements made the blood gush harder. I took the opportunity to stab him in the shoulder blade. He screamed and tried to shake me off. Again I was able to pull the knife out as easily as taking a fork from a roast.

He crawled into the living room and saw my friends for the first time. First he saw Monica, sitting proudly with Brad and Vicki's heads in her lap. Then he looked up at the Angel with Screaming Shrew, his old girl-friend, tiny and spinning in the breeze.

He looked over at my jars of piccadoggy and picca-vicki. His underwear, his lighter, his books, his bathrobe, his sheets . . . so much of his stuff was lovingly displayed. He coughed up big clumps of blood as he tried to speak.

"You've been stealing from me. . . ." he gasped. "It was you the whole time. . . ."

"It's not stealing, it's building my collection. I was preparing for the day you finally came to me."

"What . . . what do you want . . . from . . . me?" he asked, laying his head on the floor, blood pouring from his mouth.

I don't remember how many more times it took to silence him. When I was finished, I dragged him into my bedroom. I wanted to feel him inside of me at least one time while he was still warm.

I had my way with Johnny . . . uh . . . Jimmie, and I think he was grateful that he went out the way he did. Knowing that I loved him. I finally felt his lips against mine, his arms around me. I finally knew how he smelled when I hugged him tight. I rubbed myself against his mouth, his body. My scent, my love, was caressed into him, once and for all.

Now no one can hurt him again. The irony is that he and Miss Squawkyface are together again in the same place. But not really.

Jimmie is mine.

CHAPTER EIGHTEEN

Thursday, February 2

They speak to me. Not how normal people speak. It's high-pitched noise. It echoes around my head and pokes into my ears, though I try to keep them stuffed with cotton to protect them.

I find the days go faster when I don't wear my glasses. I can't see them glaring at me.

I spend most of my days in bed reading.

Friday, February 3

Mavis did the knocking-squawking routine again today. I ignored her. Maybe the wolf scared her away.

Saturday, February 4

The door opened today, and it was the landlord. Luckily my hands were smart enough to have the chain locks on. He hollered at me that the rent was due and my mailbox was overflowing.

I hollered back, "OK."

He shut the door again.

My heart was nearly slamming out of my chest. I actually got out of bed and stumbled into the living room. I had a wicked head rush, so I sat down and had to face the accusing eyes—or lack of eyes, I guess really just holes—staring at me.

How can holes be accusing?

I never really thought about it, and now I've decided that it's not true. They are just holes, and holes are bottomless voids with no expression. If they all sprang to life, then they would be operating on some distant memory and more likely manipulated by an outside force. A skull has no memory because there's no brain. But maybe the bone cells, even though they are dead, maybe they have a memory.

It hurts my head to think about it.

I'm just glad the landlord is gone. Though he'll be back when the rent doesn't appear.

Later

I realized today that I'm a real mess. Depression consumes me, and I stared forlornly at my friends all day. I even put on my glasses. At first my eyes protested, since they weren't used to it, but soon my vision became clear and I was fine except for this stupid throbbing pounding in my head.

Sunday, February 5

Monica was my good friend for a long time. She was the best lover I ever had. The first time I laid eyes on her, I knew she was special. My heart ached whenever I saw her. She often sat in my section with her friends, and I would dutifully bring them beer after beer as they laughed and gossiped and picked up men.

For many months this went on, but since I was a girl too, they often included me in other outings. At least after the time I caught a couple of them smoking up in the parking lot. Instead of turning them in, I took a haul too, and we all bonded.

Monica and I became friends and not long after that, lovers. I thought the sun rose and set on her.

Then came that fateful day. I came home from work one afternoon and caught her in bed with a man. She tearfully told me that she missed the strong arms of a man. It turned out they had been having their little rendezvous while I was at work from practically the time we met.

My rage had been so black, so complete, that Monica didn't make it through the night after her tearful confessions. My heart was truly broken.

What had felt like fulfillment of the void inside of me had been an illusion. She had never loved me as I thought she had, or she would not have betrayed me.

When my hands tightened around her throat and I felt the last gasps of breath from her kicking, flailing body, there was a moment of relief.

But that relief didn't last.

It seemed only right that I didn't throw away the one that I loved. With great love and care, I stripped the flesh from her bones and created my first art piece.

I had kept her to remind me to never fall in love again.

But how foolish I had been.

How foolish I had been to lose my heart to Jimmie. Why hadn't I paid attention to the memory sitting right there in front of me all this time?

Now both Monica and Jimmie are there to remind me. There is no love to be had with either sex.

Monday, February 6

I can stand the ache of loneliness no more. The walls are closing in. The wolf howls now and again. The whispering follows me through dreams and into the real world.

Tuesday, February 7

Selling petals on the streets. Singing songs of blood and charm. Pennies fly into my hat. Who will listen to my next yarn?

Wednesday, February 8

Where there is truth, there is light. Where there is light, there is fire. The depths of hell beckon to me, and for a moment I glimpse the brightness of what I could become. In that world beneath worlds, I could become queen. So close it is. I can taste it. I can feel it. Hell longs for me as much as I long for it.

Thursday, February 9

There is no light. The light is out. The lights are out all over except for my candle. The night is long and cold. I made fifty-five dollars today begging on the streets. It bought me food, and I nearly have enough now for the rent.

If I can get one more month out of here, then the wolf will leave me alone.

She hasn't got me yet. When I leave my apartment, I know she's there. She follows me. There are glimpses from the corners of my eyes. Shadows flicker on the streets. People staring at me, always staring at me. Knocking on the door, on the window.

They want to get me. They always are after me. It doesn't matter who.

The e-mails pile up; I can't bear to read them. I guess there must be a way to find e-mail addresses online, because there are e-mails from people at work. Mostly Mavis. I don't look at them, though. What are they going to say? Nothing. There's nothing anyone can say. It is enough to drag my ass outside in this weather to make a few bucks. Some days are better than others. It's so cold. The icy rain slaps my cheeks like salt blowing in a fan against my face. I can imagine desert sand pummeling me with equal force.

Why don't I live in the desert? Or at least Arizona, where it is warm and dry and things shrivel up. I wouldn't need a coat. I wouldn't have cold, aching feet. My nose wouldn't always be running and my hands too stubborn to wipe it. My hands don't do much good for anyone anymore. At least they still hold the pen now and again, but sometimes I wonder how much longer it will be before they decide to stop.

Writing down my thoughts is the only thing that reminds me that I exist sometimes. I haven't had a conversation in a long time. When I'm on the street, I don't talk; I pretend I'm mute, which is fine because my ears don't know the difference between the snow blowing and people talking. It all whirls together in my ears, and my brain puts up roadblocks so that I can't hear or understand the jumble of noises.

My mouth doesn't have a clue what's going on, so I try to keep it shut tightly. However, sometimes snatches of song will fly out, but that's OK. Lot's of people sing to themselves. I never realize I'm singing to myself until my ears finally hear it. Then my hands clamp over my mouth to remind it to shut up. Sometimes the gloves have to come off in order for my fingers to catch my slippery lips. But in the end, the mouth finally shuts up.

As I wrote this, my other hand was playing with my hair. Twisting a strand around and around my finger. Now it's caught, and my stupid finger is turning purple. Stupid hair is wound all around it, and I can't get it off. My finger gets mad and pulls at it, tugging though my hair refuses to unwrap itself and get on with life. It pissed me off while they fought, but I'm trying to keep writing.

Stupid hair.

The hands always win. When will anyone ever realize that?

The stubborn, stupid clump of hair is now on the

table. My hands ripped it right out. Decided that it didn't deserve to live; it should die. So die it did, or does. I don't know how long it takes for hair to die once it's ripped from your scalp. I saw on some sex show that sperm dies nearly instantly once it hits the air or water. This is why you can't get pregnant if some guy is jerking off in the Jacuzzi and comes in the water.

Yet stupid sperm can live long enough to get a stupid teenager pregnant. Or a one-night stand. Sperm is so stupid that it won't do its job for people who try for years to have a baby, yet will work like crazy for those that don't want one.

If sperm would listen and take direction, then everyone would be happy. There would be no accidents. No heartache of empty eggs. But I can't even get my hands to get along with my hair, so who could ever tell a million sperm what to do?

Stupid hair was getting on my nerves. I put it in the ashtray and am burning it with a cigarette. The clump goes up quickly and then sizzles out. There is nothing left.

Maybe that's what I will do. Burn. Burn and burn until there is nothing left. I could start it on the earthly plane and continue on into eternity. Burning and burning, anticipating the day when I am finally ash.

The darkness welcomes me, for in the darkness, beyond the darkness, there is my own personal fire of damnation waiting for me and me alone. The fire in the demon dog's eye. The peephole that shows another land. A world where munchkins twitter and jabberwockies lurk.

The doorway can open anywhere. Every time I turn

the knob, I see that something lurks beyond the corridor. So far it has only been the corridor and the familiar choice of creaky old elevator or stairs. I almost always choose the stairs, instructing my feet to tappa-tappa down them very lightly, like a little elf.

The door will one day open somewhere else. Either there will be a pack of wolves there ready to consume me, or there will be the fiery pits of hell. Or there may be other options, but none of them are going to be much fun.

I just checked the door. It still opens into the corridor. I'm still able to access the outside world and buy another month of home for my friends.

Sunday, February 12

They are like petulant children. Maybe they are mad because I sold a couple jars of piccadoggy to silly tourists. I made some really cool-looking labels on my computer, complete with pictures of dogs like Lala and Angeline in a big heart, only I called it Abby's Piccalilli, Secret Southern Recipe.

Since it's a billion below out there, I couldn't dress up or anything, but I did bring a little portable TV tray and set my five jars of piccadoggy out on it. I kept my eyes out for cops, because you aren't supposed to sell without a permit. It was pretty crowded despite the crappy weather. I guess the fact that it was nearly Valentine's Day really helped push things along. I sold those damn dogs for twenty bucks a jar. One hundred bucks I made, and I now had enough altogether for another month of rent.

My good luck continued. I ran home and changed into stinky, crusty beggar gear and found a few stir sticks from Ooolala and pasted red paper hearts on them. My hands remembered some calligraphy from an art class in high school, and they scratched the words "I love you" with a fountain pen dipped in a special mixture of ink and blood.

Well, goddamn, didn't those things go like hot-cakes too. I made another fifty bucks selling stupid paper hearts, even though they wouldn't last in the snow.

Tourists will buy anything. Many of them noticed they were Ooolala stir sticks and were glad to get one without having to spend a million bucks on drinks and dinner.

So off they went, happy with their treasures, while I sauntered off with yet another wad of bills.

Later

The guy on the corner always has good weed, and this time was no exception. I think he knows I do the beggar shtick, but he says nothing. What's he gonna say? He's dealing on the corner, man. That's way worse then someone who has no job going begging.

Later

Pictures leap and fly like popcorn heating up. No sooner do I put them back on the walls than they leap away again. Stubborn children. Most of them have no glass anymore.

I had tried to fix a few of the pictures of my J.D., but most of them were bad.

My hands kept putting off printing out more, though my eyes were very upset.

Later

A big red heart under the door.
   Was it from my Jimmie?
   Maybe it was from my wolf.

Later

Hearts of paper, hearts of flesh
   Hearts that mock you when you rest

CHAPTER NINETEEN

Tuesday, February 14

They still act like they are babies, even though I paid in advance for another month when I finally paid this month's rent. Don't want that landlord to think I'm moving out. When I was taking my shower to get ready to go and see him, I realized it had been a long time since I had last washed. My nose blocked itself off and my stomach fought hard not to let the stench of myself throw me into total convulsions. How could I not notice the rot of my own flesh and dried dead skin cells clinging to clothes that hadn't been washed in forever? I guess if I'm outside I don't notice because I'm too fucking cold, and if I'm inside I'm either asleep or burning scented candles.

I stood under there for a year and a day wondering why I had been too tired to wash before this. It felt so good. I lathered my hair and soaped and shaved, the whole works. I wondered briefly if I would see Mr. Johnny Depp Look-Alike at work today, and then remembered that I didn't work anymore and Jimmie was right here in my living room.

I missed the strong arms of a man around me. I missed his arms around me. I had slept with his arms wrapped around me for a couple of days until I knew I couldn't do that anymore.

He looks jaunty in his dressing gown. I put a cigarette in his hand; it just seemed to need it.

I closed my eyes and dreamed of him wrapping his arms around me. I wanted to feel him, to taste him, to touch him. I wished it so hard that it was true for a moment. For a brief and shining moment, I felt him squeeze me and kiss my head. Then he was gone. I finished my shower and stepped out.

I got all normal looking, putting on makeup and clean clothes, though how I found any is beyond me. I guess that's why in the end, when I looked in the mirror, I was wearing a little miniskirt, stockings, and a clingy blouse. Mr. Landlord can't have any idea of who I really am and that I'm going to hell.

No, he has to see a nice normal tenant, and that's who he saw.

I explained to him how I was between jobs and how I managed to get together some money through friends, and I gave him the money for next month too. He couldn't take his eyes off my tits, and my mouth almost had something to say about that, but I didn't let it.

As I walked back to my apartment, I had a spring in my step. I felt proud that I had managed to come up with money for another whole month just by begging on the streets and selling piccadoggy.

My pride was short-lived as I saw the glares of my friends when I walked into the living room to tell them my good news.

Even the stupid tsantsa was spinning in the Angel's hand again, though I don't recall putting her back in the Angel's hand. In fact, everything had moved a little bit.

Maybe I had forgotten moving everything around. It's happened a lot when I'm stoned, and I've been stoned a lot lately. Even before I get stoned, I feel stoned.

At any rate, they were bugging me, so I went into my bedroom and tried to find something on TV that my stupid antennae could pick up. Some sitcom keeps sidetracking me, so maybe I'll just watch that.

Everything is a Valentine's Day special. Every show has the theme of a couple experiencing miscommunication but working it through. Maybe while I listen to the TV through the headphones that my hands put on my ears a few minutes ago, I can give out the valentines I made for them. They will realize then how much I love them. Well, except for the tsantsa.

Saturday, February 18

Where there's smoke, there's fire. More hair in the ashtray. This time it refused to disengage from my hairbrush. So my hands lost their patience and ripped it off. I burned it in an offering to my friends. To let them find peace in themselves and stop taking their anger out on me. No wonder I roamed the streets from dusk till dawn trying to escape them.

I slept with dark fitful dreams. They whispered their accusations to me while the wolves howled.

Monday, February 20

My arms have little circles all along them.
　My hands think they are in charge of everything now.
　They take the cigarettes and touch them to the flesh.
　Never forget
　Never forget. . . .
　There is no love
　There is no sanctuary

Tuesday, February 21

　Fingers and toes and lips and eyes
　When they mock me babies cry
　Flying pictures in the stream
　He will love me when I wake from this dream

Wednesday, February 22

When I woke up—no, before I woke up, while I woke up, during the time I was trying to wake up, my left ear was sore. There had been panting in it all night. The hot breath of a wolf slobbering in my ear.
　She had somehow come into the apartment while I slept. I could feel the sticky goo of her spit on my ear.
　I looked out the peephole and heard growling.
　The corridor was red. As if the time split was coming.

Thursday, February 23

Cold cold cold cold . . . stupid hail *tappa tappa* at the window.

318

Wolf's breath on my pictures, making them bend and bleed.

Tsantsa doesn't want to play with the Angel. She flung herself into Jimmie's lap.

No matter how I separate them, she always goes back to him.

Friday, February 24

Tied tsantsa up in a pair of Jimmie's boxers and thought about throwing her down the garbage chute. That would teach her. She has one last chance.

Saturday, February 25

Tsantsa mocks me from a pile of glass and shredded pictures. The wolf scratches at the door and moans and groans. I flung tsantsa out the door, hoping the wolf would eat her.

Sunday, February 26

Burn the pictures that have fallen. That will teach them.

Monday, February 27

scratches and howls
Beep-beeps from e-mail box
Tappa tappa from door
What big eyes you have

There's too much for my hands to keep up with. My hands filled my ears with cotton so they wouldn't have to hear anymore.

My hands put tape on my mouth so my lips wouldn't flap around and make more noise. My hair keeps filling up the ashtrays; it's in the way.

Always put the book in the tin box so the fire can't eat it.

Tuesday, February 28

Flames reach high. The hair did its job for good this time. Jimmie laughs as his bloated lips smile. Tsantsa snuck back in to see, but I flung her into the center of it all. Her screams amuse me. Her hair crisps right up.

Goodbye canopy circus tent. Goodbye Johnny Depp underwear.

The flames are delicious and high.

The ghost wolves morph from the smoke and pace around my living room. They wait for the golden one to appear.

I wait for the golden one to appear.

It's exciting knowing that at last I'll have the secrets.

This book must live in the tin box. My hands will put it away, and then my lips will talk to the wolves.

Fire burns and my feet step into it.

Fire consumes me.

Lovers, take my hands and begin the dance.

AFTERWORD

Mavis

When I found this journal of a lunatic's ramblings, I hid it in my purse before the cops could go through everything.

Abby was my friend. Or at least I thought she was.

That fateful night a year or so ago, I happened to be sitting in the back of a car giving a handsome young man a blow job when I heard the news on the radio.

A fire had broken out, and I recognized the address as Abby's building. As handsome as my little man was—and how it pained me to leave him high and dry—I bolted up and out of the car before he knew I was gone.

It was only a couple of blocks to the apartment, and fire trucks were everywhere. People stood on the street staring up at one of the floors, where thick smoke billowed out. It didn't take long before firemen reemerged and huddled in a clump. Rumors whispered through the crowd that there were people inside. Sitting. One was hanging from the ceiling.

I managed to find out that the fire had been on Abby's floor, and I ran towards the apartment.

Even though they tried to keep me from the scene, I snuck in a side door and up the rancid smoke-filled stairwell until I reached her floor. That was no small feet in those shoes, honey.

The door had been axed and ripped from its hinges. It hurt me to see that, as if some sort of horrible scene had unfolded, although I knew it was just the firemen trying to get in. The scene as I first saw it was pretty unspeakable. Pictures were being taken; video cameras were whirring. Firemen and police were already scribbling notes and talking to each other in puzzled astonishment.

While they were pondering the significance of the bodies, I managed to whip from doorway to bedroom unnoticed.

I started combing through the rubble of her bedroom while they stood around musing at the macabre collection of bones and skulls smoldering in the living room.

Most of the room was destroyed. I don't know if it was a mess before or after the firemen came through, but garbage and burned clothes and papers were all over the place. In the black and brown charcoal ashes, I saw something gleaming. It was a tin box. I didn't know what was in it at the time, but something told me to take it.

Luckily I always carry a large purse, so it wasn't too difficult to hide it and carry it home.

In reading through this diary, I'm not sure if half of

what Abby says is true. She didn't talk about so many things.

Talk about your poetic license. She totally lied about the events of New Year's Eve. She practically chased Jimmie away with her drunken jealousy. She accused him of staring at this girl and that girl. At one point, I took her aside and politely told her that a lady doesn't complain if a man looks at another woman. She didn't want to hear about it. She thought that if she was on a date, then he should only have eyes for her. Poor thing doesn't realize that it's never that way. Only if you are one knockout dame can you capture any man's attention for more than minutes at a time.

If anyone was trashed that night, it was Abby.

And we both were busted and thrown in jail. We were fucking in the bathroom when the cops came, but does she mention me at all? I know she went to that place a few times, so maybe she got them confused.

She never mentioned any of the times we were together, and that can make a girl feel insignificant. I knew she was sweet on Jimmie, but I had no idea of her obsession. If I knew then what I know now, I would never have gotten involved with her, and I don't even mean the murders. I mean, just her obsession with that greasy writer dude is enough to turn my stomach. No human is worth that kind of adoration.

Her boss gave up on her after a week, saying waitresses often flake out after a while; the stress gets to them.

After a while, nearly everyone at Ooolala had forgotten about her. How fickle the bar crowd is, and what incredibly short attention spans. Waitresses come and go. But I never forgot. I went to her door. I phoned her. I e-mailed her. She wanted nothing to do with me. I figured she was depressed; she had been looking worse with each passing week. She was getting a bit gaunt too. There's such a thing as being too thin. Especially for someone as voluptuous as her.

I asked her many times about what happened to Brad—partly out of concern for Brad and partly out of my own nefarious yearnings. It never really occurred to me to ask about Vicki, since I never liked her to begin with and still don't know why Abby tortured herself with such a bitch.

Now I wonder, where is Abby? Her body wasn't found in the rubble. The fire wasn't so out of control that it ruined the building. Smoke residue would have to be dealt with, but the fire was pretty much contained to her apartment.

The most grisly part of her journal is that the bones really did belong to the people she said they did. At least the missing New Yorkers. I never told them about Monica and Kimberly Evans and Billy Fishmen. I don't know who the others might be.

Brad's parents claimed him and gave him a burial. They wouldn't tell anyone when and where it was, but I know now that Brad can finally rest in peace.

As can her other victims, who were claimed by worried families. There were so many lives she touched and shattered. I wonder if she ever thinks of the magnitude of the ripple she caused when she jumped into the current of our lives.

When I walk down the street, I look at beggars and

wonder if she decided to hide herself among the homeless. Or did she take what was left of her money and hop a train somewhere? Maybe she went back to that little New England town she loved so much.

She had mentioned drowning herself in the ocean. If she wasn't shark bait, her body might wash up onshore one day.

She was a strange girl, an enigma. Her beauty was rare, and I never minded her glasses.

I wonder where Abby went, and what she's doing now.

BORROWED FLESH
SÈPHERA GIRÓN

Poor Alex. She thought she would have some fun, take a chance, maybe fool around a little. Instead she's lying dead in her own blood, cut open like a slaughtered animal. But the worst is still to come. Her tender young flesh will soon be used in an unspeakable act, an unholy ritual that few sane people could even believe.

Alex was not the first, nor will she be the last. Not as long as Vanessa is alive—and she plans to be alive forever. Vanessa's unnatural life has become a search for victims, virgins to satisfy her body's need for eternal youth. But Vanessa doesn't know that there are things in the world more powerful, more terrifying even than herself. . . .

FINISHING TOUCHES
THOMAS TESSIER

INCLUDES THE BONUS NOVELLA
FATHER PANIC'S OPERA MACABRE!

On an extended holiday in London, Dr. Tom Sutherland befriends a mysterious surgeon named Nordhagen and begins a wild affair with the doctor's exotic assistant, Lina. Seduced and completely enthralled by Lina, Tom can think only of being with her, following her deeper into forbidden fantasies and dark pleasures. But fantasy turns to nightmare when Tom discovers the basement laboratory of Dr. Nordhagen, a secret chamber where cruelty, desire and madness combine to form the ultimate evil.
